## NINA B.

was born in London in 1925 and
the war. She was educated at Ilford County High School
and at Somerville College, Oxford.

Her first novel, *Who Calls the Tune*, appeared in 1953. Since then she has published nineteen other adult novels including: *Tortoise by Candlelight* (1963); *A Little Love, A Little Learning* (1965); *A Woman of My Age* (1967); *The Grain of Truth* (1968); *The Birds on the Trees* (1970); *Afternoon of a Good Woman*, winner of the Yorkshire Post Novel of the Year Award for 1976; *Walking Naked* (1981); *The Ice House* (1983) and *Circles of Deceit*, which was shortlisted for the Booker Prize in 1988 and filmed by the BBC. Her most recent novel is *Family Money* (1991).

Nina Bawden is also an acclaimed author of sixteen children's books. Many of these have been televised or filmed; all have been widely translated. Amongst them are: *Carrie's War* (1973); *The Peppermint Pig*, the recipient of the 1975 Guardian Award for Children's Fiction; *The Finding* (1985), *Keeping Henry* (1988), *The Outside Child* (1989) and *Humbug* (1992).

For ten years Nina Bawden served as a magistrate, both in her local court and in the Crown Court. She also sat on the councils of various literary bodies, including the Royal Society of Literature – of which she is a Fellow – PEN, and the Society of Authors, and is the President of the Society of Women Writers and Journalists. In addition she has lectured at conferences and universities, on Arts Council tours and in schools.

Nina Bawden has been married twice and has one son, one daughter and two stepdaughters. She lives in London and in Greece.

Virago publish eight of Nina Bawden's works of fiction. *Familiar Passions* and *George Beneath a Paper Moon* are forthcoming.

VIRAGO

MODERN

CLASSIC

NUMBER

387

*Nina Bawden*

# THE GRAIN
# OF TRUTH

# To my Mother

Published by VIRAGO PRESS Limited 1993
20–23 Mandela Street, Camden Town, London NW1 0HQ

First published in Britain by The Longman Group 1968
This edition offset from Macmillan, London Ltd, 1979 publication

A CIP catalogue record for this book is available from the
British Library

Printed in Britain by Cox & Wyman Ltd, Reading, Berks

# 1. *Emma*

Someone listen to me. *She* never did.

He was fourteen and he got a tumour on the brain. His name was Gordon and he had a sister called Sylvia who was my best friend. They lived at the bottom of our garden. This was a long time ago.

Their garden was bigger than ours: it had a hard tennis court with weeds pushing up through the cracked surface, and a shrubbery where we made a camp and cooked on a primus. After Gordon had the first operation and they thought he was cured, we played together most afternoons. That was a long, hot summer. Once, when Sylvia wasn't there, he threaded a daisy chain and put it on my head for a crown, and kissed me. In the winter he went into hospital again and he wrote me letters, first in ink and later in pencil and his writing got wobblier and in the end he didn't write at all but on Valentine's Day he sent me a pink card with a raised gold heart and inside it said, From One Who Loves You Truly. Even after he had stopped answering I went on writing to him, beautiful letters with bits of poetry and descriptions of nature that made me cry as I wrote them. I loved him more than my life and longed to prove it. I had a dream that the surgeon came to me and said, 'If you will let us have a piece of your brain we can graft it on to Gordon's where we took the tumour out, and he will be well again.' So I went to the hospital and lay in the bed next to his and the surgeon said, 'You are the bravest girl I have ever known, greater love hath no man.' He did the operation and all the time there was organ music playing and we were both conscious and smiling at each other and the surgeon said, 'Now you are one flesh.' Gordon was wearing a white gown. He was the handsomest person I had ever seen, with dark hair and very dark eyes; not brown, but blue-black, like sloes.

He came out of hospital in the spring and I couldn't wait to see him. I swallowed my tea so fast that a lump of biscuit stuck halfway down and gave me a pain. I scrambled through the fence and he was sitting at the back of his house, in the sun. There was a bandage all round his head and he had got dreadfully fat: his cheeks had swelled up so that his eyes looked like black buttons, or raisins sunk in white dough. He said, 'Hallo, Emma,' and then something else, but his speech was fuzzy and I couldn't understand. Sylvia said, 'He wants you to kiss him, Em.' She was sorry about that, I could see, but he was her brother and she didn't want him to be hurt. So I kissed him, to please her, and he caught hold of me and made me sit beside him. He kept touching me and trying to stroke my arm.

He could only walk in a lop-sided way, staggering like someone drunk. Sylvia was supposed to look after him when she came home from school and see he didn't fall. Their mother was dead: there must have been a nurse or a house-keeper, I suppose, but perhaps after tea was her time off. We tried playing *Happy Families* with him but he kept drop-ping the cards and forgetting what family he was collecting. He didn't seem to mind whether he won or not; he had this sloppy grin on his mouth most of the time, but now and again he looked puzzled, as if he didn't understand what was happening and it worried him. I was sorry and sad when I thought about him, at school or at night in bed, but when I was with him he disgusted me. He was always patting and stroking me and I hated that: it was like maggots crawling

6

over my skin. Sylvia said I was stupid to mind, he meant no harm. 'I let him play with my titties sometimes,' she said once, and giggled.

When we got bored with amusing him, we'd play hide and seek, running away to tease him, and he'd shamble after us, calling and wagging his head from side to side. Sometimes we kept it up too long and he'd cry because he couldn't find us and then we'd feel mean and let him sit between us and touch us to make up for it. I felt like a Christian martyr then, but Sylvia liked it: she'd go red in the face and throw herself about.

One day she was ill and lay in a deckchair. Gordon wanted to play ball, so I threw for him on the lawn. He couldn't catch or aim properly and the ball went into the shrubbery. I went to get it and he came after me. I was bending over and he put his hand on my bottom. I turned round and pushed him in the chest and he fell over backwards. His legs went up in the air and then he lay still. I ran out of the shrubbery and threw the ball up high, trying to clap my hands ten times before I caught it again. After a minute or two he came out of the shrubbery looking no worse than usual; my heart slowed down and I said to Sylvia, 'Come on, for heaven's sake, why should I be a bloody nursemaid all the time?'

He died that night, or the next night, I can't remember exactly. The light clicked on in my room and my mother was there, holding Sylvia's hand and saying she had come to sleep with us because poor Gordon was ill. Sylvia had been crying, her face was puffy and pink, and when my mother had gone she said she was sure Gordon was dead. She had woken up and gone into his room and her father was there, leaning over the bed. He had sent her to fetch a mirror and he had held it in front of Gordon's mouth to see if he was still breathing.

I knew I had killed him. I cried a lot and I couldn't eat and my mother said it was natural for me to be upset but I must

7

try to think of myself less and of other people more. Think of poor Sylvia and her father! They had loved Gordon so much, this was a terrible time for them. I said I had loved him too, I was *in* love with him, and she said, what nonsense! I was a little girl, only twelve years old. I said, what about Romeo and Juliet, she hadn't been much older than me, and my mother said that was a hot climate where girls matured earlier. I read too many stories, she said, real life was different. I said Northern Italy wasn't much hotter than England and she told me to fetch the newspaper and look up the temperature in Turin.

I lost weight at that time and she made me take a tonic. It tasted filthy and I spat it out and smashed the bottle on the kitchen floor. I knew it was only iron for my blood, but I screamed out that she was trying to poison me; I knew she hated me and wanted me dead. I tried to cut my hand on the glass to make her sorry, but she stopped me. She took hold of my arms and made me sit down and drink a glass of water while she cleaned up the mess.

'Now what was all that about?' she said a bit later on, but I couldn't tell her. I never could tell her anything. I quarrelled with her a great deal at that time, but not about anything real. Sometimes it seemed to me that no one talked about anything real, ever.

Emma stood on the landing. Though it was two o'clock in the afternoon, the house was dark. Through the lead-paned window over the stairs, she saw massed clouds, solid as battleships, bare trees black against them.

Below, in the hall, a patch of white glimmered. Emma went down the stairs. The banister was cold under her slippery palm. She was afraid of falling. The man lay on his face in the dark hall; she knelt beside him and said aloud, histrionically, 'Father.' She was afraid to touch him. She said, 'Oh God, help me.'

He was making a snoring noise. He lay face down, heavy,

inert, one arm trapped beneath him. The letters had scattered over the floor. One rested under his free hand, his right hand with the gold ring on the fourth finger. Emma read her own address, her own handwriting. Dear Lucas, my darling Lucas.

*Darling Lucas. Oh my love, help me. . . .*

He was breathing harshly, a long, terrible pause between each breath. She couldn't move him, though when she pushed at his shoulders the solid flesh seemed to slip under his white silk shirt. She thought – Like when the clouds move and it seems as if the house is falling.

Joints creaked as she got up. The telephone was on the consul table in the hall, beneath the Italian gilt mirror. Both were valuable, both belonged to William Rufus Lingard, her husband's father, now dying on the floor of the house he had built soon after he married. He had been an antique dealer. Emma thought – *Had been.* The house had six bedrooms, two bathrooms, a croquet lawn and a two-car garage: this was expensive, tree-lined suburbia. *As good a limbo as any other,* Henry had called it, when his father had the first stroke and they moved from Islington to look after him. *It will be nice for the boys to have a decent garden,* Henry had said, remembering his own boyhood: bicycles and summer afternoons and borrowing Daddy's car to take his first girl to the tennis club party.

Emma rang the doctor's number. It was engaged. She put the receiver down and waited, seeing her ghostly face in the speckled mirror. She watched her face and saw the mouth move. She dialled again: the number was still busy. There was a *ting* as she replaced the receiver and then silence. He had stopped breathing.

Emma thought – I know what to do. She ran into the kitchen for her handbag, on the formica work-top beside the dish washer. She fumbled with huge, stiff fingers: the shopping list fell out. Harpic, coffee, steaks. She thought – I suppose we shall have to eat something this evening. She

9

took out the small mirror. She thought – But poor Emma was a child then, not responsible. Carrying the mirror, she went into the hall and knelt again. His head was heavy as a cannon ball. He had white, silky hair, growing in a fringe round a pink, monk's tonsure; it grew long at the back, over his collar.

Emma's mother always said that Henry's father reminded her of Lloyd George. Was it because of his hair, Emma wondered now, and at once rejected this simple explanation: her mother's judgements were more mysterious than that.

She turned his head sideways on the cold floor and held the mirror to his lips. In profile, the strawberry nose, the mottled cheeks, the flesh drooping like wattles beneath the jaw bone. She had read somewhere that at the moment of death the blood rushed from the eyes, but his lids were closed. No breath misted on the mirror.

Emma sat back on her heels. She felt enormously tired. An immense lethargy. She yawned till her jaw cracked and her eyes misted; then bile rose in her mouth. Rising, she stumbled up the stairs, into the bathroom. She retched into the basin, wiped her lips and went into the bedroom to ring the doctor from the extension. The house was lighter now. Through the wide, bay window, the sky stretched above the houses opposite, streaked with yellow in the west, the clouds rolling back like a carpet. The pavements were wet. The rain had come and gone, while he was dying.

On the other side of the street was a terrace of modern houses, built with featureless good taste in the Georgian style. Holly and Felix Craven lived in one of them: while Emma watched, Holly came out of her house and slammed the front door. She was wearing a white, tightly belted rain-coat with military flaps on the shoulders. Like a film star.

'Holly,' Emma called. She rapped on the glass. Holly halted on the pavement, looking up vaguely. 'Holly', Emma shouted, beginning to cry as she pushed at the window frame which had swollen in the damp weather.

Holly waved and ran across the road, straight hair swinging.

Emma left the bedroom. Halfway down the stairs, she saw the letters her father-in-law had dropped when he fell. Seen through tears, the white sheets bobbed up and down as did Holly's silhouette, visible through the frosted glass of the front door. Emma dived at the letters, crumpling them in her hand. *Darling Lucas.* . . . She moved the old man's limp hand with her foot and picked up the letter beneath it. That she could do this, shocked her. She gave a high-pitched groan to distract herself from her own behaviour, ran into the drawing-room, pulled open the drawer of the Queen Anne bureau where she kept the household bills, and stuffed the letters inside. As she came back into the hall, Holly emerged from the kitchen, and Emma fell against her, weeping.

Holly sat her on the stairs and knelt by Henry's father. Emma closed her eyes. Holly said, 'Have you called the doctor?'

'Engaged. I tried twice. . . .'

Holly lifted her, led her into the drawing-room. 'You need a brandy.'

'We can't leave him lying there.'

'He's dead. And he must weigh sixteen stone. What time do the twins get back?' Holly looked at her wrist watch critically, like a gym mistress starting a race.

'Three-thirty. No. I forgot. They're going out to tea. It's the Jervis boy's birthday. Half-past six, about.'

Holly nodded. She went to the oak corner cupboard. 'For Christ's sake – it's locked. How *Victorian*.'

Emma giggled. She pulled her mouth stiff, like a tragic actress. 'Father would get at the whisky. Of course he wasn't supposed to drink.'

'No. Where's the key?'

'In the bureau. Wait – I'll get it.' She scrambled clumsily off the sofa and pushed past Holly. The key was in the drawer under the letters, on a length of red, knotted string. Emma tossed it to Holly and felt herself blushing. 'You'd never have found it,' she said, and laughed, to make this seem less ridiculous.

Holly's eyebrows lifted in a neat, dark arc. 'Not much of a hiding place. Had he been at the bottle?'

'I don't know.' Emma sank onto the sofa. Holly gave her a brandy; Emma's teeth chattered against the glass. 'I'm c-cold,' she moaned.

'I'll get something.' Holly went out, closing the door. Emma heard her running up the stairs, saw the chandelier dance as she trod overhead. Her high heels clacked down the bare, oak stairs. She paused in the hall. When she opened the door, Emma saw she had covered the body with a sheet.

She said, 'He f-fell down the stairs.' The blood was throbbing in her ears. 'He f-fell backwards and turned a sort of somersault. It was awful.'

Holly made her lie on the sofa. She tucked her legs up in a blanket and arranged a cushion behind her head. Immediately, Emma felt stifled. She wanted to get up, walk about the room, wave her arms.

She said, 'Was it another stroke, do you think? Or just the fall?'

'Both, perhaps.' Holly looked at her. 'It could have happened any time, you know that. But it's always a shock.'

She must have been a good nurse, Emma thought, surprised. Not unsympathetic, but calm and detached. Somehow she had never seen this before, envisaging Holly's nursing career as a sequence from an old war film: the beautiful, breezy nurse, nipping into bed with the wounded soldiers when Matron's back was turned. Though of course, Holly would have been too young, during the war. . . .

Holly said, 'I'd better go and phone. The doctor, then Henry, then this Jervis woman. Tell her to hang on to the boys. I can fetch them later. Is she in the book?'

'The red one, by the phone. It may be under S. I don't

know. S for Susan.' Emma grinned weakly, apologizing for this inefficient system.

'Susan Jervis. Droopy tweed skirt and a face like a flannel?'

Emma nodded, feeling disloyal to Susan, whom she liked. But she was afraid to disagree with Holly who was dogmatic in her opinions and jealous of any woman Emma seemed even temporarily close to. It was not a sexual jealousy but an adolescent one. For Holly, they had to be 'best friends' like schoolgirls, sharing secrets, shutting out the world. Emma thought – Whatever I do, Holly will stand by me. Water came into her eyes and nose and she yawned suddenly. She thought – After a shock, you feel sleepy.

She lay back obediently as if someone had spoken aloud, brandy glass clasped to her chest, eyes shut. She had drunk the brandy like medicine, emptying the glass in two gulps, and now she felt tight. She thought – Drinking on an empty stomach. Though she had cooked fish for her father-in-law's lunch, she had eaten nothing herself. The sun had come out and its heat struck through the window and onto her left hand, holding the empty glass. She thought – Alcohol is a poison. An insult to the brain. Dylan Thomas. There was a poem by Spender about Icarus falling. He had flown too near the sun. Why should she think about that? Henry's father was an old man who had already suffered two strokes and had, this afternoon, fallen down the stairs. The staircase had come from an old house in Gloucestershire. They would have chopped it up for firewood, William Lingard had often said. He had bought it for five pounds and designed his own house round it. It had owl heads carved on the newel posts and wide, shallow, polished stairs, the treads hollow with use and age. She had told Henry they ought to be carpeted, one of the children might slip. He had said Father would never hear of it. That was like Henry – to put everything off on to someone else. Grudging the expense, he blamed his father! For a moment, Emma thought indignantly about her

13

husband, forming sentences, flexing her mind for battle. Then she remembered his father was dead. Henry had loved his father.

'Henry's out,' Holly said. 'His secretary said she'd get him to ring as soon as he came in. I just told her it was important. Your chum Sue says the boys can stay the night and the doctor is coming. He'll bring someone to help move him. He's got a confinement, he'll be about half an hour.'

'Thank you,' Emma felt submissive and ashamed. Why should Holly do all this? She looked at her, standing in a dusty shaft of sun in her belted raincoat, a tall woman with dark, straight hair and a healthy colour and eyes that gave an impression of light. They were pale grey, flecked with brown round the iris, and seemed to reflect colour. Beneath gold-shadowed lids and in the sunlight, they looked tawny: a lioness's eyes.

'Why don't you take off your raincoat, aren't you hot?' Emma said.

Holly unfastened her belt in answer. Beneath the white raincoat she wore only bra' and pants. Her long, bare stomach quivered with suppressed laughter. 'I was going to London and I wanted to wear my green dress – *you* know, the one with the gold belt – but it's at the cleaner's. I thought I'd pick it up on the way to the station and put it on in the lav.'

She belted her coat again.

Emma said, 'If you were meeting someone, oughtn't you to ring? He'll wonder what's happened to you.'

Except for Emma, Holly had no women friends. All the same, Emma blushed because she had said 'he'. It seemed to imply a criticism.

'Let him wonder. Do him good.' Then, as if she suddenly felt this cavalier tone unsuitable in the circumstances, Holly's voice changed, became almost theatrically solemn. 'Emma – I ought to have said this before – I'm so sorry. You must be feeling awful, darling.'

14

Emma drew a deep breath. 'Henry's going to be so upset.' The inadequacy of this word pained her: she closed her eyes. 'When my father died, Henry and I were on holiday, we'd gone ski-ing. I felt dreadful, not being there.'

Holly sat on the sofa, shifting Emma's legs, and took her hand. 'Cry if you want to. I know it's what everyone says, but it helps.'

Emma shook her head. 'I can't. It would be hypocrisy. I'm not sorry he's dead. I shouldn't say this, should I? Though it's true. He was a horrible old man. Obscene. . . .' Holly's injunction to cry seemed to have affected her: she felt her chest heave. She gave a gasping laugh. 'Oh not always, that's not fair, just these last few months. I suppose he was going senile or something, he used to follow me about, telling filthy jokes. Only when he and I were alone, not when Henry was there.' Her face flamed. 'Holly, you can't *believe* – I suppose I'm a bit drunk or I wouldn't say this.' She looked at Holly with horror. 'He used to creep up behind me, put his hand up my skirt. . . .'

She thought Holly looked amused, but perhaps it was only sceptical. Why should anyone believe this?

Holly said softly, 'The poor old bastard.' Her eyes shone but her voice remained grave. 'What did you do?'

'What could I do?' Emma's voice was stiff. 'I tried to take no notice.'

'You didn't tell Henry?'

Emma turned her face away. 'I couldn't. I was ashamed – or something – oh, I don't know.' Retreating from this, and from Holly's withheld laughter, she began to cry softly. 'I hated him, I used to dream he would die. *Really*. Sometimes I'd wake up believing it had happened, he'd been knocked down crossing the street. Oh Holly, I've behaved so badly, I feel so *guilty*. . . .'

'You were marvellous to him,' Holly said brusquely. Taking Emma's glass, she went to the cupboard and re-filled it. Tears rolled down Emma's cheeks and she despised

15

herself for them. Did Holly despise her? Holly never cried. Emma said, 'I'm sorry to be so stupid.'

'Nonsense.' Holly gave her the brandy. 'Everyone dreams, darling. Goodness me. You mustn't be silly.' Her voice was practical and kindly, but her smile lacked warmth: Holly's patience with 'silliness' was limited. She gave Emma a handkerchief, patted her hand, but when the telephone rang she left the room with an air of relief. Emma heard her speaking in the hall. 'Henry? My dear, I'm afraid something's happened. . . .'

Emma sipped her brandy. The world seemed to be spinning. She thought – Nothing is in its place any more. Her mother was here, not Holly. She was saying – *I want the truth now, none of your nonsense, I know what you are.* Emma thought – People do terrible things to get at the truth. They pour water into your mouth, beat you with rubber hoses. They are going to hang you. This was the worst dream of all. No escape, a covering over your head, something black, suffocating. . . .

Emma dropped the brandy glass on the carpet and moaned under her breath, twisting her hands together.

Holly came back into the room and stood above her, frowning. 'Henry's getting back as soon as he can. Try to pull yourself together. You don't want him to see you like this, do you?'

'I don't want to see *him*. It was all my fault, Holly.'

Having said this aloud, Emma became calmer, though she continued to weep for a little, her eyes screwed up like a child's. It was always all right once you owned up; no one hurt you anymore. People admitted to things they hadn't done, so that the pain should stop. She said, hiccuping, 'I had a row with him.'

'With Henry?' Holly's face was blank. She sat on the sofa.

'No. With Father.' Words came more easily now. 'What happened was – I came upstairs and he was in my bedroom, poking about. This was the first time I'd actually caught him at it. He'd got a drawer open, everything all over the place, underclothes, old letters, and I got angry and he said various things. . . .'

'What?'

'Well. . . .' Emma blushed. 'Oh, just his usual nonsense. I was a promiscuous woman and he was looking for evidence. . . .'

Holly laughed – it was a sort of shout. Almost boisterous. Then she put her hand over her mouth and said, 'Oh, Emma. *You*. . . .'

Emma smiled, rather painfully. 'It wasn't anything new – that's what's so stupid – just his old game, but I was caught off balance, I suppose. I said I'd tell Henry and he turned quiet then and went out of the room. I put the things back in the drawer and shut it and then I heard him make this noise – a kind of grunt – and I ran on to the landing and saw him falling.'

Holly was staring. Emma swallowed hard. She thought – That was how it happened. Suddenly she threw herself backwards and began to jerk about, wailing. 'It was my fault, my fault. If I hadn't upset him – I *killed* him, Holly.'

'What bloody drivel, what bloody tripe.' Holly slapped Emma's face, not hard, but making a lot of noise, a blow on each cheek. Emma's sobs quietened: part of her mind noted, with surprise, that this traditional treatment worked. To her blurred vision, Holly's face appeared inflated, balloon-like. The outline wavered, but the tawny eyes were fixed and hard. Emma whimpered and drew up her legs, curling up like a small animal at the far end of the sofa.

She said, apologetically, 'No one believes this sort of thing can happen to them.'

'It hasn't,' Holly said. 'Listen, you. You like to feel guilty. For Pete's sake – you'd have felt guilty if he'd died when you were fast asleep at the other end of the bloody *country*.'

'Not quite, surely?'

'I wouldn't put it past you.' Holly smiled, a little grudgingly, but it softened the expression of her eyes. Her voice was low-pitched, professionally calm. 'Look. You've told me. Now, do me a favour, will you, and forget it? It wasn't conceivably your fault, but it might hurt Henry. Not the truth, I don't mean, but the way you'd tell it. Blaming yourself and so forth. You know what you are.'

'Do I?' Emma pondered this. *Really, Lucas, the extraordinary things people say!* She saw herself saying this, and Lucas's face, smiling. *He said – I know what you are, you are my darling girl.*

Emma felt suddenly peaceful. She stretched out and lay flat, her eyes closed. She said, 'I'll have to tell Henry.'

Holly gave a little hiss through her teeth. 'What's the point? You're fond of old Henry, aren't you?'

'Yes.' Emma opened her eyes and stared at the fuzz of sunlight round Holly's head. It picked out strands like red wire in the dark hair.

'Well, then?'

'What would you do?'

'Keep my mouth shut.' This was clipped, slightly contemptuous.

'Anything else would just make it easier for *me*?'

'If you want to put it like that.'

'Telling the truth isn't always self-indulgence.'

Holly sighed, crossed one long leg over the other. 'Oh, don't *fiddle-faddle*.'

Emma shivered. She was frightened by Holly's impatience. She said, 'I'm sorry. I suppose you're right, really.'

'I usually am.' Holly was stating a fact, without humour.

Emma smiled, to placate her. She said, pathetically, 'Perhaps I've made too much of it, I don't know. But I *did* lose my temper.' Tears came into her eyes again, moist and healing. 'Oh, Holly, thank God you were here. Though I'm sorry – I mean, to have dumped this on you.'

'*Not* at-tall! Lord – I shan't lose any sleep!' Holly looked at her thoughtfully. 'You're not to, either. It's over and

18

done, so don't torment yourself. No orgy of breast-beating, don't build it up into a great *thing*.'

'Is one likely to?'

Holly stood up and walked to the window. She could never stay still for long. She twitched pointlessly at a curtain and came to sit down again. 'I don't know about *one*. But *you* are!' She laughed suddenly, half-exasperated, half-affectionate, and leaned forward to take Emma's cold hand. 'Oh, for God's sake, I *know you*, Emma.'

## 2. *Holly*

People take sex too seriously.

Think a minute. Think of all the energy that's wasted on this one side of human activity! Wasted out of bed, I mean. All the talk – as if sex were some kind of mental exercise! All those books and plays, all that *fuss*. If one half of it was used for something else, like feeding those babies in the Oxfam advertisements or looking after poor old souls living on twopence a week and no coal in the grate, or frightened people in pain, wouldn't it be a better old world to live in?

Not that I'm against sex. I just think it should be kept in its place. A bit of what you fancy does you good, but once you've said that, you've said all there is to say on the subject, in my humble opinion. The stupid thing is, for most people *being* good is *not* having what they fancy, and since they want to be good they pretend they *don't* want it. And that leads to trouble.

Look at Emma, now. Married eight years, two children –

and bored to tears. Would she admit it? Not on your life. She's 'fond of Henry', they give cosy dinner parties, go abroad once a year – always together. Like Siamese twins.

I'm 'fond' of Felix, too. And I'm not against marriage. Felix and I are all right, we understand each other, and that's the main thing. He's got nothing to complain about. The house runs like clockwork, his meals are always on time, I even polish his shoes and lay out his clothes in the morning. Say this to Emma, and she'll tell you these things aren't important, but then she doesn't know much about men: she ought to see Felix, white in the face and spitting like a cat because there's a button missing from his shirt!

We haven't given up sex either. And as far as that goes, I treat Felix fair: I use the contraceptive. I don't with the others, I make them take the trouble. After all, it's Felix who keeps me, it's only right he should get that little bit extra.

Perhaps this makes me sound a vulgar sort of woman. But life is vulgar, isn't it? Birth, copulation and death. Why pretend? Why wrap up that middle vulgarity – and I mean that word in the original sense of 'pertaining to the ordinary run of things', I'm not *quite* uneducated – why wrap it up, I say, with a lot of irrelevant nonsense about morals which is just superstition left over from the old hell-fire days, mixed with a bit of possessiveness – *my* car, *my* wife – and a bit of plain fear: of getting pregnant, of being left alone. Being chaste doesn't protect you from that, for heaven's sake! My mother was, and my father left her when I was six months old. I'd never do that, I'd never leave my kid and neither would Felix. Divorce, if you've got kids, is the really wicked thing.

Not if there is cruelty or drunkenness or something – if Felix took to drink, you wouldn't see me for dust! But because of sex, because someone has a bit of what they fancy on the side – well, I think that's disgusting. As if marriage was nothing but sex and breeding, like animals. You have to come to terms with the facts of life, which are that no two people can possibly want to go to bed only with each other

20

for ever and ever, Amen. And since that's the way God made us, it can't be wrong, can it?

I believe in God. Emma thinks that's quaint, though she's far too polite to say so. But believing in God has nothing to do with the way you behave. It only means you're sure, whatever you do, that there's someone who goes on loving you like a father. *Underneath are the everlasting arms.* I think those are the most beautiful words in the English language. God has nothing to do with whether you go to bed with someone you're not married to – I shouldn't think He gives a damn about that. But to hear some people, you'd think it was the only thing He did care about. You'd think immorality meant illegal sex, nothing else at all.

That's another trouble. People are so concerned with sex that they forget it's also called the act of love. And for my money, it's better to love people than to drop bombs on them.

Felix says I'm a sentimental Christian, and that they are the biggest pretenders of all.

Felix can be a fearful old tabby at times. For instance, when he told me about Henry's joke index. Henry used to keep a whole filing cabinet of jokes, catalogued under Clean, Faintly Blue and True Blue, cross-referenced with where he'd heard them first and which parties he'd told them at. Apparently he started this when he was a young naval officer and stammered so badly that he could barely get a word out in company. Felix says when they were stationed at Malta it was the funniest thing in the world to see Henry rehearsing two or three jokes, owl-eyed and solemn as a clergyman chanting the litany, before they went out for the evening. He even got Felix to practise feeding him the right cues so he'd be sure of getting his jokes worked in.

I can just see old Henry! It would never occur to him that what he was doing was the biggest joke of all, he has no sense of humour. All the same, I despise Felix for telling me this. Henry is supposed to be his greatest friend, they were in

21

the Navy together and then up at Oxford and one of the reasons we bought our house was that he and Emma were living opposite. Felix says he would never have told anyone else, but we were married, for God's sake, weren't we? That's no excuse, to my mind. I might tell Felix some things, like who's sleeping with who, but never, *never* that sort of shameful, private thing. After all, no one minds being thought a bit of a dog – though a lot of people will pretend they do – but there are some things you'd *die* rather than have anyone know.

Not me, mind you! I'm the original Old Rhinoceros Hide. Tell the truth and shame the devil. But not everyone can be the same and there are some things even pretty honest people can't bear to admit to. (I bet if you asked Henry about that joke index now, he'd lie in his teeth.) That's why I'd never let Emma down – and didn't, even when Henry asked me straight out. I believe in being loyal to my friends.

And old Emma needs someone to be loyal to her, though looking at her from outside you mightn't think it. She'd just seem cool and organized, a clever girl who's managed to combine culture and cooking and get in a bit of do-goodery on the side. Felix says he can't understand why we get on so well together, we're such poles apart – which is his charming way of saying I'm an uneducated bitch and he can't see how an educated saint like Emma puts up with me – but he's only ever seen one side of her. Henry might know a bit better but I doubt it, and not just because he's the sort of man who only sees what suits him when he looks at other people. It takes a woman to understand a woman.

Look at that time Emma and I went to Sicily! Two girls on the loose – well, not girls, exactly, but the happier for that, say I. I wouldn't be eighteen again for all the tea in China.

I'd had a miscarriage. A couple of weeks afterwards, I was strong as a horse again, but I couldn't stop crying. I cried all the time, in bed, in the street, sitting on the stairs. I cried for my lost baby, for the world, for the sake of crying. I don't remember that I was particularly unhappy in myself, as they say – in fact, in some odd way I felt as if I was beginning to understand something and if they would let me get on with it and cry, I would find out what it was, very shortly – but Felix insisted I needed a holiday. He couldn't leave his precious job, of course, so Emma came with me.

Taormina is a cliff village, very pretty, with orange trees and jasmine and a long, rocky walk down to the sea. At night, the young men hunt in packs through the streets; the girls stay at home. The Sicilians are honest about sex. There's none of that nonsense about letting boys and girls run around together and then complaining, shocked eyes raised to heaven, that the illegitimacy rate is going up. This has nothing to do with morals, just that virginity, in that part of the world, has a clear market value. So while the young men parade, the girls sit outside the dark little houses, doing embroidery. You can tell the unmarried ones, because they sit with their backs to the street. (Not that it stops them taking a look, mind you, when Mama isn't watching!)

We drank at the pavement cafés and watched the boys go by. Until they are about seventeen, they are marvellous to look at, slender, with slippery brown skins and profiles like something on an old coin. After that, they seem to change almost overnight into runty, middle-aged men with bad complexions.

It was early in the season and there was no one in our hotel except a boiled-looking English couple in shorts and a pair of bald-headed queers, torn between the prospect of local delights – all those pretty boys – and jealousy of each other. Meal times, we sat in the dining-room at our separate tables, whispering and trying not to rattle the cutlery. One rollocking evening, the English couple stopped at our table. My heart almost stopped with excitement. 'We're going tomorrow,' the woman said, 'and we haven't seen Etna once.

In the clouds all the time we've been here. I'm so disappointed. . . .'

And that was all the social contact we had, all that first week. . . .


I thought Jules and Guy were Italian at first. They arrived in an open Fiat and I heard them talking Italian at the desk when we came down after breakfast, ready for the beach. Emma went onto the terrace to look at the view, but I stopped to fasten the strap of my sandal while the clerk got their room key. The dark one – Guy – gave a formal little bow as they walked past me and I smiled at him.

They turned up about half an hour after we had settled on the beach, which wasn't golden sand, as I'd expected, but fine, grey gritty stuff. They hired an umbrella about fifteen yards away, settled on towels and watched us sidelong.

I looked all right, and Emma looked marvellous. She is a pint-sized blonde with soft, brown eyes and the sort of delicate face that is at its best without make-up – lipstick or eyeshadow would take away from that look of dewy morn! Not many women could have got away with that look at twenty-eight, which is what she was then, but Emma did. Partly small bones, of course – look at Emma's wrists and ankles, or the back of her neck when her hair is piled up, and you are reminded how breakable people are. Men rush to carry suitcases and open doors for her. That would drive me mad, I can carry my own suitcases, thank you *very* much, but Emma accepts it as her natural due. When she notices, that is: a lot of the time she is pretty oblivious of what is going on around her. Or appears to be. This morning, she lay on her stomach, reading. Not one glance at our two swains under the next umbrella!

After a little, they went in the sea and did a bit of fancy diving from the rock in the middle of the bay.

'I like the dark one,' I said.

'Dark one? What dark one?' Emma put down her book

and looked vaguely out to see, screwing up her eyes as if she were short-sighted. (She isn't.) She loosened the straps of her bikini and began to oil herself – we were both tanning up nicely – then let her hair down and brushed it and coiled it up again. When she had given a fair exhibition of her charms, she lay down again, head under the umbrella's shade, and went on reading. She was reading *Light in August* by William Faulkner.

I didn't say anything. I didn't even point out that since the gentlemen were almost certainly foreign, they would not be impressed by her reading an eminent American author. Emma would only have been indignant, though under the pretence of not knowing what I was talking about, and once she had got into this act she would have felt duty bound to keep it up and we'd have trailed back, up the long climb to the hotel and a big, starchy lunch and a nice lay-down with cream of our faces, and that would have been that. For the rest of that day, anyway.

So while Emma pretended to read, even turning over the pages, I kept my thoughts to myself and watched the two in the sea. When they came out of the water, shaking themselves like dogs, the dark one smiled in my direction. He had a nice smile with a flash of gold in his back teeth and a firm, stocky body. A bit heavy, perhaps, but I didn't mind that: I have never liked boys. The other one was thinner, with a shy, rather blurred-looking face, more intellectual. Emma's type. They sat down and began oiling themselves and after a little a man came along with a basket. He was selling what looked like purplish hedgehogs – tiny balls of prickles. Guy bought some; he spread them out on a napkin the man provided, and cut them open with a knife. Then he glanced at me over his shoulder and held one up, questioningly. I called out, 'What are they?', as if I was really anxious to know, nothing else, and he got up at once and came over to us. 'Sea urchins,' he said. He was holding an open one in each hand; there was moist yellow stuff inside. His legs were knotted and sturdy

25

with a lot of curly black fuzz: the hair on his head was finer and receding a little. 'You eat them with lemon juice,' he explained, and I was relieved to hear he spoke reasonable English. 'Will you accept one?' Emma rolled over, smiled, shook her head and went back to her classy book. 'But they are very *good*,' he said in a disappointed voice.

His chum came up then, dug out some of the yellow stuff with a plastic spoon, squeezed lemon juice over it, and gave it to me. It didn't taste of anything much. I pulled a face and he laughed. 'You are English?'

They were French. In the hotel business. This was a business trip, Guy said, and winked. Jules laughed as if this were a joke. His English was not as good as Guy's: he often stopped mid-sentence and laughed. 'Nice business,' I said wittily, waving my hand at the gorgeous sea and the painted boats and making a mental note to do my nails that evening. Guy began to explain. They were here to recruit staff for a chain of hotels; wages were low in Sicily. It didn't sound very interesting. We talked about Etna – they called it Et-en-a – and how nice it was to see it out of the clouds this morning: two puffs of smoke, one white, one black, like a power station. We ought to visit the crater: it was very cold and dangerous for people with chest trouble because of the sulphur fumes, but very interesting. It was like talk at a party, leap-frogging, sparring, showing-off; no one really listening except perhaps Emma who had closed her book and was clasping her knees, not talking much but watching. They asked if we would lunch with them at a café on the beach. When they went to shower and change in the cabins, Emma said, 'If you don't mind, I'd rather go back, really.'

Sometimes Emma exasperates me. She has this look, as if we were all beneath her. 'Oh, for God's sake,' I said. 'We came to enjoy ourselves. Not to sit on the beach like two old hags at Brighton, admiring the scenery and bored to tears.'

'But we've nothing – well – nothing in common with them.' She looked embarrassed, saying this.

'You've been asked to lunch. It's not a proposal of marriage.'

She frowned, and then said, in a tone of pure surprise, 'Have you really been *bored*?'

'Haven't you?'

For a moment she still looked surprised – or puzzled, perhaps – and then the blood came up in her cheeks. 'Oh Holly, I *am* sorry, I didn't realize.'

It was all right after that. She put on her hair shirt and determined to be pleasant, for my sake. We had a good lunch. Emma and the boys drank a lot of wine and I had a citron pressé. Guy was astonished. People always are, when I say I don't touch alcohol. 'I'd rather drink dish-water,' I said. His English wasn't up to that, nor Emma's French, and by the time she had finished explaining and he had said, 'But why should one wish to drink the water the plates have been washed in?' we were all laughing. Even Emma – all eyes and soft mouth and strands of hair coming out of the thick coil. Like a picture come to life. The sun spiked through the woven roof over the terrace, and out in the flat sea, a motor boat shot over the water.

We went back to the hotel. Jules drove, and Guy sat in the back with me. On a bend, we swerved past a three-wheeled cart loaded with cherries and I fell against him, not quite accidentally. His hand wandered a bit, but I slapped it away. 'I don't know you well enough,' I said, and he laughed and extended his hand along the back of the seat, touching my shoulders with his finger tips. He said, 'After you have rested we will go up the mountain to the castello.'

When I woke, Emma was sitting on my bed, looking grave and brushing her hair. The sun had bleached it barley-colour. She said, 'I don't want to get involved, Holly. It's not fair to them.'

'Prudish women have such dirty minds,' I told her, getting up and making for the bathroom. 'Wait till you're asked and then say no if you feel like it. Don't cross bridges – didn't your mother ever tell you that?'

(And then remembered that the only advice Emma's mama was likely to have ladled out, was not to get in a railway carriage with a man alone, or she would have a baby. And though she would have explained exactly *how* babies were born – and pointed out that legitimate babies were beautiful and holy – she would never have got around to explaining *why*, except that it was something to do with getting into that railway carriage with one man and no ladies present. Presumably Emma knew better now, but early training lingers.)

I put the light on over the bathroom mirror and tweezed a few hairs out of my chin. 'My God, I'm growing a beard,' I said.

Emma came in to shower. 'You're right, Holly,' she said seriously, 'it seems awfully presumptuous – I mean there's absolutely no reason to suppose they want anything other than our company for the evening.'

I looked at her, standing under the shower. White breasts and a white triangle at her crotch and brown in between. Like a layer cake. 'Of course not, plug-ugly,' I said. I knew she didn't like to be looked at naked – though she would never admit it – so I turned back to the mirror and went on tweezing. 'I needn't worry about my old age at this rate,' I said. 'I'll have a long white beard and get a job as Father Christmas.'

Out of the shower, a towel wrapped round her, Emma said bravely, 'As long as you know where I stand.'

'You trust your Aunt Holly.' I gave her a quick look. 'Of course, we needn't go out with them. We can say we've changed our minds.'

'Isn't that rude?'

'Well – you've got a headache. We've both got a headache. Or if that's unlikely, I'll go, you stay.'

She wrinkled her nose, considering. 'That seems a bit –

28

well – unnecessary. Excessive. But if – I mean, if we don't
come back to the hotel for dinner but go somewhere else,
couldn't we pay for ourselves? Go Dutch?'

I sighed. Life is difficult for Emma. Every day is a sort of
obstacle race between imaginary alternatives. What I think,
what *they* think, what they think *I* think. . . . Playing her
game, I made my voice silky and patient. 'If that makes you
happier. Of course it looks a bit as if you're putting up a sign
saying *Not For Sale*.'

She blushed at that as I knew she would. 'All right,
Machiavelli,' she said, in such a droopy, resigned voice that
I could have shaken her till her teeth rattled.

Emma likes to be forced into things, so she can't blame
herself for them.


We had a cheerful couple of days and no, what Emma
would call, nonsense. Swimming, walks up the mountain,
walks in the moonlight, drinks on stone terraces with lizards
flicking over the edge. We went to Syracuse so that Emma
could see the Greek theatre and the gold coins in the museum,
and drove miles inland so that she could visit a Roman villa.
Hill towns perched on craggy mountain tops – built there
because of the malarial plains, Guy said. Shuttered streets,
smelling of dust, cement, sheep and coffee. Marvellous
children, daisy sweet, wearing white socks, loved and cos-
seted: all the time we were there, I never heard a child cry.
'Sicilian young men are terrible,' Guy said. 'Their mothers
teach them they are the lords of the earth.'

Jules had a wife in Lyons. Guy was a bachelor. They were
about Emma's age, a few years younger than me.

We went to a church somewhere and looked at vestments
embroidered with gold birds. Inside that church it was high
and cool and white. Afterwards, we sat at a café above the
sea. There was a little breeze blowing, a roof of climbing
flowers over our heads; and beside us, a group of dark men in
suits and flat caps were drinking bottled beer. 'Mafia,' Guy

said in a whisper. 'You know one of the things they do now? They rob the ancient tombs. They watch where the archaeologists go and then they come at night with drills and periscopes and sell the pots to the antique dealers in Taormina.'

We sat knee to knee under the table and the mafia drank their beer and shouted at each other, under the canopy of morning glory. And I knew it couldn't last much longer.

I felt a very pleasant sadness. This was the best time, of course, it always is. I'm not sex mad. I'm no nympho. I like the beginning of things best, looking at someone across a room, touching hands by accident, being a couple in a crowd. The small change, if you like, of love. When that stage comes to an end I always feel this sadness. Like saying goodbye to something.

A boy rode up on a Vespa. His white shirt billowed like a sail. He stopped outside the café in a cloud of grey dust and revved up his machine, for pleasure. He sat in a dream of bliss, opening and closing the throttle.

'I think we should go,' Jules said, looking at Emma and worrying in case the noise was offending her delicate ears. Jules didn't speak much, he was shy and his English was bad. Sometimes Emma talked to him in French; when I asked her what about, she said modern French novelists and General de Gaulle. 'How exciting,' I said, though of course it hardly mattered what she talked about. Jules would have listened if she had recited a laundry list.

At night, Guy and I danced in small, hot rooms, closed in like cellars. Jules and Emma sat drinking, watching us in silence. 'Tell him the story of your life,' I said, this evening, and Emma laughed. Jules had one arm round her shoulders. He bit her ear gently and Emma laughed and leaned against him. It was marvellous to see her so relaxed, so happy. With Henry, she often had a wary look as if she were afraid he was about to be angry with her.

'Well, that seems to be working out all right,' I said, as

Guy and I rocked together. He looked questioning, stroking my spine very pleasantly, and I told him not to worry. 'Miss Fix-It,' I said, 'that's me.'

Our rooms were on the first floor at opposite ends of the same corridor. Guy winked when we said goodnight at the top of the stairs. I went to shower and got into my gown. Emma was on the little balcony, looking at Etna. 'It's erupting,' she called. 'Holly – do come and look!'

I went out, shutting the door softly. Guy was in his pyjamas, grinning. I can't remember much about him now except that engaging grin and the gold tooth and the fact that his hair was receding and he was self-conscious about it, always fingering the strands when he thought no one was looking and spreading them carefully across the bald patches. Jules was fully dressed. For some reason, he had put on dark glasses. I gave him our room key. He looked sheepish and I gave him a push and said, 'Get along with you. It'll be all right as long as she knows she's got no option.'

I honestly believed that.


That was a very agreeable night. *Très agréable*, Guy said, and laughed. The bed was too soft, so we made love on the floor. (A lot of marriages are ruined because the bed is not hard enough.) Guy was a good lover, but not so expert – or so concerned – that he was absorbed in his own performance. We laughed a lot, both during and afterwards, and when I woke in the morning, I felt like a million dollars. The sun was streaming in and Guy was still flat on his back, snoring. I slid out of bed quietly, not waking him, and went onto the balcony.

I saw Jules below, on the terrace. He was hunched over the rail, watching the sea. I went along to our room. Emma was sitting up in bed, eating breakfast. Her front hair was in rollers and there was white cream splodged unappetizingly over her face. She gave me one look, buttered a roll and stuffed it into her mouth.

'I see Jules is up,' I said.

She buttered another roll and dipped it into her coffee.

'Dirty continental habit,' I said, but she didn't laugh. I might have been a piece of furniture in the room. 'Oh, all right, if that's how you want it,' I said, and took my clothes into the bathroom. When I came out, she had her suitcase on the bed and was packing neatly, smoothing out tissue paper.

'I'm going home,' she said.

'For Heaven's sake. . . .' She didn't answer. I sat on the bed and said, coaxingly, 'Emma darling – it's all right. Really. Maybe you'll feel guilty for a bit, but it'll wear off.'

'I have nothing to feel guilty about.'

'Well. . . .' I grinned. '*I* don't think so. I just thought you might.'

'Not even I could feel guilty about last night.' She enunciated clearly and primly and looked me straight in the eye. 'Jules slept in your bed. You didn't leave him much alternative, but I hope you don't mind, all the same. I daresay they'll change the sheets if you're really fussy about it.'

'Oh, *Emma*. . . .' I thought I saw a glint of laughter. 'Come off it. Don't tell your Aunt Holly such tales!'

She said calmly – she was enjoying this – 'I told him to go back to his own room but he said that would be embarrassing in the circumstances. He offered to spend the night in a chair on the balcony, but it had started to rain by then. I don't expect you noticed. So I told him to sleep in your bed. I don't know whether he had a good night or not. I took a sleeping pill, myself. When I woke up, he'd gone.'

'But didn't he *try* . . . ?' It seemed too fantastic for words.

'I suppose you could say he did. But he gave up quite soon and cried.' Her voice changed. 'Oh Holly – how *could* you?'

I was indignant. Justifiably. 'I thought it was what you wanted. You know you'd never *say*.'

Her eyes filled. 'I l-love Henry.'

'What on earth has that to do with it? For God's sake,

32

girl, you were all over the poor man last night. D'you think I'm blind? If you wanted to be faithful to old Henry, you'd never have behaved like that.'

'There's a difference,' she said, only half-believing this, so I didn't bother to argue the point.

I said witheringly. 'Do you think Henry's always been faithful to you? How long have you been married?'

'Eight years. And I believe he has.' She blushed, either because she thought this was an embarrassing thing to admit to, or because she was afraid he hadn't been.

I wouldn't know about Henry. I can usually make a pretty accurate guess about this sort of thing, but Henry is the sly type who might well be, in fact as well as appearance, some people's idea of a model husband, performing his conjugal duty Saturday night and mowing the lawn Sundays, but could equally well have a pert little blonde tucked away somewhere. If he had, she would be a convenience only and not allowed to interfere with the orderly running of his life, or to cost too much – I can just see old Henry sitting down with a pen and paper and solemnly working out how much he could afford to spend on this little, personal luxury without depriving his wife and family!

Since it seemed better to keep these speculations to myself, I ignored Henry and said, 'Emma, tell me. As a matter of interest. Last night – you *did* want to go to bed with Jules, didn't you?'

'Would you pass me my bikini? It's on the chair behind you. Thanks.' She folded it as carefully as if she were laying her mother's wedding dress away in camphor; took the rollers out of her hair and tucked them down the sides of the suitcase. Then she said, quite unemotionally, 'All right, if you must know. Yes. I suppose I was scared.'

'Jesus, what of? Having a baby?'

She looked at me thoughtfully. 'I suppose that's possible, too. But I meant just generally scared. Of myself, perhaps. Of you, partly.'

I was terribly, terribly hurt. 'Don't you know me better than that?'

'Oh, I knew you wouldn't *tell* anyone.' She dismissed this casually – as if it were *nothing* – and then smiled. 'Perhaps I just wanted to keep your good opinion. Or my own good opinion of myself.'

Anger bubbled inside me. This monstrous superiority – *I am better than that old whore, Holly*. Then I saw she was looking miserable. Utterly miserable and ashamed, as if she were despising, not me, but herself, and I went off the boil. Poor old Emma. She's so confused, such a bloody muddle. It makes me mad sometimes, but it makes me feel protective as well.

Tears came up into her eyes now, and she said, 'The awful thing is, maybe if no one had known what I was up to, I might have done it,' in such an agonized voice that it was more sad than funny, and though she was being ridiculous, making such a fuss about nothing, and turning what should be fun into torment and misery, I couldn't help feeling sorry and wanting to comfort her.

I said, 'Look, love, be sensible. You don't have to run home to Daddy. There's no need. Jules is going to Palermo today. Guy told me last night. He did say he might be able to arrange to stay on for a couple more days, but I'll tell him that's just not on. He can push off too.'

She fished in her case for a handkerchief and blew her nose. 'Don't be silly.'

'What's silly? Two's company, three's none. Do you think I'd expect you to play gooseberry?'

She said awkwardly, 'It doesn't seem fair. To you or Guy, I mean.'

There was a funny look on her face. An idea came to me. 'Would you rather have had Guy?' She said nothing, so I guessed that was it. I said, 'Oh, Emma, I'm truly sorry. Why ever didn't you say so? I wouldn't have minded.'

Which wasn't strictly true, but never mind: I'd have acted on it.

To my astonishment – I can never tell how Emma will take things – she began to laugh. Peel after peel of laughter. 'Oh, Holly,' she said, 'I do love you.'

So of course we stayed on. Guy left with Jules on the plane and we spent the rest of that week doing what Emma liked, poking round antique shops, visiting ruins, and not spending too long on the beach. Not exactly a riot from my point of view, but I tried to enjoy myself for Emma's sake: if she had thought I was bored, she would have blamed herself for sending Guy away. And she felt guilty enough already about what had happened that night. It had been a kind of false *naïveté* on her part, she said; she had known what was going on and had, in fact, played along, cuddling up to Jules and letting him get her drunk, but she had refused to acknowledge this at the time, and, what was worse, had been angry with me for what was really the result of her own lack of straightforwardness and honesty. This seemed pretty peculiar reasoning to me, and pointless, too, to go on so over something that was over and done and not even important at the time, but I kept my mouth shut. Emma is very sensitive, not like me.

We met Lucas when we changed planes in Rome. I liked the look of him in the Departure Lounge: he wasn't exactly handsome, but he had a friendly, teddybear look, big, square, rather clumsy. When they called our flight, I made sure we were right behind him in the queue and manœuvred Emma so that we sat in seats facing his on the plane.

After we had taken off, we ordered drinks and talked. He was a little shy at first. We exchanged names and Emma blushed and said she thought they had been up at Oxford at the same time. 'At least, I remember *you*,' she said quickly, as if it would have been the most utter presumption to have expected him to remember her. She chatted away after that, about Oxford and people they both might have known there, and he listened politely, not saying very much. I said once, 'People at Oxford! It's like some kind of secret society,' and he laughed then and looked at me in an interested way, but most of the time I had the idea that although he was glad of our company, he was really thinking about something else.

Emma said, 'I must tell you – I do admire your work so much,' looking rather nervous as if this were a daring remark. He made some vague reply, nothing to give me a lead, and when he went to the Gents, I asked Emma what his work was.

'He's Lucas Bligh,' she said, 'oh, *Holly*.'

'A television comic?' I said. 'Or an astronaut?' She shook her head, sighing elaborately, as if my ignorance would be the death of her. 'All right, I give up.'

'He's a *novelist*.'

'There are thousands of novelists,' I said, rather crossly, but she looked so happy at this moment – giving off a kind of gentle sparkle – that I relented. 'All right, all *right*. I'm just an uneducated loon.'

'Oh *Holly*,' she said, very affectionately, but her eyes were watching for Lucas coming out of the loo, and it struck me, suddenly, that the trouble with Jules had not been her conscience – or not entirely, anyway – but just that he wasn't her type.

## 3. *Henry*

People are attracted either to their own type or to opposites. One seldom makes generalizations without thinking of particulars: I am thinking of Holly and Emma. They are so different, almost like people from different planets: there is no point of contact, of judgement. Emma is fascinated. She cannot explain this fascination. Instead, she says, 'Holly had a terrible childhood.'

I said, 'We all had terrible childhoods. That's the way to duck out from under.'

We often discuss Holly. This was one summer evening, sitting in deckchairs and watching the boys play croquet on the lawn. The philadelphus was in blossom: starred white flowers and a heavy scent. I remember thinking – Why do we always talk about other people?

'I'm sorry for her. She's not happy, you know.' Saying this, Emma looked like her mother, who believes unhappiness gives you a moral advantage.

'You only say that because you wouldn't be, if you were her.'

Emma blushed. She blushes very easily, even now. The first time I saw her, at a party, I spilled my drink down her dress and she blushed as if my clumsiness were her fault. My stammer came back and I couldn't get out an apology. She said, 'You don't have to say you're sorry, but if you really want to, stop and start again,' – so practical and serious and concerned, that I think I fell in love with her then. I say 'think' because I cannot recognize this emotion now, only the actions that sprang from it. I love Emma, I cannot imagine life without her, but that is a different matter. Falling in love is something you forget, like pain; there are only irrelevancies left, the hospital bed, the girl at the party with long, mermaid's hair. But I know I felt drunk, though I had arrived late and it was my first drink I had spilled down her dress. I said, 'That's the first time I've stammered for years, what have you done to me?' She looked shy and I wanted to give her something. I told her how I had cured myself and she smiled in the right way and asked, 'Were they good jokes? Did people laugh?' I said I couldn't remember. 'I've never told anyone before. Now you know the guarded

37

secret of my soul.' She looked at me with her truthful eyes and I said, 'I tell a lie. I always tell girls I like the look of.' This was a lie, too. I said, 'Let's leave this dreadful non-party and go and have supper.'

Emma said, 'I can't imagine being Holly.'

'You couldn't.' I chuckled: this evening I was an extremely successful young man, very pleased with himself and with his beautiful and honest wife. I said, 'Holly hates men.'

This is true. Holly sees each sexual encounter as a fight to the death. At parties, she is like someone going into battle. Gladiator's eyes. I tell myself – I am sorry for Felix.

I said, 'She wants to humiliate them. She's getting her own back because her father left her mother.'

Emma put back her head and laughed. Gin – her own gin this time – splashed into her lap. She looked about fifteen with her hair coming down. I threw her my handkerchief and she dabbed at her skirt. I said, 'It really is true, you know.'

She said, 'I was laughing at *you*. First you say it's the easy way out, to blame one's parents. And now you say this about Holly. You say I'm guilt-ridden because of my mother. You try on arguments like *hats*.'

Her expression was triumphant. I said, 'I didn't say one couldn't explain people's behaviour that way, just that one needn't excuse it. You can't help what you are, but you can help what you do. That's what's important.'

I thought – How smug!

The philadelphus glimmered in the dusk. The boys had vanished from the lawn, leaving the croquet mallets on the grass. I said, 'Shouldn't they go to bed soon?'

Emma said, 'You think it's only what people do that's important?'

'Ultimately, yes.'

'Not what they think?'

'That only determines how they behave.'

'Not always. People have fantasies – secret lives. They don't act on them.'

I was bored with this conversation.

'You mean, shop girls and pop stars?'

'Not necessarily. Why do you say *shop girls* in that silly way?'

I said, 'I didn't mean to be snobbish. It was just shorthand. Meaning a kind of fantasy that's so remote from reality that it can't possibly affect it. Wasn't that what you meant?' Her face was turned away. For some reason, I thought she was angry. I reached out and took her hand. I laughed, teasing her, 'I'm sure I never said you were guilt-ridden because of your mother!'

Emma's mother is a large, calm blonde; a dogmatic and dynamic personality whom I am fond of and admire, but cannot get close to. She has too many defences: to attempt an intimate conversation with her would be like besieging the walls of Acre. We discuss certain set topics: the children, my father's health, the misfortunes of her friends, the iniquities of the Government. One avoids any personal problem – 'whining' – and any remark which has the slightest whisper of sexuality – 'that sort of thing is so tedious.' This was a lesson I learned early in our acquaintance. I discovered that she always carried a drum of pepper in her coat pocket when she went out. I said, 'To keep off the rapists?' 'No, Henry, to stop dog fights.' She spoke calmly enough, but her eyes were glacial: my mild little joke was 'boring'.

My mother-in-law would certainly feel it her duty to interfere in a dog fight. She is not a woman to pass by on the other side. She teaches botany to sixth form girls and, in her spare time, does a great deal for other people. Not fund-raising or committees, but personally, with her large, fair, capable hands. As a result, she possesses a kind of sinking fund of disaster on which she can call in order to rebuke the more fortunate. Once, when Emma went to Sicily with Holly, her mother came to look after the boys. She arrived hot foot from caring for a neighbour who had just had her left lung removed. 'Poor Mrs Jones, *she* can't afford any help

39

in the house, let alone a holiday. You're a lucky girl, Emma, I hope you know how lucky. . . .'

In a comic way, a splendid woman. Emma has inherited her conscience.

When my father had his second stroke, Emma said, 'We'll have to look after him.'

We had been visiting him in hospital and were driving home.

I said, 'It would be too much for you.' She had been having headaches recently and had to rest in the afternoons. I worried about her. I said, 'We'll have to find a nursing home. Some of these places aren't too bad, more like hotels, really.'

'He'd hate to leave his house. You know that. *We* could live there.'

'Could you bear to?' We had this house in Islington. It was cramped now that the twins were growing; the plaster was cracking on the walls under the gay travel posters and damp was rising in the basement. We were happy there. I disliked my father's house. It was haunted by my mother's complaining ghost. Her spiteful anger.

'It would be nice for the boys to have a garden,' Emma said. 'And anyway, we haven't any choice. Have we?'

My father was paralysed down one side. It was thought he would recover to some extent, but he would never work again. I said, 'The business will have to be sold up. I suppose that's enough of a blow to be going on with.'

I wanted to make amends for this. I was a disappointment to my father who had hoped I would take over the antique business he had built up, with his own energy and my mother's money, from a second hand shop in Kilburn. My mother had wanted me to be a solicitor: she reverenced the professions and thought my father's occupation common. She was a brigadier-general's daughter, a quite remarkably cold and stupid woman who believed she had married beneath her. I never understood why she had: when I was adolescent, I was convinced she must have been pregnant and went through her desk, one afternoon when she was out, to look for her marriage lines. I had been born two years after the ceremony in Marylebone Registry Office. She had been over thirty then, so perhaps it had been an act of desperation.

I knew, even when I was quite small, how much she regretted it, and why. She insisted that I go away to school. 'Otherwise you'll pick up your father's accent.' She persuaded him not to visit me there. 'I don't want to embarrass you with your friends, dear.' She refused to go to restaurants with him. 'Because he will speak in that loud, common voice, and use toothpicks.' It was a kind of madness, of course, but at the time it seemed part of the natural order of things. I loved my father but I learned to be ashamed of him.

I joined the Navy when I was seventeen. This was a little after the war. I believed this was what I had always wanted to do. In fact, as I realized quite soon, it was an easy option: I had run away to sea to escape from my parents' different ambitions for me. When I tried to resign, five years later, my captain refused at first to forward my application. 'You want to go to Oxford?' he said. 'You've been elected to the finest gentleman's club in the world and you want to leave it to go to *Oxford*?'

I was a grown man then, and I was ashamed because I thought he was sneering at my father through me. I thought he must have heard him talking, one time when he came down to the ship to visit me.

Class was important – or fashionable – then. People wrote plays about it; they don't now. I am getting to the age when I will soon begin to think times are changing for the worse, but this is one way I know they have changed for the better.

Another thing that happens as you grow older, is that your personal life diminishes – not in quantity but in quality.

When Felix and I went up to Oxford, we were both very inward-looking. What we did was less important than why. We discussed emotions, morals, relationships. We had ambitions which were nothing to do with jobs, with earning a living. Our crises were spiritual, not financial; we could not imagine worrying about money. Felix wrote poetry; I had finished two acts of a play. I kept a polished skull on my desk and believed the most important thing about life was to learn how to die. We were very wise and sad. Now – at what point did this happen? – my work is serious, my private life is not. I go home at night and fall asleep in front of the television.

I work in a large firm of solicitors. I handle the divorce side. All day I listen to tales of betrayal, anguish and despair. There is occasionally comedy on the surface, seldom underneath. Now and again, women cry: I give them a cigarette and send out for a cup of tea. I think – Would Emma behave like this if I left her? Sit in some man's office and cry? I cannot imagine it. It is always other people who lead extraordinary lives. I tell myself – I am glad mine is so successfully dull. While the tea and the cigarette do their work, I stand with my back to my client, looking out of the window.

My office looks out onto a courtyard where there are reddish cobble-stones set in patterns and a modern fountain: pinnacles and blunt, round shapes. The pinnacles spurt blue water. They are made of some non-organic material that has a sparkly surface, imitating granite. This fountain is much admired. To have a room facing it, is considered a sign of success.

Lucas Bligh came to my room one afternoon. A big, untidy man with lumpy features and limp, boyish hair. The name and the face raised a stir in me, like a half-forgotten smell.

We had been at Oxford at the same time. Acquaintances, not friends. I was an ex-Naval officer, smooth, affectedly cynical; he was fresh out of school, an ingenious, rather grubby, loutish boy with a common accent. Now he wrote novels, intellectual thrillers with exotic backgrounds. He was a success: I had seen his name in the newspapers. The accent had changed a little; his appearance hardly at all.

I said, 'I'm afraid I don't have much time for reading.' I was half-apologetic, half-vindictive: novelists think they are so special. I thought – If he can't sew on his own buttons, at least he could wipe the egg off his tie. To make up for thinking this, I smiled at him. (My charming, lop-sided smile.)

He smiled back. He was too successful to mind this kind of remark. He had been recommended to my firm by a friend who had recently gone through a particularly messy divorce.

He said, 'I'm afraid mine is very straightforward,' as if I might think he was wasting my time.

'That's how we like it.'

He was nervous at first: he had had to screw himself up to this. He smoked small cigars, stubbing them out halfway through, like cigarettes. He spoke in short, deliberate sentences; his face had gone stiff. He said, at the end, 'I didn't know this would be so difficult.'

'As you said, it seems very straightforward.'

His wife had left him for an American film producer, two years ago. They were now living in Rome. There were no children involved.

He wanted to know how long it would take. I told him. He said, 'This seems very unreal.'

'It usually does.'

He said, 'It must seem comic to you, the way everyone thinks their own case so exceptional.'

'Not at all. It is, to them.'

'Do you have to keep reminding yourself of that?'

He seemed genuinely interested. It was flattering. I said, 'At first, perhaps. Now I just respond in the right way, without thinking. Like an actor, I suppose. After a long run in the theatre.'

He lit one of his cigars and held it between his spread knees, leaning forward like a workman sitting on a bench. I opened the cigarette box on my desk and closed it again. I sat, cracking my knuckles. He said, 'I started a novel the day she left. Not a thriller. It began, *The day my divorce became absolute, I was thirty and feeling my age.*'

'Did you finish it?'

'No. I never get beyond the first sentence. I didn't know how it would go on.'

'Will you write it now?' This interested me. Sometimes I thought – I could write a novel about some of the things I hear in this office, if only I had the time. I was only half-mocking myself.

'I don't know.' He looked up. 'I'm sorry, you're too busy for this.'

'No. It's all right. I've no one else coming this afternoon.'

He rubbed the palm of his hand over his chin. Gingery bristles, at least two days' growth, glinted in the sun that came through the window. A forest of tiny needles. He said, 'I've not talked about this much. I didn't want to at first. I suppose I hoped she'd come back. My friends might have told me the truth.' He smiled suddenly. 'I felt humiliated, too. That's always hard to admit.'

'Most people don't try. They get angry instead.'

'Do they?' He seemed surprised. I thought – For a novelist, he's remarkably innocent. But then I don't know many novelists.

I said, 'When did you make up your mind that it was all over?'

'Last week. I woke up one morning. . . .' He stopped. 'I ought to have known before. I went to see her in Rome, over a year ago. It was all very calm. My – my wife is a very calm person. Not the kind of woman who makes scenes. She never even talked much. We sat in a restaurant and she asked me to divorce her. She might have been saying she wanted to buy a new hat. She said she would stay with Walter whether I divorced her or not, but it would be more convenient if they could get married. It was all in such a low key, I couldn't believe it. By the time I got on the plane, I didn't believe it.' He looked at me shyly. 'I suppose this sounds foolish.'

'No.'

His air of simple, sad bewilderment depressed me. My job forces me – or is this a game I play? – to act different parts with different people. With some I am a priest, or at least a kindly, avuncular figure; with others, simply a technician called in to repair an irritating defect in the machinery of their lives. For Lucas Bligh, I could see I was to be the undertaker, assisting at the last rites. On the whole, this is the role I like least. Mourners tend to be passive, even, sometimes, mutely reproachful, as if it were I and not they who had ordered the funeral.

I said, after we had arranged a few details, 'By the way, my wife's an admirer of your's. She's read all your books.'

His face lit up with such unselfconscious pleasure – this second-hand compliment might have been the one thing in the world he most wanted to hear – that I felt ashamed, as if I had spoken patronizingly.

I said, 'I'm sure she'd love to meet you. But I imagine you're busy . . . ?'

'Not at all. I fact, I'm a bit lonely. I've only just moved to London – we had this house in Gloucestershire and it seemed absurd to go on living there alone, it's a great barn of a place – but it's not only that. I've been avoiding people, as I said. If you do that long enough, your friends drift away.'

He wasn't moaning, simply stating a fact. It was absurd to be irritated by the honest, easy amplitude of his answer. False pride is despicable, after all. I thought – Maybe, but it protects us from each other. Why should I care if he's lonely?

I reminded myself that I was on edge just now because I had given up smoking. I was afraid I had been irritable with this man, because I had had to watch him, puffing away. I wanted to make amends. I said, 'If you're doing nothing this evening, would you like to come and have supper?'

We walked from the station. He said, 'You're sure your wife won't mind, my turning up like this?'

'She sounded pleased enough when I rang her.' It struck me that perhaps his own wife had been difficult over this sort of thing, the kind of incompetent woman who can't cope with unexpected guests, the house in a mess, nothing in the larder. 'Emma never makes a fuss,' I said.

It was a fine evening. Sun after a brief shower of rain, and a smell of grass.

'It's a nice suburb,' he said.

'When I was a boy, there were fields all round. And a stream with trout in it.'

'It's still nice, all this green.' He sniffed the shrub-scented air like a dog. 'I grew up in the East End. Miles of rabbit-hutches, not a tree in sight.'

I thought – Am I supposed to be impressed by this? I laughed and said, 'I'm afraid my father's house isn't exactly a rabbit hutch.'

Built of Cotswold stone with turrets and mullioned windows, it is of no recognizable architectural vintage and merely expresses my father's personality. 'Tradesman's Gothic,' I said, when Bligh paused at the gate and surveyed its façade, astonishing in this suburban street: the studded, baronial door and the flight of steps flanked by small stone lions. This was a term my mother had overheard at a charity coffee morning. I had been about nine, then. She had come home and cried all afternoon, lying on her bed with the curtains drawn. I had been frightened, alone in the house with her. Our maid – we had had a series of maids – had gone away the day before. She was a kind and cheerful girl who had taught me to play Racing Demon. She had left suddenly, I did not know why nor dared to ask: the most innocent question could, I knew, provoke one of my mother's 'states', seeming to spring some trap inside her mind and releasing either tears or anger. Both were equally inexplicable, but the tears terrified me more. I sat on the stairs most of that afternoon, listening to her sobbing which seemed to me not pitiful but pitiless, and longing for my father to come home.

When he did, he persuaded her to come downstairs and have a glass of sherry. She lay on the sofa, exhausted with grief, looking like a drowned bird. He sat beside her, patting her hand and calling her 'old lady'. He was always gentle with her, almost guiltily so, as if in some humble area of his mind he had accepted her preposterous princess-and-barrow-boy assessment of their marriage and wished to make amends for the social damage he had done her. Or perhaps it was simply that he was naturally tender towards women, romantically respecting weakness and tears as a sign of proper delicacy. 'Your poor Mother suffers with her nerves,' he said, when I was in bed that evening and he came to say good night. 'It's a great affliction.' He seemed tolerant and cheerful, flushed with whisky and smoking a cigar. But several times after that I saw him standing at the gate and staring up at his house with an air of bewildered concentration. I say 'several times' and 'after that', but I have no occasion into which I can fit this memory. Only the picture recorded on my nine-year-old retina and the feeling that went with it, of my own impotent, immeasureable sadness. My euphoric, jolly father wrung my heart. I cannot remember once feeling sorry for my mother.

Lucas Bligh stood at the gate where my father had stood. 'It has a lot of character.' He searched for a word. 'Panache.'

'So had my father.' *Vulgarity*, my mother called it. In an era of bowler hats and dark suits, he had worn brocade waistcoats and ruffled shirts and buttoned spats. He had been proud of his hair, which he wore thick and unfashionably long, and he always used a brand of very highly scented

47

toilet water. 'Of course, he's an old man now,' I said, as we walked up what should have been, considering the general conception of the house, a sweeping carriage drive, but was, in fact, only a short, crazy-paving path between standard roses.

In the drawing-room, the windows were open onto the terrace. Emma was wearing a white dress that I had not seen before. White is a bad colour for her, it makes her look washed-out. Only dark women and very young girls should wear white.

She said, to Lucas, 'It's lovely to see you again,' and then, quickly. 'We met on the plane from Rome. About fifteen months ago.'

'Of course,' he said. I was sure he did not remember this. But he sounded warm, pleased: a nice, good-natured man. It was unreasonable of me to resent this. His eyes went past Emma to Holly, helping my father in from the terrace. I thought – *Now* he has remembered.

Holly is unforgettable.

Emma and I went to say goodnight to the twins. They have the room in the tower. I used to play in this room when I was a boy, but my mother refused to let me sleep there. There are windows all round, impossible to curtain. My mother had said, *Someone might see you undressing*.

Rufus was wearing orange-peel teeth. Fangs. 'I'm Dracula,' he said, leaping on William with a gargling cry. 'I'm going to suck his blood.'

William smiled bravely but his eyes pleaded. I picked Rufus up, tickled him until the orange peel dropped out of his mouth and said, 'You know, your feet are *filthy*.'

'I thought they could do without a bath tonight,' Emma said. 'There wasn't much time.'

'I'm sorry. Did you mind my asking him? I thought you'd be pleased.'

'I am.' She was picking up the boys' clothes, folding them.

48

She was wearing her hair down this evening; it fell forward, parting at the back, and the nape of her neck looked small and vulnerable.

I said, 'Have you got Mrs Thing in to wash up?'

Rufus said, 'It's rude to say Mrs Thing, isn't it, Mummy?'

'Yes. Daddy wasn't thinking. No, I didn't bother. She's got her husband and son to get a meal for. I think there's a lodger as well.'

'Why did you ask Holly?'

'Felix has a Talk to write. And I thought she'd like to meet Lucas again. I did *tell* you – we met him on our way home from Sicily.'

'I don't remember.' I had a preposterous idea. *She's using Holly as a bait*. Emma blushed as if I had said this aloud, but she was thinking of something else. 'You don't mind her coming, do you?'

'Why should I?' I laughed, over-acting astonishment.

'Well. . . .'

I wondered – Does she ever think, *this myth that Henry dislikes Holly*? She was looking at me, her lower lip caught by her teeth. She looked so young, about twenty, and tired. I said, 'You look tired, Mouse.'

'Do I?' She frowned in the mirror over the wash basin, touching her hair.

'I didn't mean plain.' I put an arm round her and pulled her against me. I thought – I love my wife.

William and Rufus groaned together. William said, 'All this love nonsense.'

Emma laughed. We kissed them goodnight. I felt calm and cheerful. We were a happy family, living in a mildly eccentric house and looking after an old man whom some people might have put in a home, pushed out of sight. That was how Bligh would see us. I thought – Why should I care how he sees us?

On the landing. Emma said, 'I'm afraid we've run out of whisky.'

'Father?'

She nodded, looking guilty. I patted her shoulder and said magnanimously, 'You can't watch him every minute of the day. I suppose we ought to lock it up.'

'It seems awful.'

'That can't be helped. We can pretend we've lost the key or something.'

We went down the stairs. I could hear my mother's voice in my mind. *Your father must have been raving mad. Building a house round a staircase. I never heard anything so ridiculous in my whole life.*

My father was talking in the drawing-room. This must be one of his good days. Lucas and Holly were laughing. I said, 'Well, what have we got left?'

'Gin. Sherry. I think there's some brandy. Not much.'

'I'd better get something from Felix.'

I rubbed my hand up and down her back. Her shoulder blades sprang out like wings. She said, 'Don't *do* that, Henry, you'll make my dress dirty.'

Felix's house is very modern and compact, full of light wood and trailing house plants and low, streamlined furniture. A rising young executive's house, of the kind that is photographed in smart magazine's: not the sort of house I would have expected Felix to buy. He has a study upstairs. It opens out of the bedroom which has a white, deep-pile carpet and an enormous round bed, very low and voluptuous. There is a large mirror on the opposite wall. I thought – Emma would find that inhibiting. As I passed this mirror, I pulled a face at myself, elongating my jaw; and straightened my shoulders. I am tall and thin and have a tendency to stoop which I sometimes try to correct and sometimes exaggerate: I have a picture of myself, striding along like an animated pair of scissors, my scholarly head poked forward. An eccentric with a shy smile.

Felix was sitting at his desk, typing away. He was wearing

very large, horn-rimmed spectacles, like a disguise. He said, 'Of course, Henry. Take whatever you want. Downstairs. You know where.' He took off his glasses and sucked one end, frowning. 'What a bore about your father.'

'Emma can't watch him all the time.'

'Poor girl. It is a bit hard.'

'I suppose we'll have to get a nurse, in the end. But Emma's against that, before we have to. Another person in the house, you know, and she thinks he won't like it. She's very fond of him.'

Felix said nothing.

'Women have a lot of patience,' I said. 'I'm sorry you can't come to dinner.'

His brown eyes had a liquid gleam. Sad, like a monkey's. 'I've got a Talk to write. And this report to finish.'

I said, 'You work too hard.'

Felix worked for the Overseas Service of the B.B.C. as Georgian Programme Organizer. He had had a Russian grandmother who retained all her long life the Georgian accent she had learned at her nanny's knee. When he was first appointed, Felix used to say, 'This is the sort of thing that passes for a qualification in my neck of the woods.' At that time, he was shy of admitting he took his job seriously. Now it was rapidly becoming the only thing he talked about.

He said, 'No choice, just now.' He frowned. 'This damn committee.'

There was always some damn committee. This one had been set up by the Foreign Office who had recently produced the opinion that minority language broadcasting was neither useful nor particularly desirable. 'It's suddenly supposed to be tactless to broadcast to the Soviet Union in anything other than Russian,' Felix said sourly. 'Very convenient, since the Government have decided they want to economize! And on the surface, so plausible. They say – after all, if Georgian, why not Armenian, Mongol, Kazakh?'

'Well. . . .' I pulled a face.

'Georgian is an historical *accident*. Some B.B.C. bigshot had an affair with a Georgian girl in Paris in 1932. Not much of an argument, exactly. Nor is the general principle that one is against the sudden axing of any service, because one knows what will happen.' He looked at me indignantly, as if I had denied this. 'You close a service down, dismiss all your unfortunate chaps, and – hey presto! There's an international crisis and they're all screaming for it to be started up again. As if it was like turning on a tap. But you've lost your staff. And your *audience*, for Christ's sake. Since you've gone off the air, they're listening to Moscow, or Peking, or Cairo! But it's a waste of time telling them that. They want facts and figures, they say. Practical men. . . .'

He sighed, rubbed at one eye with the heel of his hand. 'Cost per listener. Some loon worked it out at one-sixteenth of a penny per day. All pretty bogus. I mean – how can you apply cost efficiency to this sort of information service? Do you measure it in advertising terms, or defence, or national-political interest, or what? Bloody ridiculous.' He peered at me. 'I'm sorry. *Boring*. Particularly when you've heard it all before.'

I had. Some similar crisis, anyway. And since other people's job-obsessions always seem slightly ludicrous, I had assumed his work was an anodyne. I thought – But if I ask him if this is true, he will only look surprised, rub his eyes, make some gesture with his spectacles. He has retreated behind – has *become* – a series of mannerisms. Camouflaged for protection.

I thought – I used to know what he was like. If I had to describe him now, I could only say: he is my greatest friend, a small, fattish, rather foreign-looking man in his middle thirties who frowns and makes gestures. His parents were musicians. His English father played the bassoon, his half-Russian mother, the French horn. A pale, willowy, shy man with an old-fashioned, upper class voice; a small, soft, ripe woman, like a Goya painting. Felix speaks like his father and looks like his mother. But he is not musical. He is an expert in Russian history and he works for the B.B.C. And he loves his daughter: this is about the only way to get through to him now.

There was a photograph of Ginny on his desk. A beautiful, dark child with a wistful air. She was at an unbelievably expensive boarding school in Kent. I sometimes wondered how Felix could afford it. He earned a lot less than I did and there was no family money. His parents had lived in an old house in Hampstead that was rather grand in a derelict way – the walls of the music room were lined with pale, rotting silk – but when they died, within a month of each other in our second year at Oxford, the sale of the lease fetched only just enough to cover their overdraft.

I said, 'That's a new picture, isn't it? You can see she's your daughter, all right,' and immediately wished I had put it differently. I thought – Does Felix ever need to be re-assured about that?

'I hope not. If she does, it's rotten luck, poor kid.' His eyes were suddenly alive, unguarded. 'Do you know what she said in her last letter? I've got a new friend this week, but I'm keeping Angela on for a bit. She'll do as a spare tyre.'

I said, 'Kids have no false shame.'

We laughed.

Felix said, 'Boys all right?'

'Fine.'

He grinned at me. 'How's the will power holding out?'

'All right, so far.' I had a theory that if I told people I had stopped smoking, pride would stiffen my resolve. Felix had stopped last year. I said, 'The trouble is, not smoking takes up so much of one's mind that it becomes a full time occupation. Then you think – This is a fat lot of good if I can't work! I may live longer, but I'll be out of a job.'

'Wife and children starving in the streets. I remember all that. It wears off in the end.'

'You're a stronger character than I am.' This was something one said: it struck me now that I had once believed it to be true.

'Oh, yes?'

Felix put on his glasses. They were slightly tinted and made him look mysterious. He had sounded defensive. I believed I knew why, but it was something we couldn't talk about. I thought – We used to be able to talk to each other, ask questions. How do you feel about being – do people use the word cuckold nowadays? – about *your position*, old chap? Do you get a ration, say Tuesdays and Thursdays, on that vulgar Hollywood bed? Do you have a girl yourself? Skinny secretary, or plump widow? I thought – Henry, my boyo, you're becoming a sly, prurient, old man.

I said, 'What's your position? If you can't convince this committee. Will you lose your job?'

He put the tips of his fingers together and leaned back in his chair. 'I suppose I can get another. I'm an administrator. There's something on the cards as a matter of fact. It's the linguists who'll be in trouble. Who wants a Georgian translator? We've got one chap who's been with the programme twenty-five years.'

This was the sort of thing that would worry Felix. Keep him awake at night.

He said angrily, 'That's supposed to be irrelevant, of course.'

'Everything can be made to look irrelevant. That's the great trick. The way to stop people fighting.'

'Yes.' He looked, suddenly, much more cheerful. He said, 'Well, I'd better get on with it. Defending my cabbage patch.'

I thought how fond I was of him.

I said, 'I'll go and forage, then. You will get something to eat, won't you?'

# 4. *Emma*

Dear Lucas,

How kind of you to write; people don't often nowadays. We enjoyed the evening, too. My father-in-law was so *pleased* to meet a real, live author, he reads a lot now he can't get about anymore. You'll be amused to hear that when we made our weekly expedition to the library this morning, he got out two of your boks and boasted to the librarian that he knew you! Such is fame! *Do* come and see us again – and not just for his pleasure, for ours, too!

Yours,
Emma.

Dear Lucas,

What about Friday next week? We're having a small firework party – for the boys' birthday *ostensibly*, but for any adult, too, who is still childish enough to enjoy fireworks. I must admit I do! Catherine wheels especially – so magical! And Roman candles! My mother would never let me have fireworks when I was a child, she said – quite rightly, I suppose – that they were a shameful waste of money when people were starving all over the world. But oh, how I longed for them all the same! I do hope you can come. Don't bother to ring or anything, there will be plenty of food for anyone who feels like turning up. Holly is making a goulash – that alone is well worth the journey!

Emma.

My dear Lucas,

I'm glad you enjoyed the fireworks. And sorry I didn't have much chance to talk to you – always difficult at one's own parties. Still, Holly looked after you nicely. She told me afterwards about your divorce. I'm so sorry. Henry told me you'd come to see him so I knew there must be something like that, though of course he didn't discuss any details with me. I *am* sorry. What else can one say? It must be such a terrible shock when someone you've loved and trusted lets you down.

Do come and see us whenever you feel like it. Don't wait for an invitation, just come. I'm almost always here because of Father, and there will always be a welcome for you. I really mean it!

Emma.

*Dear* Lucas,

How sweet of you to come down and bring your new book for Father! I'm *so* sorry I missed you. My own silly fault – I should have explained that *Thursday* is the one day I'm not here, I go to London where I work with this committee in Islington and Holly keeps an eye on my poor old pa-in-law for me. She's marvellous with him, though you mightn't think she'd have the patience; bullies him and flirts with him which he enjoys quite tremendously. He's always very skittish when she's coming and fusses over what tie to wear, poor old chap! Holly says she gave you lunch after she'd put him down for his nap, so I'm glad it wasn't *quite* a fruitless journey, though I wish I'd been here all the same. Come another time – any day except Thursday!

Yours,<br>Emma.

My dear Lucas,

*What* a nice idea! We'd love to come to your party. Henry may be a bit late though, he has to go down to the *wilds* of Essex to see a woman who can't come to see him because her husband has knocked her about so badly. He actually broke her front teeth and fractured her jaw – a terrible story! Our combined baby-and-father sitter can't get here until six, so I won't arrive until seven. But Holly says she'll come a bit early and give you a hand with what she called the 'bits and pieces'.

My pa-in-law sends his regards. He says you must have had a very *interesting life*. He says this entirely with reference to that scene with the blonde in the Russian hotel. People's choice of euphemisms is very curious. My mother says 'boring' when she means 'sexy'; my father-in-law says 'interesting'.

I thought that particular scene had a flavour of wish-fulfilment, if you don't mind my saying so!

I am so looking forward to the party.

Emma.

Dear Lucas,

A lovely evening! I'm so sorry we had to leave early. But Henry did seem so tired and though I suppose I could have stayed and come home with Holly, it seemed a bit mean not to drive him back after he'd had that awful time in Essex. It was foggy going home, we had to *crawl* all the way. Henry kept going to sleep and waking up and saying, 'Aren't we home *yet*?' as if the weather was my fault! Who was it said that the main point of getting married was to have someone always on hand to grouse at?

Father was very grumpy when we got back. He *said* because the sitter had boiled the milk and there was skin on his Horlicks, but it was really because we'd been to a party and he was envious. I think he envisaged scenes of *unimaginable vice* – when Henry was out of the room he kept saying, 'Well, what did you get up to, eh?' – winking and leering. I suppose it's a bit hard, when you've been a gay spark all your life, to have to give up and sit in the chimney corner!

Thank you for a splendid party. I *loved* that queer woman with piebald hair – dark at the back and growing out white in front – and that strange, wild face. Like a painting by Stanley Spencer. I talked to her a lot – or rather she talked to me – but I can't remember a word she said because I couldn't take my eyes off her. She must be a poet or a spy or at least a romantic novelist. If you have a minute, do let me know. I'm *fascinated*.

With affection,<br>Emma.

Lucas my duck,

Well, who'd 'a thought it, eh? A typist, living in Ealing! Even if she's lucky enough to type *your* books, it must be a dullish life! Perhaps she looks the way she does as a kind of compensation? Of course it would 'amuse' me to meet her again, how sweet of you to think of it! I'm afraid I'm not actually free for *lunch* on Thursday because of this committee – I don't know whether I told you or not but it's to do with setting up adventure playgrounds in Islington and thereabouts. We lived in Islington before we moved here. The recreational facilities are absolutely shocking, there is *nowhere* for children to play. Not a patch of green, not a blade of grass! When we lived in Islington, the only thing that grew in our street was a laburnum tree and the man it belonged to cut it down because he said it kept the light out of his bathroom! And the children run wild in the streets and people are surprised when they steal and smash things!

No lunch, then, because I *do* take this seriously and think it worth-while. And it's all I do, outside running the house and looking after Father. I suppose you could call that a full-time job, really, particularly lately. He won't let me out of his sight! He likes to talk and Henry's often too tired in the evening, and though I try to be a good listener there *are* other things to be done and when you have heard a story twenty times it's difficult to listen on the twenty-first occasion with the same *rapt attention*.

I could come for tea, or if that's no good, a drink about six? Do say if this doesn't suit, I shan't be in the least put out!

Emma.

P.S. I didn't mean to *moan* about Father. He's really a dear old boy and I'm *tremendously* fond of him.

The potatoes were peeled for supper, the casserole in the oven. Old Mr Lingard sat on the terrace in the pale sun, waiting for Emma to take out his tea.

While the kettle boiled, Emma stood at the kitchen window. Her private eye saw, not the autumn garden, but the white-capped waves of the Solent. She and Henry were spending the weekend with the Cravens; Henry and Holly were sailing the Craven's boat, a shred of blue sail, far out to sea. She and Felix were watching. A storm came up in the Solent: standing helplessly on the pier, they watched the boat capsize. Emma turned to Felix, weeping, and he put his arms round her. He was a smallish, pale-skinned man, with thick-fingered, capable hands.

The kettle began to sing. Emma gave a short, embarrassed laugh, made the tea, put the pot on the tray with milk, sugar and a plate of digestive biscuits, and carried it out to the terrace.

'You're sure it's not too cold for you, Father?' She fetched a rug and tucked it round his knees. As she bent over him, his hand darted forward and caressed her thigh. She moved away quickly and poured his tea, not looking at him, and the old man chuckled.

'Stay and have a cup of tea with me, Em?'

His speech was slightly slurred, but otherwise, sitting down, he showed no signs of disability: his heavy, handsome face was mottled but looked younger than his years, his eyes, set in their soft, yellowing pouches, were sharp and knowing.

'Henry's going to be late,' she said. 'I thought we'd have an early supper with the children, then you can have a nice evening watching television.'

'What's he up to? Got a bit of skirt somewhere has he?'

'I shouldn't think so, Father.'

'I shouldn't think so, Father! You're a prissy miss, aren't you? Why do you always call me Father when you're annoyed with me?'

'I don't think I do. I'm not annoyed.'

'Don't you wonder what he's up to?'

Emma didn't answer. She sat in a basketwork chair, gazing across the lawn and picking bits of fluff off her woollen skirt.

'A woman ought to wonder when her husband comes home late night after night. She ought to be jealous, it means she's got a bit of spunk. I like a woman with a bit of spunk.'

'There's no need to be jealous. Henry's just busy at the moment. He's got a lot of work.'

'Dipping his wick. Precious hard work, that is!' The old man laughed; tea and biscuit crumbs dribbled from the corner of his mouth. 'Tell you what, Em. Why don't you ring up – round about seven, say? Catch the young devil out?'

Emma said nothing. She could feel him watching her. Her stomach muscles were tense.

'Where's your friend Holly, then? I'd keep an eye on her if I were you. In and out all the time, all her goods in the shop window. Nothing on under her sweater, not even a what-d'you-call-it. Nice big bubs like pears. More than flesh and blood can stand, even for an old has-been like me. Henry's not made of stone, you know.'

'Henry doesn't really like Holly. She bores him. You know it as well as I do.'

'Why d'you think he bothers to tell you that? Eh?'

Emma stood up. Immediately, the old man began to whine, 'Don't go, Em. Have another cup of tea.'

She stood with her head averted, denying him the pleasure of seeing the tears in her eyes. 'I don't want to discuss Henry's mythical adventures.'

Mr Lingard sighed. Emma turned to him and saw his eyelids were drooping. Gently, she took the cup from his hand and sat down again. He fell into a doze, his lips faintly parted and twitching into a smile from time to time, like a sleeping baby.

Emma's hands, clasped tightly in her lap, still trembled. He was growing senile, it was foolish to be distressed by the senile drivel of an old man. She should treat it light-heartedly, behave like a brisk, good-humoured nurse. Did he ever talk this way to Holly? Emma decided not: Holly would have told her, made a joke of it. *She* couldn't tell anyone. Henry would be so hurt and ashamed on his father's behalf and worried on hers. He might even insist that the old man should be put in a nursing home. In her mind, her mother's voice said, *You wouldn't want that on your conscience, would you?*

Emma shivered. Thinking of her mother, reminded her of a worse possibility: Henry might not believe her. Backing away from this, she made a curious ducking movement of her head, like a shying horse. . . .

It seemed a bit unnecessary to drown Henry and Holly, just so that she and Felix could go to bed together. Perhaps to believe them drowned would be an adequate enough excuse. A couple of days with Felix would be pleasant. Then Henry and Holly could appear again safe and sound, having drifted for twenty-four hours clinging to the upturned boat, until they were washed up somewhere. The Isle of Wight? The Channel Isles? She and Felix would stay in Southampton while the search was on. There was a comfortable hotel in Southampton where she and Henry had once spent a night. They would drink a lot the first evening, both grieving, so

61

beside themselves with grief that they could not reasonably be held responsible. . . .

'Emma,' Felix said.

She looked up, blushing.

'You look startled,' Felix said.

'Not surprising.' Emma thought about the sinking yacht and the Southampton hotel. Felix did not own a boat and, as far as she knew, was not interested in sailing. Nor was Henry. 'I mean, I wasn't expecting you,' Emma said. 'Do you want tea? I can make some more. This is cold.'

'I like cold tea. No – don't go, I can use your cup,' Felix said.

They both spoke in whispers because of the old man, sleeping.

Emma poured tea. Felix munched on a digestive biscuit and told her that coal miners always took cold tea underground with them. It was so refreshing. He said he was taking a few days' leave. 'I want to get the garden tidied up a bit before I go off at the end of the week.'

'Where this time?' Emma asked. 'It's stupid, you must have told me.'

'Eastern Europe – Yugoslavia, first. As a matter of fact, it's a bit of a try-out – I'm in the running for a new job. Assistant Head of Slavonic Broadcasts. But it won't be a long trip. There a bit of a fuss on. . . .'

He explained why. Emma, half-listening, narrowing her eyes against the slanting sunlight, thought that a couple of days with Felix would certainly be enough, and perhaps it would be better if they met somewhere more exotic than Southampton. She might be flying somewhere and miss a plane and be stranded in Rome or Paris: they would meet by chance at the airport or in some softly-lit bar. Felix, sitting disconsolate in front of his lonely gin, would look up and see her. *Emma, darling.* . . . Though it was not very likely that Felix would be disconsolate, Emma thought. He enjoyed travelling, he was very wrapped up in his job.

'The trouble is, this new committee,' he was saying now. 'It's supposed to investigate the efficiency of the various services, but they're really trying to see where they can make cuts without causing too much of a row. It's absurd, of course, because broadcasting costs so little compared to other forms of national expenditure – on defence, and so on – but there it is, they're out for our blood. Very disheartening.'

'Ridiculous,' Emma said. 'When you think that the whole of the European Services cost less than one armed cruiser.'

Felix never appeared to notice when she fed back to him things he had once told her: he saw it as a sign of intelligence on her part. Now he nodded appraisingly, looking, in his dark suit, with his dark hair and eyes, curiously Byzantine in spite of his white skin. Felix never tanned, however fine the summer. His skin had the smooth, thick, slightly damp texture of a magnolia petal.

He said, 'The other reason I'm not so keen on going away just now is that Ginny's got a free weekend, and I'm not sure that I'll be back in time.'

'I expect she'll spend most of the time with the boys in the tree house. She'll be happy enough. Don't *worry*, Felix.'

'Is the tree house still safe?'

'Henry keeps an eye on it.' Emma smiled patiently, reminding herself that Felix's obsession with his precious daughter was really rather touching. 'And after all – if it holds Will and Rufus, it'll hold Ginny!'

'I suppose so. She's light for her age. I do wish she'd put on a bit of weight.' Felix looked fretful. 'I usually manage to arrange things so I'm here when she's home.'

Emma thought that the conversations she had with Felix in fancy were a good deal more satisfying than the ones she had in fact. And even in fancy, he had recently become less attractive to her. Recognizing this, she felt faintly sad. *It's over*, she said inwardly, and then, *really, this is all very funny*. Felix said, 'What are you smiling at, Emma?', looking at her with a sudden, sharp curiosity that recalled the young man

63

he had been when she first met him, so much in love with his beautiful wife that it had been painful and wonderful to see, but not so absorbed in this love that he had cut himself off from his friends. He had been so interested in everything and everyone; understanding and affectionate and kind. Remembering that Felix, Emma had a sudden impulse to answer him: *because we've been having an affair for the last eighteen months and you have never known it*. In imagination, she saw a gay and intimate discussion; Felix flattered, but recognizing – with perhaps a sigh or two – that this was in no sense an invitation: the perfect, undemanding friend. 'I'm happy with Henry,' she would explain; 'I'm not sexually frustrated or anything tedious like that, it's just that life is not terribly engrossing just at the moment. I'm so tied with Father, and it is a kind of outlet that gives me amusement and pleasure without in any way interfering with the actual conduct of my life. You could even say it's a simple and harmless outlet for a stifled creative imagination.'

*You have too much imagination, Emma,* her mother used to say, as if this was some minor disease that sensible people took prophylactics against, like Vitamin C in winter. 'But make-believe is something different,' she would say to Felix, 'it may pre-suppose imagination but it doesn't involve a real situation, nor, in a sense, real people. The Felix in Rome or Southampton is not you, nor do I really want to go to bed with you. At least,' – this might be hurtful – 'not in real life, only in this dream.'

She said, 'Was I smiling? I didn't know. . . .' He was still watching her, slightly puzzled. She thought – If I were sophisticated enough, I could tell him. She laughed and said, 'I ought to wake Father up. He gets chilled if he sleeps too long.'

'It's still quite warm,' Felix said. 'Marvellous autumn weather.' He looked baffled as if they had been talking about something quite different and she had inexplicably changed the subject. 'You're very good to him, Emma.'

64

'Nonsense! He's a dear old man. I only wish life were a bit less boring for him.' She felt a sudden excitement. 'Actually, he's been very cheered up recently. You missed Lucas Bligh when he came to dinner that evening, didn't you? Well, he was very sweet to Father – in fact, he took the trouble to come down one day and bring him a book. Father was delighted, of course, he talked about nothing else for days. Lucas is very thoughtful.'

Speaking his name made her heart thump.

Felix said, 'Bligh?'

'He's a novelist. *The* novelist, I should say.' Emma heard herself laugh lightly. 'He's well known enough.'

'Not to me. You know I don't read modern novels.' Felix spoke with a mysterious air of self-congratulation.

'What a frightful affectation, Felix!'

'Is it?' He looked amused. 'Why should it make you so indignant, Emma?'

*Dear Lucas, my darling Lucas,*

*I'm sorry for all my letters, my stupid, stiff, silly letters. But of course you know why I write like that, don't you? Only because I can't write the way I want to you. Dear Lucas, I say, and then I write my chatty letter full of terrible shriek marks and Victorian underlinings and silly jokes because all the time all I want to say is my darling, my beloved, my sweet love. You know that, don't you? Of course you do, I don't have to tell you. Perhaps it seems childish to say that no one can feel like this without it being reciprocated, but I think it's true. It is a kind of chemistry – you may be attracted to someone but unless they are attracted to you there is no reaction and it dies a natural death. Does that sound silly? You won't mind if it does, you'll only smile in that sweet, slow way that makes me so happy I want to laugh. I want to laugh all the time, anyway. I am so happy because I love you. I sit with a foolish grin on my face. Last night, Henry said, 'What are you so cheerful about?'*

*It makes me happy just to hear your name spoken. We had*

some people to dinner the other evening and I dragged the conversation round to books, just so I could mention yours and say 'Lucas Bligh'. I even talk to Father about you, though I have to be careful because he's sharper than you might think. I ration myself – once every other day! I could talk to Holly – it's a great temptation – but I won't. She couldn't possibly understand. I don't think she has ever felt like this. Or is capable of it.

I am living for Thursday. I'm sorry Miss Paul will be there, and yet, in a way, I'm not. I long to be alone with you but I love you so much it scares me and you know that, don't you? And you feel the same way yourself, or you wouldn't have asked her to come and told me she would be there. If you'd felt nothing, you wouldn't have bothered to mention it.

Look after yourself my dearest love, please don't die,
                                                    *Emma.*


Darling, darling Lucas,

Was I nasty about Holly? I didn't mean to be. She's a dear, sweet, loyal girl and I'm very fond of her. I only meant that she falls in love so easily that she might not realize how precious this feeling is for you and me.

You'll like Holly — I know you've met her once or twice – I mean, when you really know her. She's not – as she'd be the first to say herself – your type, but you'd like her, appreciate her. Henry doesn't. I think he secretly feels she's a sort of threat. He's never said he's afraid Holly will 'lead me astray' but I suspect this idea does lurk somewhere on the edge of his mind, though he'd hate to admit it, even to himself. He can be a bit pompous, though. He once said, 'Holly inhabits a moral wilderness', which is arrant nonsense, of course. She is a very moral person, in the sense that she never does anything she doesn't believe in. And after all, sexual morality – which is what Henry was talking about – is only behaving the way your society finds it convenient to behave. It has nothing to do with real morality which is laying down a course of action that would be right at all times, for all men. A universal law, didn't Kant say?

*Not that Holly thinks like that. She simply does what she wants when she wants. A kind of natural force, like the wind. And there's absolutely no malice in her, and so much kindness. I used to be a bit shocked by her, but now I think that wasn't so much a distant rumble from my Puritan conscience, but a straight-forward cover-up. Perhaps I wish I was more like her! Do I? You would know. You are not only my love, but my wise, my understanding friend. . . .*

*Your Emma.*

*Dear Love,*

*Thank you, thank you for a lovely time. Poor Miss Paul, I hope she didn't feel too much like a chaperone – though I thought once or twice that no one could possible be in the same room as we were and not know how we felt! She really is funny, isn't she, all wild glances and jingling bangles. Like a fortune teller. But much less of a poor mouse than I'd thought. A character. If she wasn't so odd to look at, I'd almost be jealous, my darling.*

*I'm terribly jealous of you. I've never been jealous before. The other evening, I asked Henry how your divorce was going. He was a bit reluctant to say anything, he's very ethical about these things, but he did say your wife's solicitors were being a bit slow. When he said 'Lucas's wife', I felt quite faint and sick.*

*Do you feel that way about me? Perhaps you wouldn't say so if you did. You've been hurt once, it's natural to be afraid, but you will always be quite safe with me.*

*Oh my love, I felt so natural sitting in your flat on Thursday. As if I'd always been there and this was where I belonged and so it didn't matter Miss Paul being there, because we had all the time in the world before us.*

*Bless you,*
*Emma.*

*P.S. I love you.*
*P.S. I love writing to you. It makes me feel alive.*
*P.S. I hate leaving you, even in a letter.*

Emma opened the drawer of her dressing table. The other

letters were in a large, brown envelope, labelled *Receipts*.
Emma folded this one, slipped it inside and sat for a minute,
smiling at her reflection in the mirror. Her eyes were very
large and dark. She said, aloud, 'Goodness, your hair is a
mess.' She smoothed the loose strands, holding pins in her
mouth. She was trembling and her hands felt sticky.

Her father-in-law called from downstairs. 'Em. *Emma.* . . .'

He was sitting by the fire in the drawing-room. He had
been asleep and was red-faced and crotchety as a woken
baby. 'Window's open, draught down my neck,' he grumbled
as she came in.

She shut the window and made up the fire. Then she
turned to him, brightly smiling. 'Did you have a nice rest?
Would you like your tea now?'

Instead of answering, he said, 'What have you been up to?'

Emma kept her smile fixed. 'Nothing, Father. Just dull
things. Letters, bills. . . .'

'You don't look like that. Too cheerful.' He sat upright,
belched, and contemplated her with sudden malice. 'You
look to me like a girl who's just had a nice, jolly time in bed!'

Dear Lucas,

So nice seeing you Thursday and I thought your Miss
Paul such fun! I could have stayed all evening listening to
her stories, but alas, duty called! Poor Holly had had
rather a tough day with Father, so she was glad to see me
back. She says we ought to put him in a home, but I can't
do that to the old boy. Could you?

Felix – Holly's husband – will be home next week.
You've never met him, have you? Each time you've come
down he's been busy or off somewhere. He can be a bit
pernickety sometimes, but he's a darling, really, and I
think you'd like him. Would you like to come to supper
on Friday or Saturday week? We'd so like it if you could,

Yours,

Emma.

# 5. *Holly*

If I'd thought for a minute that Emma was really keen on Lucas, I'd never have taken up with him. I have a few principles. No married men – washing lipstick off handkerchiefs and disguising your voice on the telephone gets tedious in the end however much fun it may seem in the beginning – nor the men my girl friends have their eyes on. There are women who are only interested in a man if he belongs to someone else, but I'm not like that. If Emma had given me the least hint. I'd have stood on one side at once and said, 'Bless you, my children.' Trust Aunt Holly.

I don't mean that I wasn't fond of Lucas, just that it wasn't a great, groaning, earth-shaking passion – and thank God for that! But of course I *liked* him. He was a very likeable type – one of those big, clumsy men who seem confident enough on the surface but are really terribly shy and humble underneath. I hate the cocky ones who assume they are doing you a favour: the first time with Lucas he suddenly gave a great shout of laughter like a schoolboy and when I asked him why, he said he just couldn't believe in his own luck. We were on the floor in Emma's drawing-room and he lay on his back, stomach quivering like a jelly and laughing in great, helpless snorts. I put my hand over his mouth and reminded him that the old boy might be asleep but on the other hand he might not, and though doddery, he wasn't actually *paralysed*: if he heard Lucas yelping like that he'd be panting downstairs in a trice, eyes out on stalks to see what we were up to. That scared Lucas: he scrambled up as if he'd been stung and got into his clothes in such a hurry that he

69

left his shirt hanging out at the back. I didn't tell him then, but later on when I'd got Poppa up and we were all having tea, I tucked it in for him when the old chap wasn't looking and Lucas went red as fire, covering up with a tremendous fit of coughing and nose blowing until Poppa said, 'You've got a real nasty cold there, Mr Bligh, and no mistake.'

'Comes of sitting in draughts with your shirt tail hanging out,' I said, and though Lucas frowned at me, he couldn't help laughing too, reaching out to touch my hand accidentally on purpose as I poured the tea. (One of the best things about the early stages is this laughter that seems to come bubbling up from nowhere like a spring of fresh water, washing everything clean and new and making nonsense of guilt and sin and all that sour old rubbish.) We sat there giggling like a pair of adolescents, and though the old man glanced at us once or twice in a puzzled way, he was too dozey, still, to wonder what was up. I had given him two Amytal tablets instead of one when I tucked him down for his nap.

Lucas wanted to know if he could come the next Thursday but I said no. It wasn't really safe: Felix doesn't work regular hours and sometimes, if he got home early, he came across for a cup of tea and a game of bezique with the old man. I don't believe in taking risks if I don't have to. Some women enjoy this side of things, get more fun out of the intrigue than out of the affair itself, but I think that's perverted. I always tell the truth as far as I can: it's the easiest policy. When Emma came home that afternoon, I told her straight out that Lucas had dropped in to bring her father-in-law a book and that I had given him lunch. She said, what a pity she'd missed him, he was so interesting to talk to, and I took that at its face value: Emma's idea of a marvellous time with a man is a good conversation across a dinner table, and I had no reason to suppose she meant anything different on this occasion.

Naturally, I didn't tell Lucas that Felix might easily have turned up that afternoon! It would have worried him stiff! Lucas was very inexperienced in what he called 'this sort of thing'. He told me he had never been unfaithful to his wife before, and though this is one of the lies men often tell, I believed Lucas: he was such a great, innocent baby. Since he was divorcing his wife he wasn't really being unfaithful now – not to my mind, anyway – but I didn't argue this point because he seemed to be getting such an enormous amount of pleasure out of what he thought of as wickedness, that I wouldn't have spoilt it for the world. At least, not at first. He was so sweet and grateful and diffident that I forgot that it is almost always this type of man who is more demanding in the end.

It was a mild-ish autumn, but he kept the temperature of his flat up to eighty degrees. For me, liking open windows and a bit of healthy chill, it was like going into a Turkish bath. Lucas worked in his shirt and a pair of shorts, sitting at his typewriter from nine to three. I had always thought writers worked when the mood took them, but Lucas said he was naturally such a lazy man that he had to make himself keep regular office hours. He had a part-time secretary, a Miss Paul, who came for a couple of hours three days a week and took home what he had done, to make a fair copy. She was older than he was, about thirty-seven, but she looked like an overgrown schoolgirl with large breasts and buttocks and a giggly laugh. If it hadn't been for her extraordinary clothes – dirndl skirts and peasant blouses and pottery ear-rings – you would have thought she was just about to set off for a good game of hockey. She doted on Lucas. Whenever she came, she brought him something: a cheese tart she had baked herself, a bottle of home-made wine, a jar of some noxious, instant drink from the Health Food Store. One day it was Peanut Butter Crunch. Lucas lay on his back after we had made love, chewing away and fishing for bits that had got wedged in his back teeth.

71

I said, 'You know she's dotty about you, don't you?'

'Because she brings me food? She's just afraid I don't eat enough.'

'She can't have looked at you.'

'Certainly not like this. She's a very modest woman.' He peered down at his naked stomach and patted it complacently. 'Just a pleasing rotundity, I thought. The sort of shape that inspires confidence.'

This was only half a joke. People think women are vain because they make up their faces and worry over their figures and their hair, but in my opinion this just shows that the opposite is true: they have so little confidence in the way they look that they are always trying to improve on it. Men, on the other hand, make hardly any effort at all. Think what most of them look like on the beach! Thin men, fat men, parading flabby stomachs and knobbly knees and leering at young girls in bikinis, quite confident that it'll be no trouble at all to persuade them to fall for their paunchy charms!

Not that Lucas was fat, to tell the truth, just large-framed and not particularly muscular. He had one of those pale, freckled bodies that look somehow more naked without clothes than dark-skinned ones do, and show the effects of cold more. This afternoon, in spite of the heat of the flat, there were goose pimples on his arms.

I leaned over the edge of the bed, grabbed the eiderdown and pulled it over him.

'Thank you, dear Holly.'

'You're welcome. Any little thing.'

'Just one.' He got his arms round me and nuzzled my neck. He smelt of Peanut Crunch. 'You never ask me if I love you. Or say you love me.'

I groaned. There had been rather too much of this sort of complaint lately. I knew it was only his conscience – he had to find an excuse for having it off with another man's wife and love was the only one he could think of – and this

72

annoyed me. After all, if he really thought it was wrong, he didn't have to do it.

He bit me. 'Say, I love you, Lucas.'

'I love you, Lucas.'

'It hasn't got a very convincing ring.'

'You wouldn't like it if it had.'

'Wouldn't I? You might give me a chance to find out.' He sighed gustily. 'Why are you angry?'

'I'm not.'

'You've gone stiff.'

'I'm *very* sorry.'

He removed his arm, reared up on one elbow and looked down at me. 'If you said you loved me, it would give me a hold over you, is that it?'

'*Not* at-tall!' He smiled as if he knew different. So I said, 'It's just so unnecessary. Just a kind of greediness, really. Like people who must have this sauce or that with their food, instead of simply eating because they're hungry.'

'Jaded appetites,' Lucas said. 'Sedentary people like me need a bit of spice with their food, it keeps the bowels moving.' He giggled at his own piercing wit, then his eyes switched to solemn and he took hold of my chin with his fingers, forcing me to look at him. 'Holly, listen. . . .'

'You're hurting me.' He let me go at once and I pushed off the eiderdown and stood up. He looked up at me reproachfully. I said, 'Would you like a drink?'

'Quite.' He rolled onto his back and stared at the ceiling.

There was a bottle of gin on the window sill. As I reached for it, stretching over the desk, I saw a letter tucked into the blotter. Emma's handwriting. I said, 'Emma been writing to you?'

He said quickly, 'Leave it alone, love, will you?'

I stared at him. He sat up, looking embarrassed. 'I'm sorry. I don't know why I said that. You can read it if you like.'

'No thank you. I don't read other people's correspondence.'

I went into the kitchen. I made a pink gin for Lucas and a lemon drink, with ice, for me. I felt angry and hurt as if he had slapped me in the face. Not because I was jealous, or anything stupid like that – jealousy is something I simply haven't got time for. It was just the way he had spoken, as if he didn't expect me to have any decent standards of behaviour.

When I came back, he was half-dressed. I handed him his drink and started to put my clothes on. He said, 'Don't be huffy, darling. It was only a note she wrote to thank me for the party.'

'I didn't think it was a love letter.'

'Then why . . . ?' Lucas grabbed at my arm. 'You're a funny girl. So tough and casual, a sort of female buccaneer – and yet I say one slightly abrupt and stupid thing and you curl up into a bundle of prickles, like a hedgehog.'

I shook off his hand and went on dressing. He sat on the bed and watched me, smoking one of his small cigars. At last he said, 'If you must know, I only told you to leave it alone because I thought she might be embarrassed. Not that there was anything in it, for Christ's sake. Oh, I don't know.'

He sighed, rubbing his hand over his chin.

'I wouldn't have read it.'

'No. I don't suppose I thought you would. It was just an automatic thing. I really am sorry.' He smiled boyishly, crinkling up his eyes, pleased with himself for apologizing so handsomely.

I said, 'Do you like her?'

'Emma? Of course. She's a pet.'

'I meant, do you find her attractive?'

He considered that. 'I suppose so. One doesn't put the question, somehow. I mean, one thinks of her as Henry's wife.'

I could have punched him. 'Why do you say *one*?'

'I mean, *I* do.'

'I've got a husband too. Remember?'

'I've not met him, though.'

'Would you mind if you had?'

He lifted his shoulders. He had a habit of holding his cigar with the end turned into the palm, the way a workman does.

'I don't know. I'm not sure that I really like the idea of a *menage à trois*. I don't know. I haven't really any *attitudes* to this sort of thing.' He chuckled, still mightily pleased with himself and the world. 'I haven't your experience, you might say.'

I said, cold as ice, 'I'm not a whore.'

'Holly, darling. . . .' He looked less smug now, I was glad to see. 'I never meant anything of the sort, you know that.'

'One thinks of *Emma* as Henry's wife,' I said, mimicking his slight cockney accent, and saw him flinch.

'Would you rather I made a pass at her?'

'It wouldn't do much good. What makes me sick is that you wouldn't think of it.'

'How do you know?' Suddenly, he was smiling again. 'Don't let's quarrel. Or do you want to? Poor love – is your period due?'

Until he said that I was more or less in control of myself. But this typical male attitude – she can't help it, poor dear, it's the time of the month – brought me properly to the boil. What cheek, and idiotic, too! Why should what you feel be less important because there's a physical cause for it?

So I let him have it. If he despised me, I said, I was glad to know it, though what right he had, I didn't know. I'd gone to bed with him which was what he wanted, wasn't it? If he thought he'd done *me* a favour, he could bloody well think again, he wasn't so marvellous a lover. One of the advantages of 'experience' as he so pleasantly put it, was that at least you had a point of comparison, and he could take it from me, he didn't compare very well. The few little skirmishes we'd had were nothing to write home about, and if he thought he could make up for that by a lot of soft talk about 'love' he had another think coming. Love and pregnancy

75

were the two things women had to watch out for, and it was the first they suffered from most. Children grew up and left you free but love tied you hand and foot, there was no one so trapped as a loving woman. I'd watched my mother grow old waiting for my father to come back; her face would light up like a beacon when she saw someone who looked like him on a bus. She took to drink in the end and used to run after men in the street and call out his name.

'Holly,' Lucas said. '*Holly*. . . .' He looked very white and I began to simmer down and even to feel a little sorry: we had been happy together until now and Lucas had done me no harm except to be right about my period which was due in the next day or so. I would almost have been pleased if he had shown some spirit and shouted back at me, but instead he got up and came across and took me in his arms and said, 'Oh you poor child, you poor baby,' and made me sit down on his lap while he rocked me backwards and forwards, which was ridiculous, really, as I am five-foot-eight and big-boned for a woman.

And the reason he acted like this was rather ridiculous too. Because although I'd been fond of my mother and sorry for her in a way, I had always thought of her as a child who had brought trouble on herself through her own weakness and silliness and my Gran and I had always treated her like one. 'You can thank your lucky stars there's nothing of your mother in you,' my Gran used to say, 'she's got no gumption, never had.' So it never occurred to me until I grew up that her sad story might be a way of excusing some of the things I did, like losing my temper with Lucas, and though I told people about her occasionally – usually men because they are so much more sensitive and sympathetic than women – I never got over the feeling that it was a kind of cheat on my part.

That quarrel was the only one I ever had with Lucas, and though we went on for a while, giggling together and making love, it was really the beginning of the end. Perhaps I had even intended it should be at the time, otherwise I would never have said what I did about his sexual performance: I knew that no man on earth will ever feel the same about a woman once she has told him he is not up to scratch in that field. He may be ashamed to admit this, even to himself, or simply sensible enough to try and disregard it – sex isn't a competitive sport, after all – but it will go on burrowing and eating away at the heart of things like a maggot in an apple. I suppose I could have tried to put it right by saying it was just a lie said in anger – which was true, in fact – but I didn't do so. I liked Lucas, as I said, but he wasn't really my type: too much talk and analysing people. Too prying: after that stupid row, he kept on at me, asking about my father and how I felt about him and what my mother had told me, and though he was always gentle and sweet and interested, it was in a solemn, rather clinical way, as though I was a displaced person who needed rehabilitation. I'd had enough of that sort of thing from Felix, who used to say at one time that my trouble was that I had had no stable masculine influence in my youth. This had always made me hopping mad – firstly, because it was such a typical piece of arrogance to suggest that no woman can possibly manage without a man, and secondly, because of the assumption that I had 'troubles'. It was just an example, to my mind, of the way people take sex too seriously: the ridiculous belief that because you like a bit of excitement and are honest enough to admit it, there must be something wrong with you.

One of the things about Emma is that she doesn't think like that. She takes me as she finds me and doesn't criticize. I've had women friends before, but never one I could trust. They've been nice enough on the surface, but I always knew they thought themselves better than me, really.

'Probably only jealous because you do the things they'd like to but don't dare,' Emma said once.

Emma's not like that. She's no hypocrite – at least, she tries not to be. She's honest with herself, and good.

Look at the way she looked after Henry's father! It wasn't just the hard physical work, the special meals and the routine and the wet sheets, but he was a bit of an old devil in his quiet way. I'd had a taste of that on the Thursdays I looked after him – he'd run his hand up my skirt or tell me a dirty joke with a sly grin on his face to see how I was taking it. I never told Emma, anymore than I'd have told her if I'd minded her kids for the day and they'd been naughty, and it didn't bother me: I'd got used to that sort of behaviour when I'd nursed on the old chronic's ward. But Emma had never done that, of course, and from what she told me after he died, he was a good deal worse with her, probably because he could see it upset her. In fact my opinion is that he bullied her out of spite! One Thursday he said, 'I'm just a cross she has to bear,' and though I thought at the time that this was just a bit of whiney self-pity – not that I blamed him, mind, it must be hell to be old and ill and at everyone's mercy – it struck me afterwards that it might be partly the reason he treated her as he did. Emma had looked after the poor old chap out of duty, not affection, and he knew it.

So did she, of course. And blamed herself; that was why she got into that pathetic state when he died. Emma is very attached to her conscience. Whatever the facts of a situation, she'll twist them in her mind so she can blame herself. Poor girl. The truth was – or so I thought at the time – she was so horrified because she'd sometimes day-dreamed he was dead, that she had to punish herself! It was no good telling her that if people dropped down dead the moment someone wished they would, the world population problem would be solved in a flash! Bertrand Russell couldn't have argued with Emma, the state she was in.

It was lucky I was there, otherwise she would have blurted it all out to Henry the moment he came home. He couldn't have believed she was in any way to blame, of course, but he would have questioned her and worried her until poor old Emma wouldn't have known whether she was coming or going. The trouble with being a lawyer is that you see things in terms of true or false, black or white, and ignore all the grey, foggy ground in between where most people live, most of the time. And Emma's always been so self-effacing and quiet-voiced and reasonable – because this is the way he likes her, it being less trouble for *him* – that he would never have believed that she didn't know what she was saying or understood that it meant nothing, only that she was half out of her mind with grief and shame. The only thing to do was to treat her for hysterics, which is what I did.

I put her to bed. I undressed her because she was too tired and too tight to take off her own clothes, and I was shocked to see how thin she'd got. I'd not seen her naked since Sicily and I reckoned she'd lost about twelve pounds since then. I remember I felt furious with Henry. That complacent pig, letting poor Emma wear herself away to nothing looking after his father! Not that I don't believe in families caring for their old people, mind you! My grandmother was bed-fast for the last year of her life and I nursed her to the end, but then I'm as strong as a cart-horse, not like Emma, and I did it of my own free will and love for my darling Gran, which made it easier. I don't mean Henry should have put the old man into hospital, just that he should have kept more of an eye on things and seen Emma wasn't driven too far: even *he* must have known she would never complain on her own account. But I suppose that was too much to hope for from Henry who isn't the type to notice what doesn't suit him. In fact, I'd actually heard him say once or twice that it was a good thing in a way that Emma had the old chap to look after: so many women felt frustrated and under-employed once their children were out at school all day! Can you *beat* that for smugness? If he'd had to wash a smelly sheet or sit at home for one week tied to an old man's ravings, he'd have sung a different tune, but then men are like that. My Gran used to say that if men had the babies, the birth rate would go down like nobody's business.

By the time Henry got home, I'd worked myself up into a fine old rage against him, but when I saw him, standing in the hall and looking up at me as I came down the stairs, I stopped being angry. He looked white and tired; there were tracks on his cheeks as if he'd been crying, and I remembered how fond he had been of his father and was glad the doctor had been with his assistant to carry the poor old chap upstairs and lay him out in his own bed, so that he looked decent and peaceful.

Henry said, 'Oh Holly. . . .' and put his arms round me for a minute, which showed how upset he must be, because he usually avoided touching me in the ordinary way – if he handed me a drink he would hold the glass so his fingers couldn't brush against mine! (Not that I wanted him to touch me, mind. Henry's not the type to set my old hormones flickering! Too skinny for my taste.)

He buried his face in my neck and held me close for a minute and then he gave a sort of groan and said, 'Where's Emma?' I told him she was asleep but at that moment she called out to me, from her room. Henry took his arms away as if we had been doing something to be ashamed of, and I was disgusted by this and disliked him again. As we went upstairs I thought – If she's going to tell him about this row with his father, she'll tell him at once, the moment she sees him. But she didn't say a word. She seemed dazed and tired and I guessed it had all slipped away from her, like a bad dream when you wake in the morning.

I fetched the twins from their party and put them to bed in our spare room. I told them their Granpa had gone to be with Jesus and William said, 'When is he coming back again?'

I thought this was cute, but when I repeated it to Felix
80

he pulled a sour face. He disapproves of what he calls 'Stuffing children up with religion' – as if it were ice-cream and bad for their teeth!

He poured himself a whisky and said, 'I do wish you'd drink something occasionally, you make me feel such a *lush*.' He was very upset. He had liked Henry's father and enjoyed their games of bezique. I thought – Everyone was fond of him except Emma.

I told Felix that Emma had been in a terrible state, blaming herself because she had hated her father-in-law and wished him dead, but that I had warned her not to tell Henry. 'He'd make such a tarradiddle out of it, you know what he is.'

Felix said, 'What rubbish! Emma was devoted to him. Why do women have to make drama out of nothing? Much better for her to talk to Henry and get it out of her system. He'll only tell her what an idiot she is,' but when I explained how the old man had tormented her and that she had been too ashamed to tell Henry, he agreed that it was best kept quiet now.

'What a frightful thing. Emma!' He looked shocked. 'She's the last person to cope with that sort of behaviour, it must have been hell for her.' He poured himself another drink to help himself face this awful thought: Felix has always believed Emma to be a tender plant who should be sheltered from the cold winds of life.

'If you ask me,' I said, 'I think she's a fool. For God's sake, she's not fourteen! She's a grown woman with a husband and two children. She ought to know what men are like by now – it's absurd to make such a fuss.'

'You would think that,' Felix said, and then, 'I suppose her mother's coming up for the funeral?'

He meant to change the subject as he often did when he had said something nasty to me, not because he regretted it, but because he was afraid of provoking a row. Felix is rather like a cowardly small boy who shouts insults, then loses his nerve and runs away.

I said, 'Henry asked me to ring her. I think he hoped she'd come at once and give Emma a hand, but she can only manage to get up for the funeral. There are a couple of girls she's coaching for some exam or other.'

'Pity she's coming at all.'

'Emma's very fond of her mother,' I said indignantly, partly because this was true, and partly because I got on with her rather well myself. She's had a dreary life in many ways – a sad sack of a husband who hung up his hat the moment they were married and never did a stroke of work after – but she's the sturdy, no-nonsense type who buckles down and gets on with what has to be done, and no complaints.

Felix grinned. 'In much the same way as a rabbit is fond of a stoat,' he said, and though I was annoyed with him, I couldn't help laughing. I would never have thought of describing Emma's mother as a stoat but suddenly I *saw* her as one: a beautiful, plump stoat, sleek and fat and groomed in its winter coat, bustling along the hedgerows with cold, remorseless energy.

'Surely term's nearly over,' Felix said. 'I mean, these girls and the exam.'

'She's probably coaching the poor kids right through the Christmas holidays.'

Felix looked at me. 'You *have* remembered Ginny will be home at the end of the week, haven't you?'

I knew from the way he whipped up then and filled his glass for the third time with a generous ration of whisky, that this was a question 'loaded with meaning' as they say. His eyes darted at me like a pair of nervous brown mice. Then he sat down, holding the glass lovingly between his hands and staring carefully into the fire. The silly old bastard.

I hadn't told him about Lucas, but of course he knew. He said once, 'I shall always know because of the way you look,' and that was true: any woman's looks improve when she is having a new love affair and not just because she is taking more trouble with her appearance. It actually seems to clear the skin like a dose of sulphur in the spring. 'Only don't throw it in my face, that's all,' Felix had said, the last time – years ago now – that we had a row about this. I was in love – or whatever euphemism you like – with a doctor at the local hospital who had delivered me when Ginny was born. He was a sweet, very shy young man with a bit of a stutter: perhaps that was why he took to putting his feelings down on paper! Felix found a letter when he was looking through my drawer – for a collar stud, he *said*.

I say it was the last time we had a row, but really it was the only one. I had had one other lover before the doctor, and though I had not actually told Felix, I had never made any secret of how I felt about the right of married people to be free in that way. Felix pretended that he had always thought that was just talk – a kind of bravado, he said, because I resented the idea of being any man's 'property'. I reminded him that he had agreed with me and he said may be he had, but that was only *in theory*, postulating a different social set-up as they had in Polynesia, say, where sex and marriage were regarded quite separately. This was not Polynesia, and he for one had been brought up with a lot of ideals and taboos that I doubtless thought silly but that he found it difficult to rid himself of. He had gone on in this vein for some time, being sarcastic and drawling as if he were giving a lecture, and then, quite suddenly, he lost his temper and began to tremble – his trouser legs actually shook, as if he were standing in a high wind. He looked, and sounded, so ludicrous that I laughed and then he hit me and broke one of my bottom teeth. I was so astonished that I just lay on the floor, spitting blood and bits of tooth, and of course he was horrified at once and knelt beside me and wiped my mouth and begged my pardon. Perhaps because he is really part-Russian, Felix tries hard to be very English, very Public School: he thinks it a dreadful thing to hit a

83

woman, though in fact, since he is a little man and takes almost no exercise, if we had really had a good old barney I would probably have got the best of it.

Of course, I was cold as ice. I said I would pack my case and leave this minute.

'And Ginny?'

I said, naturally, I would take her with me. Whatever he could say against me in court – and I wouldn't lower myself to deny it! – there was no judge nowadays who would take a little girl away from her mother.

He was distraught. He was – is – potty about the kid. I am too, for that matter, but Felix thinks the sun rises and sets on her.

He said, couldn't we start again, and I said no, not if it was going to be like this, lies and recriminations and rows. I would live my life the way I wanted, or that was the end of it.

He said, 'Let me think about it.' He was very pale and trying to look stern and decisive, but I knew what the answer would be. Felix is the sort of man who tries to do what he thinks right, even if it goes against his feelings: however jealous he felt, he would think it petty and spiteful to divorce me just because I had gone to bed with another man, when I had been a good wife to him in every other way.

He didn't speak to me for nearly a week. This was supposed to bring me to heel, so I took no notice. I cooked his meals and cleaned his shoes and shared his bed: we lay side by side like two people on an old tomb. Then, one Saturday morning, I was cleaning out the medicine chest in the bathroom when one of the screws came loose and it slipped sideways on the wall. Something fell from behind it and I saw it was a photograph of my young doctor that I'd not seen for some time: Felix must have found it when he was poking through my drawers for that collar stud! He had made a hole through the middle of the poor man's forehead and another through his chest: I suppose he had done this in the bathroom and then pushed it behind the cabinet, either because

84

he was horrified at himself or because he heard me coming. I showed it to him and said, 'For God's sake, what is this, voodoo?' – pretending to laugh though I was really very shocked. I'm not superstitious, I hope, but you never know!

Of course Felix was dreadfully ashamed. He said he must have been out of his mind, he couldn't explain it any other way. He loved me, he said, he couldn't bear the thought of anyone else touching me, but there were two things that upset him even more than that. One was the thought that when I was with another man, I might use our private language – silly, babyish things like saying 'let's take our curlers out' when we wanted to make love – and the other, the fear that Ginny would find out about me when she grew older. 'I think I can bear anything except that,' he said. 'I don't suppose there's really much danger until she's seven or so – though of course children are much more perceptive than adults think – but by *that* time, I suppose we could send her away to school. If we do that, will you promise me that when she's home, in the holidays, you'll keep on the rails like a good, conventional Mum, and look after her?'

I was furious, of course. As if I would do anything to hurt a little girl! To tell the truth, if he hadn't put it all onto poor Ginny like that, when it was really the thing about the 'private language' that had disturbed him most – I knew this by the way he had just mentioned it and then looked embarrassed and rushed on as if it wasn't really important – I think I might have tried to behave more in the way he wanted me to do, however much against my principles and inclinations that might be. And he had talked as if I were a sex maniac, instead of a normally healthy woman who had taken a lover, not all that frequently – only twice in four years! – and both times fairly discreetly. I remember thinking, 'My God, if that's what you think of me, I might as well be hung for a sheep as a lamb!'

But I didn't show I was angry, and I promised what he asked about Ginny, for the sake of peace and quiet. And because if he *had* taken it into his little head to divorce me at that time, it would have been awkward for the doctor owing to all that nonsense about professional etiquette, and though we had broken up some months before, I felt I owed him that much, for friendship's sake.

I saw Lucas on the Wednesday. I got to the flat about four o'clock, later than usual because I had been to the dentist. He had made tea: the tray was laid ready and there were even some rather repulsive looking iced cakes set out on a tray. Lucas had on a clean shirt and tie which was un-usual, too – he wasn't what you might call a snappy dresser – and he had only recently shaved: a piece of cotton wool wagged from a cut on his chin like a nanny goat's beard.

'What's the celebration?' I said, and he looked confused and said he'd just thought I'd be ready for a nice cuppa after the dentist. 'Sit down and take the weight off your feet,' he said in a jolly, cockney-char voice. 'I think I hear me kettle.'

'What's up, *really*?' I shouted after him when he had bustled into the kitchen. He didn't answer immediately, but when he came back with the pot, he said, 'Up? My dearest girl, why should anything be up?', speaking this time in exaggerated Etonian.

I giggled, thinking that for Lucas to buy cakes and make tea was the equivalent of a guilty husband panting home with flowers and champagne. 'No reason,' I said.

He gave me a quick look, but seemed relieved. He poured tea, gave me a cake, which was every bit as nasty as it looked, and lit a cigar.

It was like having tea with a vicar. (Not that I ever have.) He wanted to know how 'poor Emma' was bearing up. 'It must have been a frightful shock, finding the old man like that.'

'The funeral's tomorrow.'

'I know. Emma rang me this morning.' He cleared his throat self-consciously. 'I didn't tell her you'd told me already. She asked me if I would give her lunch on Friday. Apparently she's bringing her mother up to catch a train. She seemed in a bit of a state.' He looked at me enquiringly.

I said, 'Oh, Emma fancies you.'

He said, 'Get away,' in his cockney voice. Then, 'No – really. Is anything wrong?'

'What could be? Of course, she's upset. You know old Emma.'

'Not *very* well, actually.' He hesitated, creasing his forehead with elaborate doubt. 'I just wondered what she wanted.'

'How should I know?'

I had seen Emma that lunchtime and she'd asked if I would mind having the twins on Friday. Ginny was coming home in the morning so I would have to get lunch anyway, wouldn't I? She wanted to take 'Mummy' up to London to catch her train home.

I thought – Sly little so-and-so. But I was amused, really.

'I just thought you might have an idea,' Lucas said.

'I expect she hoped you'd cheer her up. You ought to be flattered.'

'Mmm. Well. Have some more tea?'

'No thank you.'

It had been almost dark when I arrived and now all I could see of Lucas was his face, lit by the street outside. He gave a sort of grunt and switched on the table lamp. Then he sat, hands on his knees, and looked at me.

'You'll know me next time,' I said.

He said nothing for a minute, getting up his courage, as it turned out. Then his face reddened and he said, abruptly, 'I'm getting married. As soon as the divorce is through.'

'Well, what d'you know?' I thought about this. On the whole, apart from a slight resentment because he had been clearly so scared of telling me, the chief thing I felt was relief. Lucas and I had grown *cosy* together, like a happily married, middle-aged couple. This might suit Lucas who

87

liked sex in much the same way as he liked good food, as long as it was cooked by someone else and handed to him on a plate (if there was no one around he'd go without or munch an apple) but it had begun to bore me a little. Now we could part good friends and I needn't feel guilty.

'Who to?' I said.

'Miss – I mean, to *Lisa*. My secretary,' he explained, as if I might not know who she was.

'Well, what d'you know?' I said again, though I wasn't, really, so surprised. In fact, now I thought about it, I decided I had probably known before he knew it himself! Lucas needed a wife – some men are all right on their own but he was hopeless, dishes piled everlastingly in the sink, dirty clothes all over the place – and here was Miss Paul, ready to hand and no trouble. Lucas was the sort of man who always marries the girl next door, out of laziness, not sentiment.

'You old dog,' I said, and then something struck me. 'I suppose she *knows*?' It would be like Lucas to get things straight with me before he asked her.

He looked shy. 'I've written to her today. I think she'll say yes.'

'Written?'

'She's in Austria. She went on Sunday. She has an old aunt there.' He went on, explaining about this aunt, who was the only relation she had. Her parents had been killed in concentration camps; she had been got out of Germany under some sort of scheme and moved from foster parent to foster parent, like a parcel. 'She hasn't had a settled home since she was about eight years old,' Lucas said. He was moved by this sad tale, I could see.

Then he said, very seriously, 'You think I'm doing a sensible thing, don't you?' which made *me* sorry for poor old Lisa. I wanted to say, 'What do you mean? You'll be getting good cooking, free typing, and probably life-long gratitude into the bargain!' But then I thought – At least he's honest.

I said, 'She'll jump at you.'

He asked, quite anxiously, 'Do you really think so?' and I hoped then that all he had been telling me about her unhappy childhood was really beside the point and that he'd simply been too embarrassed to tell me straight out that he was fond of her.

'Of course I do.' I grinned at him and clapped my hands on the arms of my chair. 'Well, it's been nice knowing you.'

'Don't go.' He looked shy again. Poor old Lucas! He had hoped we'd make love but had felt he must tell me beforehand.

I laughed out loud and he dived at me, squeezing me round the ribs the way a child hugs a teddy bear. Or his mother. 'Oh you are *wonderful*, Holly. I was in such a bloody funk. You do know, don't you, I'd not been cheating or anything? I only really knew about Lisa when I took her to the plane. *You* know.'

'Love had burgeoned without your knowing it,' I said in a suitably gay, bantering tone.

He sat back on his heels. He took off my shoes and held my feet in his warm, freckled hands, not tickling, just holding them firmly and gently. This was something I liked and I was touched that he should think to do it now, to please me.

He said, 'Dear Holly, you've been so sweet, do one thing more for me? Lisa will be back next week, and of course there's no question – I mean, you wouldn't want that either, would you? But I thought, on Saturday, perhaps, we could have a sort of farewell binge. A nice, civilized ending. A slap-up lunch somewhere.'

'Ginny will be home. School ends on Friday.'

'Emma can look after her. You look after her children, don't you? *Please*, Holly.'

He sat there, holding my feet and looking so shining happy and hopeful that I could hardly say no. Even if this lunch was only to flatter his vanity, make him think what a marvellous chap he was, cock of the bloody walk. Besides, if I did say no, it might look like a fit of pique. Or worse, as if I really minded.

'I don't see why I shouldn't manage that,' I said, feeling very fond of him suddenly, and wondering, at the same time, how I would have felt if I had really loved him. For some reason this made me feel sad for a minute.

# 6. *Emma*

'Well, you certainly had a wonderful father-in-law,' Emma's mother said.

Perhaps her daughter's face (tearless, too composed) had provoked this remark? A rebuke. Or was she merely *summing up*, a habit of hers at what she thought appropriate moments? Emma wondered, blinking in the surprising sunlight into which they had walked out of the gloom of the crematorium chapel, her dazzled eyes seeing her mother only as a collection of garments: a pale fox fur slung round her shoulders and secured by a gold chain attached to its narrow, glass-eyed head; a tweed suit with a deep Vee showing a peach-coloured blouse; a dark, solid hat, like a man's. Perhaps it *was* a man's, Emma thought; her mother had never, to her knowledge, owned a hat; perhaps this one belonged to the senior maths master who lodged with her now. Emma pictured her mother in the narrow hall of her small, semi-detached house, passing the mahogany stand where ancient raincoats hung and snatching the hat up, common property like an old umbrella, and jamming it on top of her marvellous thick, coroneted hair.

Her desire to laugh astonished her, though she knew it was not unusual on this kind of occasion: standing in the chapel between her mother and Henry, she had seen Henry's mouth twitch as the coffin (remarkably small, covered with a blue cloth) had stuck momentarily, halfway down its jerky slide towards the doors. She had been shocked at Henry: this moment, for her, had been unbearable. To shut it out, she had closed her eyes and dreamed that Lucas had arrived in the chapel, slipping into a pew on the other side of the aisle. Lucas, with his big, ungainly body, his kind, clever face half-turned towards her, his mouth grave but his eyes smiling – he had come to help her face this, to hold her up. Afterwards, they would have a moment together. *I had to come, my darling girl, I knew how you would feel.* She would feel the warmth of his hand, through her glove. *Oh Lucas, my love. . . .*

It seemed strange to find herself outside the chapel, waiting with her mother while Henry, standing by the Cravens' car, talked to Felix and Holly. Beyond them was a backdrop of bare trees against a pale sky, stone plaques in the grass, ornamental dwarf conifers and late chrysanthemums in vases. Felix was wearing a very long, dark overcoat that gave him the appearance of a sinister character in an old film.

Emma's mother said, 'Mrs Craven looks wonderfully well. A good-looking girl, glad to see *she* doesn't go in for this dieting nonsense. Henry looks thin, though. Do you feed him properly? Just because you starve yourself, there's no need to deprive the poor man.'

'I'm not dieting,' Emma said.

'Then why are you so thin? You know, Emma, you owe it to your family to take better care of yourself.'

*She's like a train*, Emma told Lucas. *Thundering along a single track. Unstoppable.*

'It's clouding over again,' Emma's mother said, shunting Emma into the back of the car. 'Did I tell you old Mrs Philips died the other day? You must remember her, she taught the lower forms music. Cancer of the bowel. Her daughter nursed her to the end, a terrible illness. You were lucky to be spared that, my girl, I can tell you. Her daughter wanted the funeral on the Saturday so we could all come from the School and when she rang the crematorium they said it was a very busy day but they'd see what they could do. They rang her back in half an hour – you'll never guess what they said! They'd had a cancellation!'

'*What?*' Mystified, Emma watched Henry come towards the car, splashing through a glittering puddle. Was he thinner?

'Must have rained while we were inside.' He spoke, Emma thought, as if they had all been to the cinema.

'It turned out that the local undertaker had a block booking,' Emma's mother whispered, unwilling to leave the story unfinished but hoping, it seemed, that Henry's grief would make him deaf.

'What's that?' He turned from the driver's seat. She told him and he laughed. 'You're a tonic, Mama.'

'Cry at weddings, laugh at funerals. In the East, of course, people always wear white.'

Emma's mother had never been out of England but she always spoke with authority of foreigners and their customs. 'In China,' she said, 'death is a celebration.'

She would understand that, Emma thought. She rode life like a bucking, spirited horse: death and disaster were challenges to her, ditches and five-barred gates. Emma saw her mother galloping, seat firm, hands steady, face lifted proudly into the gale. Incredible, Emma thought, with pride and fear: she must be fifty-nine, all her own teeth, the tight skin of a girl, a plump, still supple body.

'I'm glad you could come, Ma,' she said, as the car swept out of the ornate, funereal gates, wheels crunching on gravel.

'I wish you could stay longer,' Henry said. 'We'd both like it. And Emma could do with a bit of support.'

'I'm all right,' Emma said.

'Of course she is. Henry dear, you mustn't worry over this girl. Just a bit skinny, that's all. Picky over her food, like her father. That was always his trouble. Put her on yeast and yoghourt, cut out the coffee and tea, pull her up in no time. Less meat, more fresh fruit and vegetables – the body's an engine, it needs proper fuel. Not that I'm cranky about diet, I haven't the time, but what I say is, lay down the basic rules and then forget about them.'

'Emma doesn't eat badly,' Henry said, 'but she's had a tough-ish time recently.' His eyes met Emma's in the driving mirror. 'As a matter of fact, Holly gave me a talking-to just now.'

Afraid that his good-humoured tone concealed resentment, Emma smiled at him brightly.

'Of course I'd stay, dears, if it was really necessary', Emma's mother said. 'But one must keep a sense of proportion. Did I explain about these girls I'm coaching? Well, one of them in particular, Jenny Hindmarsh . . .'

Jenny Hindmarsh had been unable to take her 'A' level exams in the summer because she had had rheumatic fever. Her mother had been killed in a car accident in the autumn and she kept house, now, for her father and two younger brothers. The father was against his daughter staying on at school and trying for a university place. Emma's mother had had the devil's own job persuading him; he had finally agreed but only on condition that she got good grades in her examinations in January. Naturally, it would suit him to keep his daughter at home; he refused to employ any domestic help and the girl had to cook and clean and wash in the evenings, before she could begin her homework.

'Can't her brothers help her?' Though she knew it was almost certainly useless, Emma felt compelled to protest against this totality of gloom.

'One is only *five*,' her mother answered in a gently ironic voice. 'And the other a polio victim. Both legs in irons.'

Emma saw Henry's grin, and knew he could hardly believe her. No day could be so dark, no wind so cold: there must be some shelter on the blasted heath. But she knew her mother was no liar and the knowledge produced the familiar weakness in her limbs, the familiar tightness in her throat. The eternal feeling that she was too lucky, so ungrateful: she should count her blessings and shut up.

She stared out of the window at the passing suburban streets, petrol stations, little houses, arcaded shops, her eyes unfocused by the tears she should properly have shed at her father-in-law's funeral, her throat aching. . . .

*She was lying in bed, terribly ill. Lucas was holding her hand, his face white and tense, but smiling to comfort her. The small ward was scented with the flowers he had brought. It hurt her to speak, but she said, she'll never come, I can never be ill enough, desperate enough. I'd had appendicitis, I was twelve and I was in this hospital, there was a woman dying in the next bed and I was frightened of having my stitches out. There were big black knots and I was afraid they would pull them through the skin and that the wound would open again. I cried and she said, goodness, what a fuss; look at that poor woman, only thirty-two, how do you think she feels, leaving five children and a sick husband? And it was quite true; the husband was sitting by her bed, so sad and thin like a scarecrow, and when I left the hospital at the end of the week it was visiting time and the children were waiting in the hall, perched on a bench like five starved sparrows. . . .*

*Lucas's face was pale, stern. He said, I'll make her come, it's my job to look after you from now on.*

Emma thought – I should stop this. Why am I doing it, why am I playing this game?

*Oh Lucas, my love, at the end of this corridor there is a dark door.*

Henry said, 'What time will the boys be back?'

'Susan said she'd bring them home about six,' Emma said.

'Granny,' William said, 'tell us about the Fuzzy Buns.'

They were playing Pelmanism. 'Finish the game first,' Emma's mother said. 'You only want the Fuzzy Buns because Rufus is winning.'

'I've won already, I've got seventeen pairs,' Rufus said. 'I always win. William doesn't concentrate.'

'It's a boring, stupid, awful game,' William said. 'I want a *story*.' His face reddening ominously, he scuffed the Pelmanism cards with his sandalled feet. Emma's mother gathered him onto her lap and rocked him, gently pulling the thumb out of his mouth.

'You're too big, too old. Rufus isn't such a baby, is he?'

'I do suck my thumb sometimes, it tastes nice,' Rufus said. 'Tell us the Fuzzy Buns, Gran.'

Emma's mother drew him against her knee. She looked like Demeter, cuddling these lusty cherubs, her fair hair coming down.

'I must help Mummy get supper. Poor Mummy's not well.'

Emma begged – Don't make them feel guilty. Aloud, she said, 'I'm fine, Ma. You tell them a story. There's hardly anything to do, really.'

In the kitchen, she put water on for spaghetti, chopped onions.

She said, to Henry, 'I'd have to be paralysed from the waist down.'

'What?' For a moment, he seemed bewildered. Then he laughed. 'D'you think that would be enough? You'd need to be a deaf mute as well.' He laid the table, clattering cutlery. He said, 'Oh no - you're not *crying*?'

'Just onions.'

She pressed the handkerchief he gave her against her streaming eyes. 'Cut them under water,' he advised. He smiled, suppressing, she thought, some irritation. 'You wouldn't really want to be in your mother's gallery of unfortunates?'

'No. Of course not.'

He looked at her conscientiously, to see she meant this. Relieved, he said, 'You know, it struck me that she didn't look so bright. Marvellous for her age, of course, but she does drive herself.'

'To help people? She needs to do that. She has to feel she's of use.'

'If she turned up on my doorstep unexpectedly, I'd be scared stiff. Wondering what was wrong with me.'

'Don't be foul.'

'Sorry. *Joke*. You know I admire your Mama, though saying so seems a bit unnecessary. Like saying one admires the Colosseum. But I meant what I said, she doesn't look as well as I've seen her. I bet she's not only coaching this Jenny Whatsername who's got a drunken father and six crippled brothers, but going round to the house and doing most of the work.'

'She's strong as a horse,' Emma said, but felt a chill: her mother was something fixed, permanent.

'I didn't mean to worry you, I just wondered,' Henry said.

Over spaghetti, Emma watched her mother. She couldn't see – honestly couldn't see – anything wrong. Was Henry, perhaps, more perspicacious than she was, even more loving? Emma knew she was less adequate than most people in most things. Her mother drank two glasses of wine which was unusual for her: she despised what she called artificial stimuli. Emma said, 'Look, Ma. You're coming back for Christmas. That's only another week. Why not stay? Not to help me, but to have a rest. A holiday.'

'A holiday? Why should I want a holiday?'

'You'll make yourself ill one of these days,' Henry said.

'Goodness me – I haven't time for that sort of nonsense.' The healthy laugh carried conviction – or did it? Emma saw a shadow under the forget-me-not eyes. Or thought she saw it.

'Stay one more day, anyway,' Henry said.

'Well . . .'

Emma's pulse fluttered. 'The only thing *is*, I've arranged with Holly. . . . I can't take you to the station on Saturday because I'm having Ginny for lunch.'

*Her mother dropped dead on the twelve-fifteen to Tonbridge. A*

96

*heart attack. Emma told Lucas – oh my darling, it's my fault, I wanted to see you and I steam-rollered her into getting this train, we got caught in a traffic jam and nearly missed it and I made her run, carrying her case down the platform. . . .*

'There's no need to take me all the way into London anyway. I'm not a cripple,' her mother said. 'But since you've arranged it, we'll leave it as it is. I'd prefer to get home on Friday as a matter of fact, there's the shopping and I like to get Mr Stevens – my lodger, you know – his supper on Friday night. He's a vegetarian, poor man, and school meals don't agree with him naturally so he goes without during the day and that's not good for him because he's only got one kidney.'

Emma began to laugh. Wine spluttered out of her mouth onto the table cloth. Then tears came.

'Salt,' her mother said, picking up the salt cellar and shaking it liberally over the white cloth Henry had put over the kitchen table to make this funeral feast more of an occasion. She stood up and came round the table and pressed Emma's head against her firm stomach. 'Over-wrought,' she said, to Henry. 'The poor child.'

Overcome by that 'poor child', Emma buried her face and howled. She heard Henry say, from a distance, 'She's been marvellous, you know, she couldn't keep it up,' and she groaned, clapping her hands over her ears.

Her mother's arm was an iron bar behind her back, propelling her up the stairs. 'Quiet now, you'll wake the children. Don't want to upset them, do we, their Mummy crying? You'll be tucked up in bed in a minute. Henry's getting you warm milk and a hottie.'

Love had always been there, Emma remembered, but it required total collapse and was always withdrawn too soon.

She was in bed, hot bottle at her feet, a cup of warm milk in her hand. Her mother said, 'A good sleep's what you need. Mind you get it, no staying awake reading till all hours. Really, you know, I'm a bit surprised, I'd no idea you were so fond of Henry's father. As a matter of fact, I'd always thought you were – well – a bit cold towards him. You know what you are!'

What am I? Cold, incapable of love. An unloving wife, a selfish mother, a bad daughter? She said, 'Oh Ma, I feel so awful about him, you don't know.'

Hope seized her. She could tell her mother.

'I feel so guilty,' she said, smiling wildly to soften this. She thought – She will be sorry for me if I tell her, is that the only reason I want to? At once she knew how the tragi-comedy would go, her mother confiding in some unknown third party: Of course the poor child was exhausted, worn out, he was incontinent, obscene, to tell you the truth I'm astonished Emma managed as well as she did for so long. I don't mean she's lacking in courage, but she has less stamina, a lower threshold than most people, more sensitive, you could say, though personally I distrust that word, it's so often an excuse for lack of will power. But in this case I think one can fairly use it: Emma minded all that filthy non-sense more than a great many women would have done, not out of prudery – another mis-used word to my mind, un-fairly pejorative, as if modesty was automatically something to be despised – but simply because she is not coarse-fibred enough to bear that sort of thing day in, day out. If her control snapped in the end one can understand it, not approve, of course, but understand and forgive on a moral level. Easier for an outsider, naturally. I think we did right to decide her husband should never be told. He has always put Emma on such a pedestal, expected so much from her – too much, in my opinion, though I've been guilty that way my-self – that he would be more shocked and distressed than if she had been someone, well, more ordinary. Not that Emma considered herself for a minute, her one thought was that Henry shouldn't suffer. . . .

'Why on earth should you feel guilty, Emma?' her mother asked, standing at the end of the bed.

Emma didn't answer. Although her mother's stance suggested no particular tenderness, indeed, merely implied impatience – there was a little frown on her fine forehead as if she were saying inwardly, hurry up now, there's all that washing-up downstairs, surely you don't expect poor Henry to do it all? – Emma felt cared for, loved, safe, as if through some telepathic process all her mother's powers of indignant, whole-hearted partisanship had been ranged on her side, a line of heavy guns against a faceless enemy.

Her mother went on, 'My dear child, you did everything you could for him, from what Henry's said, more than I realized perhaps.' This was generous, a real accolade. Emma's eyes filled. 'Of course you're feeling the reaction now, but you mustn't give in to it. That's self-indulgence.' She hesitated, softened a little. Then, 'Emma, I do know what I'm talking about. When your father died with that bout of pneumonia, I blamed myself endlessly afterwards, even though I knew there was nothing I could have done that I didn't do.'

Except let him stay in bed with his cold in the beginning, Emma wanted to say, and wondered, for a heart-stopping moment, if she was so far out of her mind that she had actually said this, the unforgiveable thing, because her mother's face clouded.

But, 'I had a terrible struggle making myself face the facts. It's such a waste of *time*, that sort of thing, believe me,' was all she finally said.

'Have a nice time, duckie.' Holly was smiling. 'What time's the train?'

'Twelve-fifteen.' Emma hesitated. 'As a matter of fact, I'm having lunch with Lucas afterwards.' Speaking his name made Emma's face glow.

'See he gives you a good one.'

'It's sweet of him to ask me at all. Actually, *I* rang him up. He was so nice to Father, I wanted to thank him. I hope he doesn't mind. . . .'

The blush was taking time to subside. Emma laughed, to distract attention from it.

'I should think he'd be thrilled. Probably even now popping into his best bib and tucker.' Holly winked. 'You'll be a nice change for the poor man, after that terrible wife.'

'You don't know his wife's terrible.'

'All men have terrible wives, love. It's axiomatic. I learned that word when Felix was doing the crossword this morning. I'm improving my tiny mind.'

'Don't diminish yourself, Holly,' Emma pleaded earnestly. This morning she wanted everyone to be happy. She said, 'Henry says you've got a very good, intuitive intelligence. Why do you have to have an inferiority complex about it?'

'Henry said nothing of the sort, but I'm glad you think so. Have fun, don't hurry back, Aunt Holly will look after the boys.' She laughed, suddenly kissing Emma on the cheek. 'Don't do anything I wouldn't do.'

'That gives me plenty of latitude,' Emma said, embarrassed by the kiss, but uplifted with affection.

*Lucas*, her heart sang. The car hummed along, sleety rain tapping the soft top.

'You're certainly better this morning,' her mother said. 'Sleep's the great healer. Try to get to bed early this next week or two. Henry could certainly do with it. He's looking tired. A lot older, I thought.' She spoke with a certain relish. 'A man gets to his age, he needs extra attention.'

'Henry's only thirty-six,' Emma said. She thought of her father. How much attention did he get, with his weak chest and his sinus condition, in the house his wife kept cold and gusty as a football field on a winter's day? Between open window and empty grate, Emma and her father had lived, chilly conspirators against health and freshness, turning on the electric fire when she was out but enjoying the comfort guiltily, listening for her latchkey. If, reading or dozing, they failed to hear it, retribution descended: her indignant scorn. *What a horrible fug, it's no wonder you have colds, it's just asking for trouble, breathing in all that stale, used-up air.* Colds and chilblains were manifestations of moral weakness; a brisk walk the answer, toning up the circulation and the character together. Poor Dad – no place he could really keep warm except the shed where he nursed his baby tomatoes; no one could send *them* for a brisk walk so he reaped the benefit of the necessary oil heater, sometimes even sitting beside it to read in an old wicker chair, but mostly just standing and warming his hands over the daisy-flower light of the stove. He always grew more plants than he needed, passing the remainder on to the young widow next door. Emma used to run in through the hole in the hedge, an important big girl, lending a hand with the babies. *That poor child*, her father called their neighbour; several times Emma saw him through the french window of her back sitting-room, talking to the fair, droopy, pretty girl, and holding one of her children on his lap. *Where's your father?*, her mother asked once, and she answered, instinctively, *I think he went to buy a newspaper*, not wanting to give him away, expose his crime – slipping in next door to get a bit of warmth by the lovely fire that the widow kept banked up so high you could feel it through the wall above their own empty grate, if you pressed your hand there. Emma's childhood had been so obsessed by the search for free warmth, hugging radiators in public buildings, inventing things to look up in the Reference Library on Saturday mornings, reading the menu in the window of the café by the station so she could stand on the pavement outside and let the hot, smelly air blow up her legs from the kitchen below, that it did not strike her for years that her father might have had a different motive for his visits.

She said, 'What happened to Mrs Hilary, Ma?'

'The girl who used to live next door? Oh, I must have told you, Emma. She married George.'

'*Uncle* George? The one who made a pass at me?' Turning right against the stream of traffic, Emma spoke without thinking.

'Made a pass at you? *Emma!*'

A stoney profile, the cheek faintly mottling.

'He did though.' She thought – I'm happy, I can't be intimidated today. She said, 'You didn't believe me.'

Her mother did not answer. Glancing sideways, Emma saw that her lips were set in a punishing silence.

Emma smiled. She said, lightly, 'You know, I never understood why you didn't believe me.'

Her mother's voice was cold, carefully unprovoked. 'I don't remember any such incident. Really Emma. . . .'

Emma said, 'Do you get on with your parents, Lucas?'

'I'm very fond of them. I see them about once a month. My father's retired – he used to be on the railway. They have a bungalow on the South Downs. They grow roses.' He smiled, as if this gave him pleasure.

They sat side by side on a red velvet bench. In a tinted looking-glass opposite, Emma saw her face reflected, smiling, slightly drunk.

'I have a bad relationship with my mother,' she said. 'She never listens to me and she has this queer, contemptuous attitude. And a selective memory. If I were to try to talk to her about something that has really worried me, she'd only say, *oh Emma, it wasn't like that.* It's as if she can't bear to admit that anything bad ever happened to me, it might reflect on her!' She could hear her voice, slightly hysterical, and laughing, grimacing at herself in the glass. 'I suppose the truth is, she makes me feel inadequate. How petty! She's wonderful, really, she does so much for other people! Perhaps I'm jealous. I want all her concern for myself!'

'If you had it, you'd complain she was possessive.' Lucas said. Though he was attentive, his eyes hinted at embarrassment.

'Oh, I *know*.' Smiling gaily, Emma moved the conversation on to a less personal plane. 'It's ghastly being a parent! Whatever you do is bound to be wrong. You try to avoid your own parents' mistakes and probably make worse ones of your own.'

'The relationship between parent and child is the most difficult one in the world,' Lucas agreed gravely. 'I suppose because it needs continual adjustment. Would you like a brandy?'

Emma shook her head. 'I wouldn't mind another cup of coffee, though. Or are you in a frightful hurry?'

'*Not* at-tall.' He sounded like Holly, Emma thought, surprised. He shifted in his seat, trying to catch the waiter's eye.

'Are you writing at the moment?' Emma said. 'Or do you hate to be asked that?'

'No. I'm finishing a book at the moment.'

'How do you start?' The ineptitude of this question flustered her. 'I mean, do you think of a plot, or the characters? Do you make a synopsis?'

'Well . . .'

Emma said quickly, 'I'm so sorry. People must ask you stupid questions all the time.'

'I'm not famous, you know. I still find it quite flattering to be asked, though not easy to answer.' Their waiter was busy. Lucas sighed. 'You see, each book is different. For me, anyway. I suppose one does develop an approach, but I'm not really conscious of it.'

'Do you dictate?'

'I make a rough copy and it's typed as I go along. I make corrections.'

'How's your nice secretary? Miss Paul,' she added, as if Lucas might have forgotten her name.

'She's in Austria at the moment.' Uncharacteristically, he reddened. 'She's due back on Sunday.'

'Funny time of the year to take a holiday.' Hearing herself say this, Emma despaired. She looked at the tinted mirror and said, brightly, 'We look like two fish mouthing at each other in an aquarium.'

He smiled dutifully. The waiter turned in their direction at last. Lucas lifted a beckoning finger.

They had eaten avocado pears, chicken in a pimento sauce, drunk a bottle and a half of burgundy. It was ten minutes past three and she was going to have a second cup of coffee. Emma wondered if she were going to cry.

She said, 'I do hope you don't mind my inviting myself,' and remembered that she had said this at least twice already.

'I was delighted, of course.' Having had practice in this answer, Lucas produced it pat and firm, though what he had to be delighted about, Emma thought, one might well wonder!

'I suppose I wanted someone to talk to,' she said. 'Outside the family, I mean. It's all been so – I mean, Henry is so upset about his father. One feels so helpless.'

This struck the right note. He put his hand over hers and squeezed it.

She said, 'It was terribly kind of you to write. That sort of letter is so difficult. Henry was touched.'

'I was so sorry.' He gave her hand a final, dismissing pat. His expression was puzzled.

She thought – this is impossible, and at once, horror seized her. He was bored. Humiliation sat like a stone in her stomach. Drinking her coffee too quickly, she burned her mouth. She looked at her watch and said, with a theatrical start, 'My goodness, is that the time?'

'It's not very late. But I suppose . . .' She could see that he felt he had disappointed her in some way. He fumbled with his wallet, paying the enormous bill – Emma felt remorseful when she glimpsed it – dropping the change. He and the waiter grovelled together under the starched tablecloth; Lucas straightened up, red in the face. 'Sorry,' he muttered, and her heart went out to him. How lovable people are when they are clumsy, make mistakes. *Dear Lucas, my love. . . .*

They came out of the restaurant into a sharp wind that made the eyes water.

'Where's your car?'

'The Embankment. I thought I wouldn't find a parking place any nearer.'

'Better get you a cab, then.' One hand under her elbow, Lucas waved the other at a cruising taxi. It stopped and he turned to Emma. 'Do you want me to come with you?'

She shook her head. He approached his face for a farewell peck. Emma closed her eyes.

'Thank you for a lovely lunch,' she said.

Ginny was tall for her age, a lean, pale child with a lot of dark, coarse hair, like a mane. She had Holly's eyes but her father's greater delicacy of feature. 'I don't think I want any lunch,' she said.

Ignoring this, Emma placed a plate of stew in front of her. She said, encouragingly, 'What are you going to do this afternoon?'

'What time'll Dad be back?'

'About four o'clock, I think.'

'I haven't seen him properly yet, he was late home last night, he missed my Coming Home Supper.' Her eyes filled. 'He didn't mean to, it was just something went wrong. Some silly *programme*.'

Hunched over the table, she stabbed at a lump of meat. Her hair flew around her, stiff with electricity; bits of stew clung to the ends.

'Who loves her Dad,' Emma said, smiling.

The child said primly, 'I love Mummy too,' as if Emma had challenged this.

'She's scared of the tree house,' William said.

'She's not scared of the *house*,' Rufus corrected him. 'She's just scared to climb up the rope ladder. She wants the steps.'

105

'Then let her use them.' Emma smiled at her sons, little boys with Henry's blue eyes and limp, fair hair, and at Ginny, whom she loved. She was competent, kind; a dream mother in a bright kitchen. But this was a pleasant dream.

'We always used to get up with the steps,' Ginny said. 'Now they've got this silly old rope ladder.'

'It was our birthday present.' William glared. 'It's more *real* to have a rope ladder.'

'Ginny likes her own way.' Rufus said priggishly.

Ginny chewed her hair. 'I do *not*. And I'm not scared, it's just that the rope ladder shakes. Dad told me to be careful.'

'Then you must have the steps,' Emma said. 'Don't let them bully you.'

Rufus said in a scornful voice, 'She wants to play *hop-scotch*.'

'Then you ought to. Fair's fair.'

'It's a girl's game.' William belched. 'Pardon my wind.'

'Who taught you that awful expression?'

'Mr Dodge. He didn't *teach* me, though, he's not a *teacher*. Just the caretaker at our school. It's what he says when he blows off, only he does it from the other end.'

'Pop, pop, pop – like a machine-gun,' Rufus said.

Both boys rocked their chairs, bellowing insanely.

'Lavatory jokes, it's a stage,' Ginny said, who had grown out of it.

'A tiresome one,' Emma agreed. She rapped the table, made her face stern. 'Eat up now, or no ice-cream after-wards.'

While Emma washed up, they played hopscotch on the terrace. She watched them through the window, the leggy girl, tossing her hair about, the fair, stocky boys. Emma was grateful that their cries sounded happy. She put the dishes away, peeled more potatoes for supper. They had a woman in for two hours on weekdays, but not on Saturday or Sunday. Emma thought – One day they will have robots to do this, will Henry notice the difference? She leaned her fore-

106

arms on the edge of the sink and shook with laughter. She could go to Lucas and nothing would change for her family. Adultery made easy. She played with this idea, smiling to herself as she put the potatoes in cold water, cut sandwiches for tea. Two Emmas; one husband, one family between them. 'It would solve all sorts of problems,' Emma said aloud, wrapping the sandwiches in foil and putting them in the refrigerator.

The children were on the lawn now, Ginny sitting on the garden roller, the boys inside separate cardboard boxes. Ginny was talking, waving her arms about: the boys watched her, unmoving. Emma wondered if they were warm enough. She opened the window a little, testing the air. It was unusually warm for December. Freak weather.

She closed the window, looked round the kitchen. There was nothing else to do. She thought – I forgot to order the Christmas tree.

She went into the hall. The telephone stood on the consul table in the hall, beneath the carved gilt mirror. She dialled the greengrocer's number. It was engaged. She put the receiver down and waited, looking at herself in the mirror. There was a faint, pink flush below her eyes: rather stagily, she put up the back of one hand to touch her cheek. Her lips moved in the mirror. She dialled again: the number was still engaged. There was a *ting* as she replaced the receiver.

She stood quite still. Fear was a knife, a sharp pain in her heart. She thought – I want to die, oh God, let me die. She gave a little cry and then moaned, hands stiff at her sides, eyes closed.

There was only one way of holding it back. *Lucas, my love. This is real. Nothing else.*

*My darling,*
    *It was wonderful being with you, so wonderful that I had to be alone, to savour it. That was why I told you not to come with me in the taxi, you knew that, didn't you?*

*I smiled to myself all the way home. Once I stopped at a traffic light and a man in a Jag looked at me as if I were a crazy woman, grinning and muttering to myself. I wanted to wind the window down and shout at him, I love Lucas, but then he might have been sure I was mad, and called a policeman!*

*You know, I always thought that if I fell in love I would feel so guilty about Henry, but I don't at all. Loving you has nothing to do with him, it is something quite different and set apart, so you need never be afraid I will use him to make you feel guilty – or myself, either. Of course I did feel guilty at first, but only in an attenuated way – rather like when I was a child eating sweets and reading a comic instead of getting on with my homework. So I gave it up – feeling guilty, I mean. It was as simple as that.*

*I love you. I could go on saying it for ever. I love you so much that I am no longer jealous, my darling. (You gave yourself away at lunch, did you know that?) But I only want your happiness. If she makes you happy in that dead, unreal time when I am away from you, then I love her too,*

*Emma.*

Dear Lucas,

Thank you so much for my nice lunch. It did me so much good, you performed a real service to humanity!

So thank you, I now feel more myself, as they say. Come and see us soon.

Yours,

Emma.

Emma put the letter into an envelope, stuck it down and addressed it. Then she opened the envelope and wrote a P.S.

And I mean *soon*. It would cheer us both up!

The envelope had torn. She threw it away and addressed another; looked in the old tobacco tin where she kept stamps. It was empty. She sighed, muttered aloud. 'For Heaven's sake, didn't I buy some the other day?'

'Who are you talking to?' William said.

'Myself. I get the right answer that way.' He was standing

in the doorway of the drawing-room, his socks coming down, shiny tear-tracks on his cheeks. 'What's the matter, pet?'

She crouched in front of him, drying his eyes. William cried very easily. 'They won't play with me, they're playing mothers and fathers and I won't be the baby all the time.' His mouth quivered at this injustice.

'Never mind. You can do something for me. Run up to the post.'

'Can I buy something at the shop?'

'You can get some crisps. A packet each. I'll give you two shillings, that'll be one-and-six for the crisps and fourpence for the letter. How much change?'

'Twopence.' He smiled; he had cried so hard that his mouth was still full of water and a bubble spluttered through the gap in his front teeth. Hugging him, Emma wanted to cry herself. She felt natural, happy.

She went to the front door, watched him hop down the path avoiding the cracks in the crazy-paving. 'Careful – don't hop on the pavement, you might over-balance and fall into the road.'

His head crushed by a passing lorry. Her stomach contracted. *I suppose all mothers are like that*, she said to Lucas, envisaging a candle-lit dinner. She would wear her white dress, jade ear-rings. *It's a kind of superstitious safe-guard, like carrying an umbrella on a sunny day.*

She went into the kitchen to put the kettle on. She was standing at the sink, the tap turned on, when the child screamed. She shouted, 'Rufus', leaning over the sink, the edge cutting into her stomach. She saw him clinging, half-way up the rope ladder. She ran out of the kitchen, down the hall, out of the back door. He saw her coming across the grass and began to cry. Emma picked him off the ladder and held him against her for a second, heavy and warm, before she put him down and knelt beside Ginny, on the ground.

'I was only wobbling her,' Rufus said. 'She was higher up

than me and I got on and wobbled her for fun and she fell off, it wasn't my fault.'

Ginny lay on her back, limbs spread, limp and rubbery as a starfish. Her eyes were not quite closed; there was a glimmer of light beneath the lids. Under her head, the grass was sparse and grey, only the moss was green. Emma felt her neck, her shoulders. Dare she move her, had she broken anything? People were fragile as china. 'Ginny,' she said roughly, in fear, and thought her lids fluttered. Cover her up, keep her warm. My God, Felix. . . .

'Is she dead?' Rufus asked, interested.

'No. Unconscious.' She glanced at her son who was sliding his thumb into his mouth. 'Gone to sleep. We're going to get the doctor.'

She caught his hand and raced him across the grass, her cheeks jolting. 'He'll make her well in a jiffy, you'll see.' She dialled, cradling the receiver between chin and shoulder; her other hand held Rufus. He was shaking; suddenly a pale stream trickled down his leg and splashed on the polished floor.

'I couldn't help it,' he wailed, and Emma pulled him against her, stroking his head while the telephone rang in the doctor's house.

'My precious baby, don't cry, it's not your fault, my pet, my apple-pie. . . .'

# 7. *Henry*

'Felix is at the hospital. I'm going to fetch Holly.'

'You know where she is?'

Emma nodded. Her face, which had been whiter than I had ever seen it, flamed scarlet. She had met me at the door, told me as we walked to the garage. Unable to believe it, I fumbled with inessentials.

'You mean she *tells* you these things?'

'Yes.' Getting into the driving seat, Emma rattled keys, turning away from me.

'Who is it?'

She didn't answer. I said, 'Heaven's above, this isn't a time to be loyal.'

She closed her eyes.

I said, 'Well, if you know, couldn't you 'phone?'

'I tried. It was out of order. Off the hook – I don't know.'

She looked exhausted. She was wearing her blue woollen coat with the fur collar.

I said, 'Poor mouse, you look awful. I could go.' I wondered about my motives. I thought – I am getting too old for this sort of thing. My heart was thumping.

'Henry, listen.' Letting the engine run, adjusting the choke, she looked suddenly better: cool and competent. 'The baby-sitter will be here in about five minutes. You go to the hospital. Take Felix's car, the key's in it. He went in the ambulance.'

'How's Rufus?'

'Better now. He's been telling William, turning it into a story.'

I said, 'Oh, Jesus.'

My son and Felix's daughter. I thought – We are too cushioned, we can't face this sort of thing. You go to work on a Saturday to clear things up before Christmas, come home tired, looking forward to telly and early bed, and walk into a fictional situation. Gladstone, weeping over the death of Little Nell, was not mawkish: he had sat by the death-bed of his own daughter. Nowadays we aren't used to children dying.

Emma said, 'Darling, don't look like that. She's not dead.'

Felix was sitting in the reception hall. There was an aquarium with goldfish swimming in brownish water, magazines in neat piles on the tables, a counter where they sold tea and biscuits. I had walked up a long ramp, past wards decorated for Christmas. The floor was covered with a brown, composition material, pitted with round, black holes.

When I spoke to Felix, his face twitched a little.

I said, 'Emma's gone to fetch Holly,' but he seemed not to hear. That bitch, I thought, that filthy bitch.

Felix said, 'They think there's a crack fracture of the skull, but her temperature's well down, and the blood pressure.'

'What does that mean?'

'That there's no evidence of haemorrhage yet. She came round in the ambulance for a bit but it wasn't too soon afterwards. Apparently that's a good sign; I don't know why.'

'What are they doing?'

'Keeping her under observation.' His voice, flat and cool, acquired an edge. 'It seems we're in luck. There's a consultant in head injuries operating at the moment. God descended from the heights of Harley Street. He'll condescend to look at her when he's finished.'

'He could hardly walk out of the theatre.'

'No.' Felix looked at me. 'I'm sorry, I just have to hate someone. They've all been marvellously kind.'

'One's in their hands.'

'Yes. Poor Emma. I yelled at her, I'm afraid. She was wonderful. God, I'm *sorry*.'

'Don't think about it. She wouldn't.' I hesitated. 'She's gone to fetch Holly.'

'Good.' He looked at his hands. White, rather plump, with well-kept nails. 'When she came round for that minute or two, she said, *I want Mummy*.'

I couldn't think of anything to say.

Felix said. 'It doesn't *matter*, for Christ's sake. It doesn't make any difference, she might just as easily have been at the dentist or out buying a dress.'

I said, 'Well, at least Emma seems to know where she is. I don't know how long they'll be.'

A nurse came into the hall, shoes squeaking. 'Mr Craven, the doctor would like to see you.' A plump woman, a pillow cut in two by a stout leather belt. Her soft downy face smiled, almost sociably.

Felix followed her. He looked very young from behind, walking very erect, his toes turning in a little. I tried to put myself in his place but I couldn't. One never has enough imagination.

I went to the counter and asked for a cup of tea. Something to do. There was a middle-aged woman with a genteel accent. 'Milk? Sugar?' This would be a voluntary job. People ease their consciences this way. I thought – What the hell do motives matter? I said. 'Milk, and two lumps, please.' She had a dried-out, yellow skin with powder lying in the wrinkles.

I sat down with my cup. My head ached. I wished I had a cigarette. There was a big clock on the wall with a red minute hand. How long would Emma be? Why hadn't I asked her? She would have told me that. She and Holly must have confidence-sessions, giggling like schoolgirls. I wouldn't have thought Emma was like that.

The tea had a milky scum on it that left a rim round the

cup. I took it back to the counter and the woman said, 'We're closing. Do you want another?'

'No thank you.' I thought – Felix has a sweet tooth. He used to eat peppermint creams.

'Have you any peppermint creams?'

'I'm afraid we only keep biscuits and chocolate.' For some reason, she looked offended.

I bought a bar of chocolate for Felix and sat down. The only other person in the hall was an old man, snoozing in a wheelchair. He had one leg in plaster. I wondered if I should go out to the car and see if Emma had left a packet of cigarettes in the glove compartment. I would just have one cigarette. I remembered that I had come in Felix's car. Felix had given up smoking. I sighed and picked up a motoring magazine. I flicked the pages and read the small ads. There was a Delage for sale.

Felix and I had shared an old Delage at Oxford, a long, low, black saloon with an aluminium body and a Cotel electric gear-box. We used to boast about it. 'It doesn't do miles per gallon, it uses gallons per mile.' Felix drove it to London at weekends to see this gorgeous nurse he wanted to get engaged to. He was terrified of asking her, in case she turned him down. He was very happy and tortured. We shared a small flat on the Iffley Road; late at night we brewed up coffee on the gas ring and I gave him the benefit of my wise advice. This was before I had met Emma and I was against marriage until one was at least thirty-five and had nothing else to look forward to. I was reading law but I was writing a play and hoped for a career in the theatre. I had forgotten what it was like to be in love: Felix could not envisage life without his nurse, whom he had met in the Casualty department of a London hospital when he got a bit of burning ash in his eye. She wasn't working now. She was looking after her grandmother, who was dying. Since she couldn't leave her, Felix spent the weekends in the grand-mother's flat, above a greengrocer's shop in Clapham. I

114

thought this couldn't be much fun, but Felix admired Holly for her devotion to her grandmother. 'She really is a remarkable person – it's an awful situation, almost no money and that terrible flat, but she never complains, she even makes it seem easy. And you know, a lot of girls would be put off by Grandma in the next room, or use it as an excuse, but she tucks her down with a hot water bottle and hops into bed, leaving the door open so she can hear if the old lady rings her bell. . . .'

I thought I saw what had happened. Felix had discovered sex. He had always believed he was too small for anyone really attractive to take him seriously, and so his girls tended to be plain and intense, tearful rather than passionate: he asked them to the flat and they sat on the sofa and wept. They were in love with their tutors, or their fathers, or some married man. Felix dried their tears and gave them drinks and cigarettes. They said, 'Felix, you are so terribly sweet.'

I pointed out that this experience had been largely his own fault. There were plenty of cheerful, carnal girls about, there was no need to go overboard over the first one he met. I said, 'Love is a biological trap.' Felix waved his hands about protesting – 'She has this astonishing *energy*' – but he couldn't really explain what was different about her. 'She'll be good for me,' he argued, 'she'll stop me getting stodgy.' He was obsessed with his 'stodginess' at this time: he was still young enough to be affected by someone else's assessment of his personality. It would be typical of Holly to make such a crude one. In fact, though he was high-principled and morally serious, he was also rather neurotic, quick to change, very humble: he respected other people's opinions more than he did his own. Holly had 'very advanced ideas'. He was shyly proud of this. 'It's marvellous to meet someone who is so completely lacking in hypocrisy, like coming out of a stuffy room into the open air.' I said, 'Well, if you must get married, at least you'll go into it with your eyes open.'

I had met Holly by this time and I think Felix wrote this remark down as jealousy, which perhaps it partly was, though I believe I was honestly concerned for him as well. He was so proud to have achieved this marvellous, mythical girl. All his defences were gone; he had lost his solemn, slightly quirkish manner. She made him ridiculous, and he didn't care. She came down to a Commemoration Ball and treated him like a mascot, like a toy she had got out of a Christmas cracker. Tweaking his tie undone and calling him 'Pussy'. Towards the end of the evening, she danced all the time with a tall, kilted Scot whose father was a Labour peer who often appeared on television. The Scot's partner was ill and lying down in a room somewhere. Holly danced with her shoes off, in a gold dress with her dark hair streaming. Felix and I sat on some steps with my girl, whose name was Faith. She was reading History and her father was a Bishop. I remember this moment: drugged, thudding music from the nearest marquee and some people laughing somewhere. I had my arm round this girl, with whom I had been sleeping all that term. We were beginning to bore each other, and she leaned against me as if I were a pillar. We watched Holly and the Scot, dancing on the silver grass, both rather drunk, swaying together. 'Doesn't she move beautifully?' Felix said. He wasn't jealous. He was in ecstasy because he was allowed to sit here, watching her.

It made me so angry. He was my oldest friend, my best friend, and I had a sentimental feeling that he was more vulnerable than I was, more easily hurt.

I wondered now if my feelings about Holly had distorted my picture of Felix – I wanted him to be hurt so that I could hate her for it – or if he had always been much tougher, much harder than I thought.

Or grown tougher, perhaps. I watched him as he walked down the hall towards me. I had been thinking of him as he had been years ago, so that his physical appearance was almost a shock, he looked so exhausted, so old. And then I thought – His child is dying.

He said, 'The consultant's seen her. He's quite hopeful though he can't give an exact prognosis, of course. Head injuries are tricky things.' He was quoting.

'Is she still unconscious?'

'Unconscious – asleep – I don't know. She's lying there. Her hands are filthy. I suppose they can't wash her, don't want to move her too much.' He sat down, thrusting his own hands between his short thighs as if he were cold. 'They've chopped off her hair at the back, Holly will be upset.'

'Damn Holly,' I said.

He seemed surprised. Then he said, 'It's not her fault, what happened to Ginny.'

'You'd have to tell yourself that.'

'That's not the point. The point is that it's true.' He looked at me. 'You know, as far as Holly goes, you might say I'd made a pretty fair adjustment to that situation.' He pulled a face, hearing this cant phrase. 'True, though. It ceased to be important quite some time ago.'

I wondered. People pretend all the time, to make life bearable.

I didn't know whether he wanted to talk about it. I thought probably not. I said, 'I wish to God I'd never bought that bloody rope ladder.'

'So do I.' His voice sounded impatient and I was glad he didn't feel he had to deny this, for my comfort. He said, 'I'm not so scared now. She looks a better colour and they really do seem quite hopeful. But perhaps my adrenalin's just stopped flowing.'

'I should think they'd say if there was really any danger.'

'Perhaps they don't know.' He picked up the motoring magazine I'd been reading and stared at the cover.

I said, 'Funny thing, there's an advertisement for a Delage, same year as ours.'

'Can't be the same one, though. This must be a museum specimen if it's still on the road.'

'I suppose so.'

He said. 'You know, I couldn't believe it at first. For years I simply couldn't believe anyone could really behave like that. Ridiculous, of course, since she'd told me. I suppose I was too used to people striking attitudes. At Oxford. I could hardly blame her for that, could I?'

'Did you ever think you might sling her out?'

'I suppose I might have done. But I felt it must be my fault, you see.'

'That's neurotic.'

'Possibly.' He sounded politely bored, as if this were something that no longer occupied him, but he felt it was nice of me to be concerned about. 'Anyway,' he said, 'there was Ginny.' He looked at me for a moment, then he put his head in his hands. I felt I wanted to smash something. I dug my hands in my pockets and found the chocolate I had bought. I took it out and put it on the table.

Emma said, 'Holly's here. The sister said you can go and sit with Ginny now.'

Neither of us had heard her come. Her hair looked darker than usual, then I saw it was wet.

'Is it raining?'

'Cats and dogs.'

Felix got up. 'Bless you, love.' He held her elbow and kissed her cheek.

She said, 'Oh Felix darling, I do hope . . .'

'I know.' He walked away, up the empty hall.

Emma said, 'Is she going to be all right?'

'They can't be sure yet.'

She put the back of her hand against her cheek.

I said, 'We might as well go home. We're only in the way now. We can telephone.'

She started walking, quite fast, as if she had a long way to

118

go and might as well start now. I caught her up and held her arm. 'Where did you leave the car?'

'At the bottom of the ramp.'

It was sleet, turning to snow. Crystals on the windscreen, like silver flowers. I was driving. The car smelt of wet raincoats and decaying vegetation. The boys ate bananas and dropped the skins on the floor. I thought – I ought to clean it out over the holidays. Five days to Christmas. I said, 'So you found her all right?'

'Evidently.'

I groped for her hand which felt small and cold. I said, 'You're frozen. Put your gloves on. Poor mousie, was it terribly embarrassing?'

She didn't answer. Of course, she would think it shameful to admit to embarrassment at a time like this. I was ashamed, too, because I wanted to know. It was none of my business.

'Tell me. Come on, get it off your chest.' Making my voice light and humorous; a kind man, comforting his shy wife. I squeezed her hand before I let it go to turn out of the hospital gates onto the main road. The tarmac was smooth, gleaming like black silk. A lighted bus roared by.

Emma said, 'Henry, I would really prefer not to talk about it, if you don't mind.' She sounded as if she were suffocating.

I said, 'Just as you like. I only thought it might help you.'

In the headlights, trees shook in the wind. The traffic began to slow. We were coming into the outskirts of our suburb; a line of shops, a garage, the cinema that had been turned into a Catholic Church. We stopped at the traffic lights. The windscreen wipers squeaked: it was snowing now.

Emma said, 'They weren't actually in bed, if that's what you wanted to know.'

Her voice punished me for a sin I hadn't obviously committed.

I said, with a fair show of indignation, 'It wasn't. I was thinking of you.'

She gave a small, moaning sound as if she were in pain. It struck me that her distress was exaggerated. It bored me. I said, bracingly, 'Come on, love, you're a big girl now.'

I drove the baby-sitter home. She was an old woman with asthma who liked the boys to be in bed before she arrived and always had to be home before midnight. This often annoyed me, but Emma said she didn't like to find anyone else, the poor soul needed the money. The poor soul didn't do too badly out of us. She sat with Ginny, too, in the holidays.

'Oh, that poor baby! And the only one, too! Poor Mrs Craven, I can't bear to think what she's going through. She worships that child, she really does, it's lovely to see them together. It'll break my heart if anything happens to her, it may sound silly but I'm like that, I take things to heart even if it's just something in the newspaper, but when it's someone you know, it makes it worse, doesn't it? You think too much of others, my husband says, you ought to think of yourself for a change, other people put upon you, but I can't say Mrs Craven's ever done that. Such a lovely, natural person, isn't she, always gives me a bit over and above and fetches me from the hospital on the days I go up for my varicose veins which makes a lot of difference because standing for the bus undoes all the good the treatment's done me. Oh, I tell you, Mr Lingard, I shan't sleep a wink tonight, thinking of that poor soul in her trouble. . . .'

And so on and so forth, the breath snuffling and wheezing in her chest. Oh lovely sadness, the warm release of someone else's sorrow. But her easy flow brought a lump into my own throat and when I dropped her at her house and saw the tears in her eyes, water came into mine.

We don't feel enough. We know so much now; we have grown cold and wary. Even when we do feel, we mistrust the reason behind it: hypocrisy is the great sin.

We don't know what is real anymore.

Emma was standing in front of the open refrigerator. She said, 'I suppose we ought to eat something.' She began to take out butter, cheese, milk. She was moving like a sleep-walker, a zombie.

I said. 'What have you been doing?'

'I'm sorry. I meant to get a meal, but I felt sick.'

'Boys all right?'

'Fast asleep. They've been making paper chains, they're all up and down the stairs.'

'It doesn't feel like Christmas. Still feel sick?'

'A bit.' She yawned. 'I don't think I want anything.'

'You ought to try. Make you feel better.' Her face looked yellow; her eyes were small, muddy holes. I said, 'Sit down, I'll heat you some milk to begin with. Or would you rather have a brandy?'

She shook her head and sat down, arms spread out on the table. I poured milk into a pan, added sugar. I wondered when we should ring the hospital. What was the time now? I looked at the kitchen clock and saw, shocked, that it was only seven-thirty.

'It feels more like midnight.' I said. 'I suppose we could ring about nine.'

Ought we to get a meal for them? Would they come home? I poured the warm milk into the cup, gave it to Emma, and looked in the refrigerator. There was half a cold chicken, eggs – I could make an omelette with minced chicken and herbs. Something – what was the word? – something *tasty*. At some point during the war, my father used to get tea for me when I was home in the holidays. His shop was closed because of the bombing and he was waiting to be called up; my mother was out at her 'war work', serving gin in an officers' club. 'We'll have something tasty,' he'd say, which meant fish and chips or smoked haddock or bloater paste sandwiches, washed down with great floods of hot, strong, sweet tea. My mother thought that kind of meal vulgar. When she was home, we ate 'dinner' at seven-thirty in the blacked-out dining-room: watery soup, small squares of grey meat, pink cornflour pudding in cut glasses, a ritual of dreary tastelessness, nothing to do with appetite or pleasure. 'I'd rather eat water toast,' my father once said to me when we were washing up afterwards. 'At least it's honest pap.'

He had been standing in this kitchen, about two yards away from where I was standing now, at the sink, wearing a flowered apron of my mother's. A stout-ish man with a handsome, cheerful face; broken veins on his cheekbones; a bristly, black and grey moustache. For a second he was here beside me, solid, alive: I could almost believe I had heard his voice.

I said, 'Do you know what water toast is?' I felt suddenly hungry. I hacked at a chicken and pulled off a leg. 'My grandmother used to eat it, she lost all her teeth and could never get used to dentures, so she lived on this stuff. You put a lump of butter on toast, lots of pepper and salt, then you pour boiling water over it.'

Emma looked at me. There was a fringe of milk on her upper lip.

I said, 'It's extraordinary, the way you think of things. I never saw my grandmother eat this muck – I hardly knew her, as a matter of fact, she and my mother didn't get on – but I suddenly remembered my father telling me about it.' My mouth was full of chicken and bread. I thought Emma looked frightened, as if I had suddenly gone mad. I said, 'I suppose it just sounded so thoroughly repellent that it stuck in my mind.'

Emma's nostrils were pinching in and out. Like a horse.

I said, 'He was very fond of his mother. He said she was a good sort. She had a house in Hackney; when he made money, he tried to move her out of it, but she wouldn't budge. She was killed by a bomb – he took me down there one Sunday to see where the house had been. I was about twelve, I suppose. He said, *poor old soul, not much of a last resting place*. He cried, standing there in the street, and I was horrified. I walked away up the street, whistling. . . .'

And had, almost immediately, been even more horrified by my own behaviour. I was old enough to be aware that embarrassment in this situation was despicable and I despised myself. I thrust my hands into my pockets and whistled louder. When my father caught me up, my cheeks burned with shame and tears rose in my eyes. Mistaking the cause, he comforted me. 'Don't take on old chap, she had a good life and there are worse ways to go. I don't suppose she knew much about it.' My tears fell. He took a red silk handkerchief out of his breast pocket and mopped my face gently. He said, 'Come on now, I know what we'll do, we'll pay Auntie Jess a visit, that'll cheer you up, won't it?'

Auntie Jess had tangerine-coloured hair arranged in a high, stiff pompadour, and wonderful breasts, jutting beneath her tight blouse like satin globes. She gave me a strawberry ice in a glass bowl. I ate, balancing on the edge of a deep, very softly cushioned armchair. She and my father sipped drinks, sunk side by side in the equally soft cushions of the sofa opposite, and watched me admiringly, as if I were doing something clever. In the hearth, an electric fire with imitation coals flickered first red, then orange. A budgerigar in a cage by the window said, 'Hallo Joey,' and pecked at its reflection in a mirror.

As soon as I had finished the ice, Auntie Jess rose. 'I'm sure Someone could manage another, couldn't he?' She bent over to take my empty bowl and her satin bosom was fascinatingly close, the nipples sweetly evident through the thin material of her blouse. I thought of the cherry, perched on top of my strawberry ice, and couldn't take my eyes away. Then my father cleared his throat, loud enough to make me jump. There was a pink flush on his cheekbones. I said, quickly and politely, 'No thank you, Auntie, I don't think I could.' My mother had taught me that it was rude to appear eager for second helpings, but I knew I was safe: Auntie

123

Jess would not take no for an answer. There would be a second ice-cream, even a third if I could manage it. My father would look on, drinking whisky and soda and beaming encouragement: the extent of my appetite would determine the length of our stay. Once I could eat no more, my father would drain his glass, wipe his moustache, get up with a grunt. 'Well now, I suppose it's Home James and don't spare the hosses.'

I knew the drill. During that early part of the war, when my father was waiting to go into the Army, I had visited a succession of Aunties. After one of our expeditions – the park, the cinema – my father would pull out his gold hunter and crinkle up his eyes with apparent surprise. 'Well, it looks as if we've got a little time in hand, doesn't it?' Then the bus, or the train ride – never very far – and the Auntie of the moment at the end of the journey, her smiling, pretty face blooming above her best blouse, her welcoming voice slightly common (my mother's dreadful standards had made me an expert on vowel sounds), so pleased to see us, so lavishly stocked with ice-cream, so kind. Each new Auntie seemed very much like the last, or perhaps that was only my desirous imagination. I used to fall in love with them all, comfortably and happily, as with a myth or a dream. . . .

Auntie Jess was the last I was taken to see. My father was called up quite soon afterwards, and though we went out together when he was home on leave, we always went to a restaurant afterwards. Though I was disappointed, I could not say so. I had some guilty embarrassment about the way I had stared at Auntie Jess, but my inhibition had deeper roots than that. My father and I had never discussed the Aunties: he had never given me any explanation of their relationship, either to me or to himself. It is hard to remember how I thought then. Growing older, we change our assessment of ourselves. We condemn or we justify. I think now that children are aware of the protection that the assumption of innocence gives them. I knew that I must not mention our visits to my mother, but I never admitted to myself why. Thus getting the best of both worlds.

I said, 'How foul kids are. . . .'

Emma said, '*Henry* . . .' She was standing up. She had one hand to her side as if she had a pain.

I said, 'Sorry. This is boring. Funny the way things come into your head. Irrelevancies. You ought to have something to eat.'

I thought – Now I've stopped smoking, I think about food all the time. I would become enormously fat, my piggy eyes glinting.

'Henry, I've got to tell you something.' Her eyes had gone suddenly huge. She said, 'I can't bear it any longer.'

I said, 'You're making it all up. Listen – no, let *me* talk for a change. You've got this mad idea in your head, God knows why, but don't you see, it can't be true or you'd have told me at the time? All right – maybe you had a row with him, though I'm not even convinced about *that*. Oh, I daresay Dad told you a dirty joke or two, teased you a bit. He was always one for the girls. Darling, I don't want to hurt you, but haven't you enlarged a bit? You say you pretended it hadn't happened – well, if it *had*, I can see you might do that – but I don't believe it *did*. Look – you had a row, I'll accept that, and the poor old man turned giddy and fell. And this has all worked up in your mind into a kind of towering guilt and this awful thing about Ginny has brought it crashing down. I can understand that. . . .'

She lay on her back on the bed, her hair spread out. A mermaid under water. I thought – I ought to take her hand and comfort her but I don't want to touch her. This frightened me. I made myself sit on the bed and stroke her arm gently.

'After all, what was the row *about*? If what you've been telling me is true, you'd be able to tell me that, wouldn't you? Even if he made a pass at you, which might be upsetting, I grant you, it could hardly have frightened you that much. I mean, he was an old man, pretty tottery, you couldn't possibly have believed he could hurt you.'

She was picking at the stuff of her dressing-gown. I caught her hands and held them against my chest, like a Victorian gentleman in an engraving. She twisted her head away, her eyes closed. Her whole body was shuddering. I wondered if I ought to get the doctor, and then I thought – Suppose she tells him? I had a moment of pure terror. Doctors, police, newspapers – the whole fabric of life falling apart. Through one, hysterical lie.

Emma wasn't hysterical. She was calm, gentle, always truthful. A sweet, self-effacing girl. My kind, intelligent Emma. I thought – I have to tell myself these things. I thought – She killed my father – and had to press my knees together to stop my legs shaking. I let go her hands and they fell on the bed, palms upwards, defenceless. Her eyes, open now, stared at the ceiling. I said, 'I'm going to get you a sleeping pill.'

I went into the bathroom, tightened a dripping tap, opened the medicine chest. I thought – What do I know about Emma? People live together for years, die strangers. I am a stranger to myself, I don't know what I am capable of. I said, aloud, 'You need a drink, old boy.'

I shook a sleeping pill into my hand, put the bottle into my pocket. I thought – Better lock them up somewhere. Emma would never do a thing like that, but one might as well make sure. I rinsed out the tooth mug – plastic decorated with pink roses – and filled it with water.

She was still lying with her eyes staring open. I said, in a nanny's voice, 'What you want is a good, long sleep. Sunday tomorrow. I'll get breakfast, you can lie in.' She sat up and took the pill, the mug juddering against her teeth. She smiled at me shakily and I felt a great bound of relief. *Of course, this is all such nonsense.*

I helped her off with her gown and turned back the covers

so she could get into bed. She lurched about drunkenly, like an exhausted child.

I sat beside her. 'Precious love, you mustn't think anymore tonight. We'll talk tomorrow. You know, it's my guess you'll wake up and it'll all seem like a ghastly nightmare. A sort of brain storm.'

She was screwing up her face. She said, in a light, breathless voice, 'Henry, I can't make out whether you believe me or not. I pushed your father down the stairs. Try and believe me for a minute. How do you feel?'

'Christ alive, this isn't a *game*.'

She began to move her head from side to side, moaning.

I said, 'I don't know. The thing is, of course, I can't believe it. I suppose if I did, I'd feel – well – pretty odd.' I stretched my stiff face in a clown's grin. 'I suppose I'd be scared out of my wits, wondering whether you'd push *me* next time.'

What I would feel – what I *felt* – was slowly rising horror, like creeping paralysis. I thought – What is the moral position? One's wife kills one's father, what does the honourable citizen do? I gave a short bark of laughter and turned it into a cough, holding my side, acting the bronchitic old man. I thought – I wish to God I could talk to Felix.

She had begun to whimper, small, squeaky sounds like a dreaming puppy. I knelt beside the bed and tried to take her in my arms but she pushed at my chest, pummelling me, throwing herself about. I said. 'All right, Emmakins.' I let her go and she rolled onto her front, her face hidden. I turned off the bedside light and went to the window to draw the curtains back. Emma liked the street lamp shining in at night. There were lights in Felix's house.

I turned back to the bed. 'Go to sleep, love. I'll be back in a minute.'

I telephoned Felix. He said, 'It looks as if she's going to be all right. She woke up and had a drink. Then she went to sleep. It seems we've been very lucky. Everyone kept telling us how lucky we'd been.'

I said, 'Felix, we're so terribly glad.'

'I was going to ring you. I saw your light was on. Thank Emma, won't you? She was wonderful. Everyone's been wonderful.' He sounded tight as a tick. 'Oh Christ,' he said, 'I feel as if I could push over a bloody mountain.'

'I shouldn't try. You might hurt yourself. Better go to bed and get some sleep.' It struck me that I was always telling people to get some sleep. 'It's a universal panacea.'

'What?'

'Sleep is a universal panacea,' I said. 'Mother Nature's cure-all.'


'Daddy. Get up.'

I rolled over, muttering. My mouth tasted sour.

'Get *up*, Daddy.'

'He doesn't know what *up* means.'

'Daddy, where's Mummy?'

I stretched out my hand, patted empty space beside me, opened my eyes. The light in the room was cold and silvery. Snow light. My sons, in striped pyjamas from Marks and Spencer, regarded me reproachfully.

'It's snowing.'

'Where's Mummy gone?'

'We thought she was downstairs getting our breakfast but she's not.'

'If you smoked a pipe, we could make a snowman with a pipe in his mouth. Why don't you smoke a pipe, Daddy?'

'We're going to make a snowman after breakfast, there's tons and tons of snow. It all came in the night.'

'A bit of the roof's come off the garage and it's hanging *down*.'

'Where's Mummy?'

'I don't know. Shopping?' I took my wrist watch from the bed table. It was nine o'clock.

My sons roared with laughter. 'It's Sunday. Shops don't open *Sunday*.'

'The little one at the end of the road. We might have run out of bread, or something.'

Emma never ran out of bread. I got up, pushed my feet into slippers, my arms into my gown.

'Go and get dressed,' I said.

They followed me onto the landing, complaining. 'It's Sunday, we get dressed after breakfast on Sunday. *You're* not getting dressed, it's not *fair*.'

'I'm going to get your breakfast. If you get dressed now, you'll have more time to play in the snow.'

'I expect Mummy's gone to the hospital,' William said. 'Rufus waggled the rope ladder and Ginny fell off and she went to the hospital.'

'I did *not*.'

'You did, Mrs Thing told Granny on the telephone, I heard her.'

'She's a fat liar.'

'You're a fat liar.'

'I'm not, *you* are.'

Rufus screamed and ran at his brother, arms flailing. William put his head down and butted him in the chest, like a young steer. Rufus sat down hard on the floor, eyes screwed shut, bawling. I picked him up and he snuffled damply into my neck.

'It was an accident, sweetheart, no one's fault, don't cry.'

'Is she dead?' William asked. The colour rushed into his face and he giggled, shrilly.

'Of course she isn't. A bit of a headache, that's all. Now...' I set Rufus down. 'Go and get dressed, double quick time.' I clapped my hands, shoo-ing them up the stairs into the tower room, like chickens.

Downstairs in the hall, the post lay scattered, a special Christmas delivery. All unsealed envelopes. Christmas cards. One with unfamiliar handwriting. A white-robed cherub blowing a golden trumpet. Inside it said, *Seasonal Greetings from Flo and Bun*. We knew no one called Flo or Bun and the postmark was indecipherable. I thought – This'll make Emma laugh. And then – Where is Emma?

Sometimes in an emergency, the body slows down. The mind crawls, action is a meaningless reflex, like a dead chicken twitching. I called softly, experimentally, 'Emma . . . ?'

In the kitchen, the table was laid for breakfast. Cereal bowls, cutlery, clean napkins, a packet of Weetabix. She had put slices of bacon ready under the grill, halved tomatoes beneath. I put the coffee on and went to the drawing-room. A scene of domestic disaster: crumpled cushions on the floor, brandy bottle on its side on the hearth rug, a broken glass in the grate. I picked up the bottle. It was three-quarters empty – surely it has been almost full when we started last night? I couldn't remember drinking so much. Had Emma come down after I was asleep? Sat crouched by the dying fire, a drunken, blonde witch, brooding?

I moved round the room, picking up cushions, emptying ashtrays. I had smoked last night. How many? Six, seven . . . ? I rubbed at the side of my nose, calculating. There was an empty packet on the open flap of the Queen Anne bureau; beside it, a brown envelope with letters spilling out. Emma's handwriting. *My darling Lucas . . .*

The door bell rang; it made me jump, as if I had been caught doing something disreputable. I stuffed the letters into my dressing-gown pocket and went into the hall.

It was the greengrocer's boy, lanky in jeans, long hair like a yak.

'Your Christmas tree, Mr Lingard, we're getting the trees out this morning. Getting ahead a bit.'

It was a large tree, going brown at the bottom. Last year, the needles had begun to fall before Christmas was over. I said, 'It looks a bit tatty.'

'Tatty? D'you think so, Sir? They're a fine lot this year,

130

this was one of the best, the lady picked it out herself.'
Already old in this game, he frowned, pursed his lips. A
studied look of amazement.

'Oh. Well, then . . .' I took the tree inside. As I leaned it
against the wall, needles rattled on the floor. The boy hopped
from one leg to the other, slapping his chest with his arms.
Like a spider dancing. Catching my eye, he grinned.

'Seasonable weather.'

'What? Oh. Yes.' My loose change was upstairs, in the
pocket of my trousers. I said, 'Hang on a minute.'

I raced upstairs, gathering the skirts of my gown round
me. My trousers lay in a heap on the floor of the bedroom.
I picked them up, shook; a half-crown fell out. Nothing else.
My wallet had a ten-shilling note in it. I went downstairs,
the half-crown in my hand, and advanced, smiling, to the
door. His bright, expectant look blackmailed me. I fumbled
in my pocket and brought out the ten-shilling note and
several of the letters with it. One lay beseechingly on the
floor. *Lucas, my love.* I could feel the colour rise in my face.
I said, 'And a Happy Christmas to you.'

'*Thank* you, Sir.' The surprise sounded genuine: one
might almost believe he had lingered for a friendly chat.
'All the best to you, too. Looks like a white Christmas.'

'It does indeed.' We grinned cheerily at each other. A
lump of snow fell with a *thump* somewhere and I remembered
what the boys had said about the garage roof. I went to the
top of the steps. There was a piece of guttering broken. The
greengrocer's boy had paused interrogatively at the gate. I
gave him a friendly wave and closed the front door.

I began to pick up the letters. Disjointed fragments leapt
up at me. I began to mutter under my breath – *this is too
ridiculous, really, what is one to do?* Felix had once had a habit
of suddenly groaning aloud whenever he remembered something embarrassing he had said or done. I shuffled the letters,
shaping them like a pack of cards. The telephone rang.

I stumbled over the tassel of my gown.

'Emma . . .'

'Henry?' Emma's mother said. 'I do hope I haven't woken you up.'

'Goodness, no. I've been up for hours.'

I was panting as if I had run a race.

'Or got you out of the bath? I'm so sorry.'

'*No.* It's all right.'

'I got the baby-sitter yesterday evening. She said you were at the hospital. How's the little girl?'

'She's going to be all right.'

'I'm so glad. I was going to ring again last night, but I thought *no* – you'll only be an old nuisance! The baby-sitter said she fell out of the tree house.'

'Off the rope ladder. Rufus was playing some silly game.'

'Oh dear. I was always afraid something like this would happen. I do hope Emma won't . . .' Her voice seemed to fade.

'What?'

'Don't let her make too much of it.'

'What do you mean?' I pulled a face at myself in the mirror.

'Well, you know what she is. I couldn't sleep a wink last night, thinking of you both. Of course, one doesn't like to say, how terrible, it happened in my house, but that's what you must have been feeling.'

'I suppose so. Yes, I suppose so.'

'As a matter of fact, Henry, I've been a bit worried in general. Perhaps you were right, I should have stayed after the funeral. Emma seemed very strained. As it turns *out*, my lodger's driving up to London today to spend the holiday with his mother. He's offered to bring me, on the way. That's why I rang last night. Would that suit you? We'd be there in about an hour's time.'

'Well . . . I mean, *yes.* Yes, of course.'

'Henry . . .'

'Yes?'

'You said, *Emma,* when I rang. Isn't she there?'

'No.'

'Oh.' She waited. 'Of course, she'll be across at the Craven's. You're sure I can be useful, Henry?'

'Of course'.

I thought – The old crow. She can scent blood, the smell of corpses.

I had put the letters on the consul table. I stared down at the words that stared up at me.

I said, 'We'll look forward to seeing you, then. I'm afraid I've got to go now, something's boiling over.'

I wanted to scream, bang my head against the wall.


'Daddy,' Rufus said. 'Is breakfast ready yet?'

They came down the stairs, in jeans and red jerseys.

I said, 'Cereal first. I'll cook the bacon while you eat it.'

'Hasn't Mummy come back? Isn't she going to have *breakfast*?'

'I expect she had it before she went out.'

'Where'd she go?'

'Just to see someone.' I knew where she must be. It seemed totally unreal. Even the bile that rose in my mouth could be a purely physical symptom: I had drunk too much last night, not breakfasted yet. 'Granny's coming after breakfast,' I said. 'When she's here to look after you. I'll go and fetch Mummy.'


# 8. *Holly*


I went to early communion and then on to the hospital: it was bitter cold, and when I got back I was dying for a pot of tea. Felix was still fast asleep, so I settled down in the kitchen and the tea was made and on the table when Henry walked in.

'Just in time for a cuppa,' I told him, knowing he liked it the way I did, a dark, strong brew with lots of sugar. 'Working class tea,' I told him once, but though he grinned, he didn't much like my saying it: old Henry's a fearful snob.

He asked about Ginny and I told him I'd been to see her that morning and she was in great form. I didn't mention I'd been to church. People are often more embarrassed about religion than about sex: sometimes I think it's because they're afraid they're missing out on something you know about and they don't. When I prayed for Ginny at the hospital, Felix actually got up and walked out of the room! Poor old Felix! I think I felt sorrier for him then than I'd ever felt; it was so terrible for him, seeing her lying there and thinking she might die, because death for him is blackness and nothingness, the end of everything. To tell the truth, I used to feel that way myself, until I saw the way my Gran went. She had been miserable and crying a lot, less out of fear, I think, than resentment – she was the sort of person who could never bear anything to come to an end, parties, outings, a good film, let alone life itself – but about a week before the end she seemed to gather up a kind of calmness and strength as if she had suddenly accepted what was coming and decided to make the best of a bad job. She had gone to skin and bone and been looking nearer ninety than seventy-five, with her poor face shrivelled up like an old apple, but during those last days she grew so cheerful, laughing and joking and talking about the days when she was a girl, that it was hard to believe she was going to die. Even the doctor was taken in; he said he believed she had put on weight and wanted her to try some new medicine. She said, 'That'll do me no good, young man, and you know it. If my face looks fatter, it's only because I've put my teeth in.' It wasn't bravado: she was really happy. We spent a lot of time looking at old photographs: her father and mother, her two brothers, who had been killed like her husband in the First World War, and Aunt Milly, her mother's sister, who had had a withered hand and whose bed my Gran had shared all her young life until she left home to go into service at the age of fourteen. When Gran talked about these people they seemed alive in the room, although all I can remember now are the little things she said. 'My dear husband gave me a pair of blue garters to get married in and Aunt Milly was so shocked she cried all the way to the Church. She thought it was too intimate a gift to accept from a man.'

It was after she had told me this, that she closed the album for the last time and said, 'All safe with Jesus now,' not in the special tone most people use when they talk about Him but as if he were just another relation who was rather especially hospitable and kind. She died about ten minutes later, and it seemed to me then – and it still does – that death was something it was stupid to be frightened of. I didn't think I would ever see Gran again, or any old nonsense like that, but I understood suddenly that death was no more than a kind of horizon: it looks like the end, but only because you can't see beyond it from where you stand at the moment. I say 'understood' but it wasn't like an idea I had worked out in my mind, more like a vision that had been given to me, and of course I was very lucky to have had this experience. It helped me to bear up through that awful evening, sitting by Ginny's bed and watching her and listening to every breath. And having been a nurse myself helped too: I could tell as soon as I walked in that this was a good hospital and that I could trust them to do their best for Ginny, whereas Felix, who has never been ill in his life, was half frantic with worry and fear that they must be neglecting her because there weren't dozens of doctors and nurses round her bed all the time.

I don't mean that I wasn't terribly afraid, and of course I prayed to God not to take my baby, but if He had, I think it would have been easier for me than for Felix, because I would have known it was His will, and not for us to question. I suppose there are people who would say what had happened to her was a judgement on me, and in fact for a little time I was in such black despair that I couldn't help feeling that way myself, but I knew, in my heart, it wasn't true: even if I *had* been a wicked woman – which I don't admit for a minute! – God would never try to get his own back in such a mean and spiteful fashion.

Henry said, 'You look frightfully fit, Holly,' in rather a disapproving way, as if he would have thought a good deal more of me if I hadn't bothered to put lipstick on or comb my hair.

I said, very quietly, 'Why shouldn't I? Ginny's alive, isn't she?' Which put him in his place pretty firmly, I thought.

He grinned in that irritating way of his (as if he knew something to your discredit but wasn't going to tell you) but he said, apologetically enough, 'I only meant you must have had a ghastly night and you look marvellous in spite of it.'

'Thank you, kind Sir.' My looks don't pity me, as they say: whatever happens I look like a blooming dairymaid. It comes of having a good skin and a naturally high colour.

I poured out more tea for us both and it struck me that Henry, on the other hand, looked wretchedly ill: white and very tired with dark, gouged-out hollows under his eyes. As a matter of fact, this improved him to my mind; made him look less like the successful city gent, a bit more human.

I said, 'You don't look so hot, though. Have some whisky in your tea?'

He shook his head. 'I'm all right. It's just that I've had rather a shock.' He watched me for a minute – a bit sly, or shy. Then he cleared his throat, stretching his jaw forward. 'Holly, I'm sorry. You've got enough on your plate. But I've got to talk to you.'

'Carry on,' I said, wondering what was coming and feeling

a little – not excited, exactly, but interested and perhaps more curious than if it had been someone else who wanted to off-load their troubles onto me. Henry usually behaved as if he thought I was too stupid to be worth talking to.

'It's Emma.' He stopped, fiddled with his spoon and stared at his cup. Then he got his courage up and brought it out. 'Emma's been committing adultery.' In such a dry, cold voice that I had to grit my teeth to stop myself laughing.

'Oh Henry,' I said, widening my eyes and looking as sorrowful and concerned as I could. 'Who with?'

'A man called Lucas Bligh.'

That stopped the laughter that was fluttering my stomach. I was stunned. It was so incredible. Not as far as Lucas was concerned – no man is to be relied on in that way. But *Emma*. . . .

'I don't believe it,' I said.

He hesitated a minute. Then he shoved his hand in his pocket, brought out a bundle of papers and pushed them at me. 'They're letters she wrote to him.'

I was really shocked. It must have shown in my face because he said, very stiffly, 'I found them lying about, naturally. I wouldn't have read them otherwise.'

'No. No, of course not.' I wanted to laugh again, he looked so outraged and red-eared at the thought! But I controlled myself. 'Do you want me to read them?'

He fixed his gaze on a point above my head. 'If you would.' His face was tight and immobile as a dummy's, then, suddenly, it collapsed – just as if the wax had started to melt – and he looked tortured. 'Holly, I can't explain, but it's terribly important. I have to know what you think about it.'

I was sorry for him then. Even stuffed shirts have feelings. I picked up the letters, though I was horribly embarrassed, with him sitting there watching me. I skimmed through them, reading bits here and there and I felt so ashamed, it was as if my skin were crawling. I had never read anything

in my life so terribly sad. Poor, poor Emma. I wanted to cry.
I put the letters down.

Henry looked at me, thin-lipped. 'She's been having an affair with him, hasn't she?'

I didn't know what to do for the best. Then it struck me that Henry must have lied, and I went cold with anger. These letters were so much more private than any ordinary love letter could possibly be, that Emma would never have left them 'lying about'. That hypocrite must have been poking about in her drawers, her desk. . . . Serve him right, then, if he'd found more than he bargained for! I said to myself, 'Perhaps it's a good thing for him to think Emma's been unfaithful, it might make him value her a bit more!' He would be furious, of course, but if I told him what I was sure was the truth, he would be sorry for her instead, which would be *humiliating*. Emma couldn't bear it. *I* couldn't bear to do it to her. It would be like skinning someone alive.

And, to be honest, at the back of my mind was the thought, *Serve the old pig right*.

I looked him straight in the eye. 'Well . . .' I said, shaking my head and sighing a little, sympathetically. Then I said, because this was bound to strike him sooner or later and it would be more convincing to produce the answer now, before he thought of the question, 'It must be over, though. He's just got engaged to his secretary – you must have met her at that party we all went to. I happened to run into Lucas the other day, and he told me. I suppose he sent Emma's letters back to her. It seems a childish thing to do, but he's rather a schoolboyish type, isn't he?'

I said all this very solemnly, frowning a little and worrying whether I was explaining too much, which is always suspicious, but Henry just nodded. I got the impression he was hardly listening to me.

He said, in a dull voice, 'Of course, I forgot you knew him too.' He picked up those tragic letters and stuffed them back in his pocket. Then he sat, staring in front of him.

I got up and cleared the tea things away, rinsing the cups and putting them in the rack. I was going to dry them and put them away – it was a relief to have something to do – but Henry came up with a tea towel and began to do it for me.

So I laid Felix's tray. He usually had breakfast in bed except when Ginny was home, when we all had it together in the kitchen. Felix is a terrible glutton for sleep, but it seemed time even he woke up: I had promised Ginny we would be in to see her at half past twelve. I tried to think of Ginny and what I could take to amuse her, but Emma's face kept bobbing up in the forefront of my mind and obscuring everything else. Her poor, pale face and the sweet, gentle way she had tried to comfort me yesterday, not showing by a word or a look how she felt! When she came to fetch me, Lucas answered the door but she didn't speak to him, just walked past as if he didn't exist and said, 'Holly, darling, I'm afraid you'll have to come straight away.' Even when I asked her how she'd known where I was, she simply said, quite calmly, that she had heard Lucas say '*Not* at-tall' in just the way I did, and once she'd remembered that, other things fell into place. I had thought nothing of this at the time, thinking only of Ginny and how quickly we could get to the hospital, but of course it should have given me a clue: people don't notice these things unless they are in love.

She must have been dreadfully in love with Lucas to have written those letters. It made me feel guilty, as if I had deliberately taken him away from her. Though I wasn't really to blame: Emma would never have told me how she felt about Lucas, not in a month of Sundays! Too proud and too ashamed: virtuous little wives don't admit to falling for other men. I know my Emma.

But *did* I? Writing letters you don't post is something schoolgirls do. There was a girl I knew when I was about fourteen who wrote to Charles Boyer and kept all the letters tied up with ribbon. And when I was a bit younger than that, I had a patch when I wrote to my father every day, a kind of diary, telling him all the interesting things that happened to me and slipping in bits from time to time about my mother and how she cried at night and slept with his photograph under her pillow. (Gran burned that photograph when my mother died; I think that was the only time I ever hated her.) I used to day-dream sometimes that I had actually sent this diary and that one day he would turn up, smiling and loaded with presents, from some faraway place like Peru; knowing all about me and with a perfectly good explanation of why he had stayed away for so long. Sometimes he had been exploring in the depths of the jungle, other times he had been lying in a mission hospital for years, having lost his memory after some frightful accident.

Silly nonsense, of course, but girls are often a bit queer and fanciful at that age. They grow out of it and no harm done. I certainly couldn't imagine myself doing anything so crazy now, but Emma is different from me.

Henry said, 'Holly?'

'Yes?'

'I'd rather you didn't tell Felix, if you don't mind.'

I looked at him. He wasn't thinking about Emma, but about himself being pitied and shamed. It struck me that he must have enjoyed being sorry for Felix so much. 'Poor old Felix' – I could just imagine the smug look on his face! – 'it can't be all that much fun being a deceived husband.' How he would loathe it if Felix were in a position to say that about *him*.

He said, 'I wouldn't mind quite so much if he wasn't such a bloody second-rate novelist. One thing I can't stand, and that's pretentious mediocrity.' He gave me a sickly smile. 'Or perhaps I mean successful mediocrity.'

'I can't see what that's got to do with it. But I assure you, I wouldn't dream of giving Emma away,' I said, very pointedly showing who *I* was concerned for in this matter. 'Not that Felix would think any less of her, let me tell you. He's not that kind of prig.'

'No,' Henry said. 'No, I suppose not.'

'After all, Henry, not everyone thinks what you do with a few inches of flesh is so important,' I went on witheringly. I am not often coarse, but his prim, tight look drove me to it!

I was really annoyed and it was absolutely typical of Henry that he should choose this moment to pounce on me. As I passed him to put the coffee percolator on the stove, he gave me a push which almost over-balanced me and before I'd recovered, he had me against the wall at the side of the sink and was thrusting his stomach at me and fastening his mouth on mine. His lips were soft and wet and rubbery, like a limpet sucking onto a rock. The comparison made me giggle. I jerked my head away but he held my arms by my side and jammed his bony knee between my legs, murmuring, 'Come on, come on, Holly,' for all the world like a keen football fan encouraging his side. This was the sort of thing that might have made me laugh in the ordinary way, and though I wouldn't have let it go any further, because of Emma, I would probably have said something like, 'Oh Henry *darling*, I didn't know you cared!' and by turning it into a joke, stopped his carry-on without hurting his feelings too much. But there was something so contemptuous and arrogant about the look of his face and his half-closed eyes and in the way he was handling me – as if he despised both me and himself but still expected me to dance for joy at the huge honour he was doing me – that I wasn't exactly worried about his feelings! I couldn't get my arms free but I swore and kicked his shins until my attitude towards this romp must have penetrated even his tiny mind. He let me go quite suddenly and began to stammer apologies.

I said, very coldly, 'I may be a tart by your standards, Henry, but I'm not a public convenience.'

He put his hands up to his face and staggered round the kitchen, groaning. Then he collapsed onto a chair, looking so white and shaken that I thought for a minute he must be

141

really ill. I went into the dining-room and got him a brandy but when I put it on the table beside him, he didn't touch it. He just looked at me blankly and said, 'I'm sorry. Oh Holly, it's all so bloody awful, you don't know.'

Then he gave another groan, sticking his elbows on the table and clutching at his hair, and I saw at once that this was all a great act put on to divert attention from the little trick he had just played on me, the way a child will deliberately fall down and pretend to be hurt when he has done something naughty.

The only way to deal with this sort of behaviour is to ignore it absolutely. I turned my back, lit the grill, and began to cook Felix's bacon. When I thought Henry had had time to recover, I said casually, 'Does Emma know you've seen those letters?'

He shook his head, his eyes sliding away from mine.

'Then if you take my advice, you'll just put them back where you found them and keep quiet about it.'

He looked at me vaguely and I could only hope he had hoisted this in. Then he said, in a slow, surprised voice, 'But I told you. She left them lying about. I don't understand why. I don't understand anything.'

Felix said, 'You're really sure Ginny's going to be all right?'

I had already told him so a dozen times. Now, I simply nodded, wriggling into my girdle and wondering what to wear to the hospital and thinking about Emma. I was worried about her, naturally, but as I was pretty sure Henry would have the sense to keep his big mouth shut (that kind of cold man always has a strong sense of self-preservation) I was able to enjoy being worried, awful as this may sound. Everyone has a certain pleasurable, ringside-seat excitement when their friends are in trouble, but what I was feeling was a little more than that. Much as I loved Emma, she had often been a thorn in my side, not because of her real goodness and sweetness which I had never denied nor disliked her for, the way some people might, out of envy, but because of the way Felix had sometimes used her against me, praising her to show me up and speaking of her almost reverently as if she were some kind of saint, too frail and good for this hard world. Frail! *Emma!* 'She's strong enough to get people to do things for her and I don't mean just carrying suitcases,' I told him once, but Felix couldn't – or wouldn't – understand this. He can be very stupid and stubborn sometimes. Slow, too. If it wasn't for me, he would never get up in the mornings, let alone get to work on time.

This morning, for example, I had taken up his breakfast, run his bath, and he was still sitting cross-legged on the bed and contemplating his navel like a fat little Buddha in blue silk pyjamas.

'If you don't hurry, the water will be cold,' I said. I got my new yellow suit out of the wardrobe, put it on a chair and began to look for a sweater, taking some time and thought, for Ginny's sake. She had a good eye for clothes, not for dotty fashions, but for colour and line, and I knew it would cheer her up to see me looking nice.

Felix said, 'Holly, do you want a divorce?'

I was on my knees in front of the chest of drawers. I turned to look at him, pushing the hair out of my eyes.

His face was screwed up as if he had a stomach ache. He said, 'I lay awake most of last night. You can go on for years and then you come to a stop. Like running up against a brick wall. There's no *point*, Holly.'

I said, 'You should have taken a sleeping pill.' Felix is always very low in spirits and scratchy-tempered if he misses his sleep, the way some men are with constipation, though most of them will never admit it.

'I looked in the medicine chest but there weren't any left,' Felix said. Then he looked annoyed, as if I had deliberately introduced this as a red herring, bounced off the bed and burst out, 'I can't bear any more *pretending* – it won't do – not

143

that I'm blaming you, I'm equally to blame – I've let things run on because I couldn't bear to admit the truth to myself I suppose – but now that I have done I can't' – he gave a gasp like a runner breasting the tape – 'can't go on – I can't just plod on for ever like some old horse in harness. . . .'

He looked so frantic, standing there in crumpled pyjamas, with his eyes showing so much white they looked like ping-pong balls and the sweat slicking his hair down so flat it might have been painted onto his head, that I had a hard job not to laugh. But I held it in, reminding myself that I didn't look so marvellously dignified either, crouching on the floor in bra' and girdle.

I said, 'You know you'd miss your home comforts.'

I was light and friendly as I could be, to show him that I didn't want to quarrel at this moment, when he had been suffering so terribly over Ginny, but I suppose he thought I was mocking him.

He said, in a pompous voice, 'Perhaps not as much as you might imagine,' and then he lost his temper and began shouting and throwing his arms about. He said what sort of fool did I think he was, he could clean his own shoes and run his own bath, he wanted a wife, not a bloody *nanny*, strapping Baby down in the pram with a nice dummy and then popping into the bushes with the first man who came along. If I had ever cared one straw for any of them he wouldn't have minded so much, but I had no *taste*, it was any Tom, Dick or Harry. And then he started on a list of men, most of whom I wouldn't even have touched with a barge pole, and even brought up some names I had clean forgotten, but I said nothing, just sat back on my heels and let him rage. There were plenty of things I could have said but I felt it was better for him to let off steam and simmer down of his own accord.

'You never cared for me,' he said, 'what on earth did you marry me for?'

'Gran liked you,' I said, and saw at once it must look as if

144

the suddenness of this question had startled the truth out of me. And though it was true, it was not the whole truth; he had been so kind, both to me and to her, and I had grown fond of him and trusted him more than I had ever trusted any man before. Or since, for that matter. But I couldn't say this, it would have looked as if I was pleading with him, which I wouldn't dream of doing, so I kept quiet and just stood up and began to put my clothes on.

He watched me while I got dressed, pulling a handkerchief out of his breast pocket and mopped the sweat off his face. I took my suitcase down from the top of the wardrobe and put it on the bed.

He shouted, 'What are you doing?'

I gave him a surprised look and said I was leaving, as he clearly wanted me to do. I was cool as a cucumber. I said he had better hurry up and have his bath and get dressed or he would be late at the hospital.

I began to throw things into the case and he slammed the lid down, almost catching my hand. 'For God's sake – what about *Ginny*?'

'You can tell her what you like,' I said. 'I shan't interfere. You needn't be afraid I shall try to turn her against you.'

'But you can't do this to her *now*.' He still sounded angry, but I knew he was beginning to be frightened underneath. He spluttered, 'What sort of woman are you?'

'I thought you'd just told me! You can't expect me to stay after the things you've just said. And as for *not now*, it's now or never, to my mind. Ginny needn't know till she comes out of hospital. I'll find an hotel and visit her every day.'

I turned my back on him and went on, taking things out of drawers and putting them in the suitcase, determined to go through with it because this was one fight I had to win. And if it seems I was hard, using Ginny as a weapon against him, I can only say that if I had been weak and admitted I was to blame, life would have been impossible between us from then on. Felix had to take me as I was, or not at all.

He was walking round the room. Round and round, into the bathroom and out again. Then he said, 'Holly, *please*.'

'Please what?'

'Stay. Please stay.' He sat down on the bed. 'I've put up with it all these years, I suppose I can go on. I don't want her hurt. That's all.' He rubbed his eyes till they squeaked and then looked at me. 'But if you could only *see*, sometimes. Yesterday – Christ, it seems petty in the circumstances – but I felt such a fool.'

He meant Henry and Emma knowing. As if they hadn't known anyway! I wondered if I should tell him about Henry but decided against it. I don't believe in making trouble between friends. 'I'm sorry about that,' I said. 'Believe me.'

'Yes. Well . . .' He sighed and stood up. 'Rebellion over, then,' he said, with a bit of a grin. 'Worm safely back on course.' And he went into the bathroom and shut the door.

I thought – Poor old Felix! That was what all the fuss was about! Felix cares about appearances. Not in a suburban way – as long as he doesn't know the man next door he doesn't care what he thinks – but his friends are a different matter: after a sleepless night and probably a bit of liver trouble – he had drunk a lot after we came home from the hospital – he had decided that this was a stand he had to take because they would think he ought to, even if it was against his own interests and inclinations. Which it was, of course: Felix is the sort of man who likes peace and order at home, so he can get on with his precious job and not be bothered. If I had been a faithful little wife, living for her lord and master's return and serving up the day's grievances with the evening meal – which I would have done, having felt all the long day that I was wasting my life and my energies – he would have been out of his mind within a month.

But in spite of knowing all this and understanding Felix so well, I felt, suddenly, very low and miserable. Perhaps it was partly the strain of keeping my temper all through this ridiculous row but what nagged at me most was the way he had ended it, with that sneering remark and no word of affection or apology for the things he had said. It wasn't like Felix. I told myself, 'If he wants to be bitter and hard, then let him be, I'm not going to be soft with him.' but I knew, in my heart, that I couldn't bear to leave things like that.

I unpacked my suitcase and rang the hospital. The sister said that Ginny was sleeping now, and I said that in that case, we would come after lunch, about two o'clock. I put down the telephone and went into the bathroom.

Felix was still lying in the bath. He is a hairy little man, not only from chest to groin, but on his back as well. Like a small gorilla, I thought, and had to bite my lip to stop myself laughing.

He looked up nervously when I came in and pulled the flannel over his genitals, as if he thought it improper, in the circumstances, for me to see him naked. I did laugh then and he grinned back, weakly. This made things easier: I sat on the edge of the bath and said, 'Felix, you know I'm very fond of you, really.'

He glanced at me quickly, as if he suspected a trap. Then he said, 'I daresay. Like a stray cat you've taken in in a weak moment.'

'No.' I was serious now. 'I mean it. I *rely* on you.'

'I'm afraid you do.' He gave a long sigh and swished the water up over his chest. The black curls stood up and waved like seaweed and then straggled flat again as the tide receded. He seemed totally absorbed in this little game.

I said, 'I meant another thing, too. If we ever did split up, I'd never take her away from you. A girl needs her father more than her mother.' I had made this statement knowing that it would soften him towards me, but as soon as I had spoken, the truth of it brought a lump into my throat.

He closed his eyes, screwing them tight as if something was hurting him.

I said, 'Darling, don't *sulk*.' He made no answer so I

147

picked up the loofah and tickled his chest. He pushed it away, pulling a face, and I leaned over the bath and trailed my fingers along his side, under the water. He looked at me then, with an odd, considering expression on his face – almost *scientific*, as if I were some strange animal he was observing for the first time. I smiled at him and tweaked the flannel away. He shouted, quite hysterically, '*No*, damn you,' and struggled up, slopping water all over me.

I stood back while he got out of the bath and wrapped himself in a towel. He looked outraged and rather sweet.

He said, 'Go away. I haven't shaved yet.'

'There's no hurry. We're not going to see Ginny until two. She's asleep.'

'All right. Please go away.'

I was terribly hurt to see him look at me like that. I said, as humbly as I could, 'I only want to be friends first,' and went to put my arms round him.

I could feel him trembling through the towel. He said, 'You'll get your nice suit wet.'

'It's wet already. You soaked me.' I couldn't kiss his mouth because he had turned his face away, so I tickled his ear with my tongue. He gave a little grunt that was only half annoyance, and said, 'Oh Holly . . .'

He put his hands on my waist and held it hard. Then he pushed me away from him and said, very solemnly, 'Look. There's one thing I want to make clear before we drop this subject altogether. I no longer care what you do, do you understand that? I may not like it, for appearance's sake, but it simply doesn't *lacerate* me anymore.'

It seemed an odd moment to make this point, but I understood why he wanted to. He needed to show his independence of me, to keep his pride. I won't say this didn't annoy, and even hurt me a little, but I saw it was better to let him believe what he liked for the moment, even if he had to pretend he didn't love me, to give us both peace.

So I said that I was truly sorry if I had ever hurt him, but he had known the sort of person I was when we married and accepted it then, and nothing had changed, really, only that in many ways I was more dependent on him than I had ever been. He listened to me at the beginning, frowning and serious, but when I said, 'Felix, I really don't want to leave you, you old fool!' – I felt at this point as if I were two separate people, one watching the effect of what I was saying and the other meaning it, quite deeply and sincerely – he gave a sort of despairing whimper in his throat and started kissing me and making love. Which was just as well, because there was nothing else to say that I could think of, except that I loved him. Which has always been a statement that stuck in my throat.

He was very quiet afterwards. We had a scratch lunch in the kitchen and he hardly spoke until I was clearing the plates away, when he came up behind me and put his hand on the back of my neck and said, 'You are an incredible girl.'

This was something he often said, I had never understood why. It always seemed to me that my behaviour was much more straightforward and reasonable than most people's, who are so bewitched and bedevilled by what they think they ought to be feeling and doing, that they charge uphill and downdale, arguing away, until they've lost sight of where they wanted to go in the first place. And it seemed particularly absurd that he should say it now, when all I had done was the obvious thing in the circumstances, which was to make life more comfortable for both of us, instead of rushing off with my suitcase, moaning and gnashing my teeth.

But there was no point in saying this to Felix who would think it disingenuous, which is a word he is very fond of applying to me. So I just smiled at him, affectionately and a little mysteriously, and said, 'Do you really think so?'

Ginny was marvellous. She was sleepy, still, and most of the time she just wanted to doze. But her mind was quite clear. She said, just before we left, 'I hope Emma isn't angry

149

with Rufus. He only meant to tease me because I was such a silly scaredy-cat.'

Felix was touched: tears came into his eyes. All the way home he kept saying what a wonderful nature she had, how generous, how naturally good. I said that might be true, but she was also a clever child who knew the right thing to say to please people.

'Why on earth should she feel she has to please *us*?'

'Maybe she feels insecure,' I said, not because I believed this, but because I knew Felix would. He said nothing, just gave me an old-fashioned look, but I knew he had taken the point and I had done no harm in ramming it home.

When we got in, the telephone was ringing. 'The hospital,' Felix said, and ran up the hall.

He said, 'Yes – Yes, it's Felix – No, he's not here – What? – All right, but what do you – *Emma* . . .'

I took the telephone from him but she had rung off.

He said. 'Really. How extraordinary.'

'What did she want?'

'Don't know.' He rolled his eyes and spread out his hands in an absurd pantomime of comic surprise. He was so relieved about Ginny, nothing else mattered. 'She said, tell Henry I'm going to give myself up. That make any sense to you?'

## 9. *Henry*

I was angry about Lucas because I was afraid. I believed Emma must be with him, because any alternative frightened me. Anger is almost always an escape from fear.

To know this commonplace changes nothing. Driving to London, I was enclosed in rage, like armour.

*Damn Emma.* The car was almost out of petrol, the warning light flickering. The first five garages I passed were closed. I had no money; I had given my last note to the greengrocer's boy. The sixth garage made a fuss about accepting a cheque. There was an artificial Christmas tree in the office window, silver branches hung with fairy lights, and a notice in Gothic script: 𝔄 𝔐𝔢𝔯𝔯𝔶 𝔜𝔲𝔩𝔢𝔱𝔦𝔡𝔢 𝔗𝔬 𝔄𝔩𝔩 𝔒𝔲𝔯 𝔆𝔲𝔰𝔱𝔬𝔪𝔢𝔯𝔰. I had to produce my driver's licence for identification, put my address on the back of the cheque. For Christ's sake, who used the car most? Couldn't she have filled it up yesterday? There was that time last summer when she had a puncture and forgot to get the tyre mended. The spare was worn smooth. It burst, driving home from a party in Hampstead. . . .

*Damn Holly.* That bitch, that whore, offering an open invitation and then withdrawing it. *Felix isn't a prig like you, Henry dear.* Waggling her juicy hips, flashing those embattled eyes. Like a Hollywood vamp of the thirties! Pretending she hadn't known about Lucas and Emma, when of course she would have encouraged her. That was her role, a *madame* in an amateur brothel.

Anyone could have her, why not me?

*Damn Lucas.* I had hated the idea of an office, of being cooped up for the rest of my life like a battery hen. Reading law at Oxford, I had hoped for a career in the theatre. Felix and I belonged to an experimental drama club. He wrote a verse play and I produced it in the college garden. We had zither music and a ballet in the second act: everyone dressed in white sheets. The national newspapers sent critics. One of them was in love with our leading lady, a Greek girl from Somerville with a beautiful voice. This critic called our play 'a brilliant production'. A new repertory company in Sheffield offered me an assistant stage manager's job at five pounds a week. Perhaps if I finished my own play, they would put it on. Or perhaps I could adapt it for television. I was marrying Emma. My mother was dying: she had always wanted me to be a solicitor. She lay in bed in the nursing home and said, 'Henry, I'm only thinking of you, I worry about you night and day.' I couldn't love her, so I wanted to please her. I loved Emma. A frail, shy girl, in need of protection. A noose round my neck, a millstone. The mortgage, the insurance against fire, death, disaster; the cheque at the end of the month, the pension scheme. She wanted a baby. Lucas's wife – this was something he didn't know yet! – was cross-petitioning on the grounds of cruelty. She claimed he had refused to let her have children. The enemy of talent was the pram in the hall. His creative life was so important. It left him free in the afternoon to romp with other men's wives.

Somewhere in the midst of this, was the grain of truth, the black core of fear. Something not to be thought about.

And perhaps even more unthinkable, the excited thrill, the hint of pleasure: *something is actually happening to me*. Or, *I am making it happen*.

I rang the bell of Lucas's flat and thought – Dear God, I am enjoying this.

Lucas's voice emerged through a polished brass grille at the side of the door. I said my name.

'Henry? What a nice surprise. Come on up.'

His voice was fuzzy, yawning. *I* had been up for hours.

The buzzer sounded and I pushed at the heavy door. This was an imposing, converted house in a terrace overlooking Regent's Park. A marble entrance hall with a great gilt mirror reflecting a bowl of chrysanthemums. Plastic, perhaps? It is so difficult to tell, nowadays. A small lift that jerked and whined.

Lucas was wearing a woollen dressing-gown stained with grease down the front and belted with a red, frayed tie. His face was pouchy and unshaven; his large, square feet pale in thonged sandals. He shivered and yawned, showing a gold cap at the back of his mouth. He was a frowsty, unappetizing man, running to fat.

I said, 'I'm looking for Emma.'

'Emma?' He blinked at me and smiled his open, apologetic smile, as if it was his fault for not understanding what I had said. 'Sorry, I'm afraid I've just woken up. I was working late last night. I don't often, but I had something to finish. Would you mind – just a minute?' He waved his hand vaguely. 'Make yourself comfortable.'

He closed a door behind him. There was the sound of running water. I looked round me. There was nowhere to sit: every chair bore its burden of books, old newspapers, literary and political periodicals. The desk was covered with ash-trays, papers, unwashed cups, glasses. There was a brown shoe with black laces on top of the typewriter. At the far end of the room, the door to the bedroom stood open. Tumbled, grey-looking sheets, dirty clothes on the floor. An untidy, over-heated lair. I didn't know how anyone could live like this. A ridiculous affectation of low-living and high-thinking? I thought – Emma is fastidious, how can she stand those filthy sheets?

There was a photograph on top of a low bookcase. I picked it up.

Lucas came back into the room. He hadn't shaved but he looked more awake. He had changed into crumpled grey flannels and a blue shirt with a darker blue scarf tucked into the neck.

I was embarrassed; I had been caught prying. 'Nice-looking girl,' I said. I meant, pleasant, kind.

'My secretary.' He smiled. 'My fiancée, too, I hope. She's coming back from Austria today. I'm meeting her plane. So I'm indebted to you for waking me up.' He hesitated. 'I think you must have met her, as a matter of fact.'

This was like an ordinary social occasion. I said, gazing at the photograph, 'I believe I have. At that party of yours we came to?'

A big woman with a good-natured smile; intelligent eyes. Neither pretty nor young – older than Lucas, surely? – but attractive in a rather outlandish way. Foreignness? Unsuitable clothes? She had puffed at her cigarette clumsily as a schoolgirl, thrown back her head at some joke I had made, been engagingly anxious to please. She had told one or two quite amusing stories. I had liked her, I remembered now, I had been very tired and she asked for nothing. I could have laid my head in her lap.

I said, 'I'm afraid I can't remember her name.'

'Lisa. Lisa Paul. Of course, I suppose we can't get officially engaged until my divorce is through.'

'I'm afraid we've run into a bit of a hitch over that.' I thought – Why mention it? I said, 'But that's not what I came about.'

'What hitch?'

'I said I didn't come to talk about that.'

He looked astonished. Then, quite suddenly, wary. He pulled at the lobe of his ear, watching me. He said, uncertainly, 'Would you like something? Coffee?'

'No, thank you.'

'Well. A drink, then?'

I shook my head. He was looking very sly. I thought – So there is something, after all, and felt, all at once, very exultant. The blood seemed to be rushing up into my head.

I said, 'Emma's been here, hasn't she?'

'Well . . .' Again that sly look, but there seemed to be bewilderment behind it. I thought – The bloody actor. He said, 'In what connection, exactly?'

'You know damn well.' The top of my head seemed to be lifting off. 'You've been having an affair with my wife.'

'With *your* wife?' He spoke slowly. The slight inflexion seemed stagey, affected. I thought I saw the implication.

'You mean, she's not my possession? That I've no right to complain? That may mean something in the fancy, intellectual circles you move in, but not in mine. . . .'

'Henry. Wait a minute. Listen . . .'

He seemed to be on the verge of laughter.

'Shut up and listen to *me*.' Lucas's face, red, amazed, seemed to have become separated from his body and be bobbing about, like a balloon. I shouted at this disembodied face. 'I'm not interested in sophisticated arguments, I haven't the time, I'm not a literary gent, not a bloody left-wing intellectual, just an old-fashioned suburban cart-horse, living in a bloody suburb and working my guts out to support my wife and children.'

I could see myself, stalking round the room, swearing, waving my arms, puffing my chest out. I thought – What a frightful act. My God, Felix would laugh! 'I'm just a simple bluff sailor man,' I yelled, uplifted by the thought of Felix into this final absurdity.

'You must be out of your mind,' he said.

I hit him. It was unpremeditated – my arm shot out apparently of its own volition – and very satisfactory. He fell. The floor jumped under my feet. I thought – This is the first time I've hit anyone since – since when? Since Felix and I got into the fight in Gibraltar. We were collecting barber's poles for our mess and there was this particularly good one. Felix had to stand on my shoulders to get it and a man came out of the dark shop, a huge man with great, long arms like an ape, and he reached up to hit, not me, but Felix, who fell on the ground with the pole in his arms. The man lifted his foot to kick him in the stomach and I hit him. Then we ran, each holding one end of the barber's pole, and my knuckles were burning. . . .

Lucas was lying on the floor, holding his jaw.

He said gently, 'Henry . . . ?'

'Get up.'

He grinned at me. 'Oh no. You might hurt me. But since I suppose I'm safe lying down, I'll take the opportunity to tell you I've never been to bed with Emma and I have no idea why you should think I have. She's been to this flat twice, once to that party I gave, and once for a drink with Lisa and me.'

I had known this, really. It seemed incredible that I could have thought – persuaded myself to think – anything else. My heart was thumping. I sat on a chair, on a pile of newspapers.

'May I get up now?' Lucas said.

He raised himself with elaborate, mocking caution. I thought – I don't like this man.

I said, 'I'm sorry, I can only say I'm bloody sorry.'

'An explanation might be more interesting.'

He'd like to know. He could put it in a book. Taking the lid off a comfortable, middle-class marriage. But perhaps that wasn't in his line. Not exotic enough.

I shook my head.

He grinned. 'Haven't I earned it?' He was putting his clothes straight, tucking his shirt in.

'I must have been raving mad. It's been a difficult time, my father dying, everything muddled.' I smiled at him painfully, trying not to over-act. 'Would you accept that?'

He nodded. He was watching me thoughtfully. 'There's one thing. Just to get the record straight. I had lunch with her the other day. She called me and said she was coming to London. It was innocent, I assure you.'

'Yes.' I felt listless. There was a pain at the side of my head. I didn't want to think. I thought – Oh, my poor Emma. Then – How can I get out of this?

I said, 'Has she ever written to you?'

'From time to time.' He stopped. His amused air had vanished now. 'Would you like a drink, after all? Only gin, I'm afraid.'

'No thank you.'

He said, 'Look, I don't know. There was no reason why she shouldn't have written. But I don't want to be disingenuous. I did wonder – well – once or twice it struck me that perhaps she was a bit lonely?'

156

'Lonely?'

Emma? A busy woman with a husband, children? We were *happy*, for God's sake. She wasn't a grass widow, or a golf widow, or even a job widow – I was home every night. She wasn't like some wives, bored with domesticity, tiresomely fretting after a career. She had been tied recently, looking after my father, but I hadn't forced that on her. Was I comforting myself?

'People can be.' He gave a short, artificial laugh. 'My wife used to complain that I never talked to her.'

She complained of other things, too. I thought - Well, he's got that coming to him. The selfish bastard.

'These letters. . . .'

He said earnestly, 'Henry, you must believe me. There was nothing in them that even the most watchful husband could object to. They were just friendly. To say thank you for a book I took your father, to ask me to dinner, that sort of thing. I was just a kind of Pen Pal!'

He smiled, tickled to bits with this phrase and his own handling of the situation. He had summed it up: the jealous brute spying on his neglected little drudge of a wife, peeking in her handbag to see who she was writing to. A suburban monster. Could he believe that? There was doubt in his eyes. He hadn't thought me that kind of man.

I said coldly, establishing this new character, 'It wouldn't have occurred to me that she could be so childish.'

'Oh, I don't know. Is it?' He looked at me now with unconcealed dislike. He was transparent as glass. Poor, innocent, little Emma, tied to me! Then he said, slowly, 'Though as a matter of fact, Henry – Oh, I don't know if it's relevant or not, but on Friday she seemed in a bit of a state. About her *mother*. Resentful, distressed – rather more so, I thought, than if they'd just had a row. I didn't understand what it was all about, but I remember thinking it seemed odd. I mean, that sort of deep involvement with one's parents is something one has usually grown out of, by now.'

He was interested, seeing this as an intellectual problem, quite ready to sit down and discuss it. Naturally, other people's lives were raw material for him. I thought – Poking about in dustbins. I had to get away before other questions occurred to this scavenger. Where was Emma? I had come to look for her, hadn't I? She was walking somewhere, in this bitter cold. Wringing her hands like Ophelia. My poor, mad girl. Writing those mad letters. A cry for help, like an attempted suicide? Like this nonsense about my father? Emma – who would never hurt a fly. I had seen her, letting the bath water grow cold, while she rescued a drowning spider. Screwing herself up to touch it.

I gripped the arms of the chair and heaved myself up. My body was heavy.

'Does one ever grow out of it?' I said.

'She's a wicked girl,' Emma's mother said. 'I'm sorry, Henry, but to put this on you when you've had all this worry! It's so thoughtless.'

The house shone as if an army of maids had been polishing. She had cleaned, made beds, lit the fire, given the boys lunch. Now I was eating mine, from a tray in the drawing-room. William and Rufus were playing in the garden, in the melting snow. It was half-past three.

I said, 'I don't understand why she rang the Cravens.'

'She may have rung here first. I did answer the telephone once, but whoever it was rang off. If it was Emma, she didn't want to speak to *me*. I suppose she knew what sort of reception she'd get!'

She sat very upright in her chair; a handsome, lively woman, flushed with indignation.

She said, 'She always had to be the centre of attention. Even when she was a little girl. Of course, her father encouraged her. He had nothing else to do. I did my best to make her think of others beside herself, but it was uphill work, I can tell you. *Look at me*. It was always, *look at me!*'

This conversation seemed incredible. But it was taking place.

I said, 'What do you think she will do?'

She said robustly, 'Well, I can tell you what she *won't* do. She won't go to the police. Not my lady! All she wants to do is to frighten us all silly. Oh *Henry* – I could tell you some tales! She once tried to cut her wrists. She was a violent child. Always some *drama*.'

I laughed. 'That doesn't sound like Emma.'

'Of course, most girls go through a stage. I hoped she'd grown out of it.'

'Why did she try to cut her wrists?'

She shrugged her shoulders. 'I really can't remember now. It was all over nothing, I expect; it usually was. She was never really in trouble, it was always something manufactured. There was a girl at her school got polio and all Emma could do was complain that *she* had pain in her legs. She had to have the limelight. It was difficult to be patient, sometimes.'

I hardly knew what this was about. We were talking of two different people.

She said, 'I'm sorry if I sound hard. I do love her, Henry.'

Admitting this, she seemed pathetic, suddenly. I thought – Even fortresses crumble.

I said, 'I know you do.'

I thought – Does Emma?

I said, 'She knows it too. She couldn't doubt that either of us love her. Don't worry about that, dear.'

She said, with asperity, 'Heaven's above, I'm worrying about *her*. I'm afraid she's gone too far this time.'

I thought – She's talking about a child. Children test their parents affection by bad behaviour: I'll be really naughty, *then* we'll see if she still loves me! But Emma wasn't a child any more.

I was frightened. I had allowed myself to be lulled, mesmerised. Now I was frightened and angry.

I said, 'Look – let's get one thing straight. Emma's not a little girl in a tantrum. She's not doing this to punish us. She's a grown woman. I don't know what happened. Only that my father upset her. Perhaps she felt ashamed because she couldn't cope. Perhaps this is all some fantasy of guilt. But it's real to *her*. . . .'

'Rubbish. Absolute rubbish.' My mother-in-law sat straight, her body rigid and proud. A ship's figurehead riding a storm. 'Henry, I can't tell you why she's lying, but I know that she is. And from first to last. You can't tell me that you really believe this dreadful nonsense about your father!' The colour crept upwards from the neck of her dress but she faced me gallantly. 'Really, Henry! I must say, in your place I would find that very hard to forgive. Oh, I know there are women who pretend this sort of thing happens. I knew a doctor once, whose career was ruined by this kind of wicked lie. But until you told me this, I would never have believed Emma was that type!'

Her face was the colour of a foxglove; her head trembled with her agitation and one thick coil of her hair snaked down. I thought – She can't believe this.

She said, 'Henry, I tell you, I'm ashamed of my daughter.'

I said, 'Suppose it's the truth.'

Felix got up from his chair and began stamping round the room and swearing.

I said, 'No, seriously for a minute. After all, it has to be *considered*. Unless she really has had some kind of brain storm.'

We were sitting in his study, drinking instant coffee. There was nothing else to do. Holly said Emma must have telephoned because she had hoped we would come to find her. Holly had gone out to look, driving round the suburb. There was no point in that except to occupy Holly. Emma might be anywhere.

'Rubbish. Bloody rubbish,' Felix said.

'So her mother says. But she sees – oh, another person altogether. I suppose we all do.'

'Who do you see?' Felix stood at the window and looked at me broodingly, through his spectacles.

'I don't know.' I put down my cup and stood up too. It was impossible to keep still. I thumped my hands on the back of a chair. 'What do you think of Emma?'

'Oh Lord. Your wife. A dear, sweet girl. Perfect. I always think, *how lucky you are.*'

I felt frightfully cold suddenly. Twitching and shivering. I crouched to turn on the gas fire. It popped, then flared blue.

Felix said, 'Sorry, are you cold?'

'Freezing.'

He said, 'Holly told me how your father had upset her. I was awfully shocked.'

I said, 'Randy old man. . . .'

I thought – Do I believe this? My father was a cheerful man, fond of children and animals and women. I tell myself he was 'one for the ladies'. This phrase has a gallant, old-fashioned ring, very attractive. Why do I use it? To absolve him? I had loved and admired my father, who enjoyed life. A trip on a trolly bus with him was an adventure. When he was at home, the house was warm, noisy, alive. He laughed a lot, and sang. *When Irish Eyes Are Smiling.* This was his shaving song: I sat on the edge of the bath and watched him singing and shaving, waiting for him to turn round and put a blob of soap on the palm of my hand and another on the end of my nose. I remember the soft, frothy feel of the soap and his deep laugh, and the sound of my own: giggly, high-pitched. I was very little, then.

Older, of course, the afternoon my mother lay on her bed and cried. We were alone in the house because the maid had left the day before and I was angry with my mother for sending her away. She was a pretty girl and I had loved her. I sat on the stairs and listened to my mother's terrible, remorseless weeping, and after a while, I went downstairs to make

161

her a cup of tea. I was nine years old, small for my age, and the kettle was heavy: I had to stand on a stool. I climbed back up the stairs, carrying the cup carefully, trying not to slop the tea in the saucer. Stood by the bed while she raised herself on thin, shaking arms, her face beaky, like a bird's; pale eyes red-rimmed and staring.

I said – forced myself to ask – 'What are you crying for?' She whispered, almost too low to catch, perhaps not really meaning me to hear. 'Oh, men are such beasts,' and was seized with such a shuddering fit that I had to take the cup back or she would have spilled the tea. I knew, then, why she was crying, why our pretty maid had been dismissed. Knew this – although of course I could not have put it into words at that age – with absolute clarity. And felt, for my weeping mother, only an immediate and suffocating indignation. I had tried to be kind, I had brought her tea! Why couldn't she stop crying? She looked so ugly. I was revolted by her pathetic, unwanted body, hideously exposed where her wrapper had slipped, showing the cavernous, yellowing breast bone. This was the kind of childish, physical horror that blacks out everything. I couldn't look at her. I stood, frightened and disgusted, holding the cup of cooling tea and staring instead at the photograph on the bedside table. My parents on their wedding day: my handsome father smiling straight into the camera, she looking at him. She had been a plain woman, even then, but the big, thin nose and protuberant eyes were softened with happiness. I was gazing at this picture when she lurched across me and slapped it face downwards on the table. '*Grotesque*,' she said. One word, meaning, I suppose now, that naked love and eagerness: at the time it terrified me with its mysterious violence. I began to whimper which shamed her into controlling herself. She took the tea from me, said I was 'a good, kind boy', and that she was 'sorry to be such a silly'. She stood the photograph up again and said, 'Goodness me, I was a lot fatter then, wasn't I? Your father used to say I was plump as a little pigeon!' She began to laugh hysterically. Red patches appeared on her sallow skin. I couldn't get out of the room fast enough. And, almost as soon as I closed the door, the weeping began again.

I thought – Why have I always pretended to believe she was crying because of that silly remark about the house? I couldn't have made this up. I suppose I must have heard her repeat it to my father. It would be in character: if my father had seduced the maid, she would attack him on some other ground. She was stupid and proud: she could not admit to jealousy. She expressed it, instead, in those terrible outbursts of spite. Insane in their irrelevancy.

I thought – How cruel. I never liked her because I loved my father and she sneered at him. *Why* she did that ought to make a difference, but it doesn't. My father was attractive to me and she was not. I loved my father who had betrayed her again and again, taken me to visit his mistresses, never once warning me not to tell her, not caring if she knew. . . .

I thought – I should try to be just to her.

I said, 'He was always a bit of a gay spark. I don't know if I ever told you, but he behaved frightfully badly to my mother. Married her for her little bit of money and then had an endless series of women – quite openly, I believe. . . .'

Felix took his glasses off, folded them and tucked them in his breast pocket. He looked astonished.

I said, 'Of course, that's nothing to do with how he went on with Emma. That was just senility, I imagine.'

Felix said, 'It must have been ghastly for her. If it had gone on a long time, I suppose it might have made her ill, produced some kind of queer, mental state. Any sign of that?'

'Perhaps she'd been a bit withdrawn recently. But that may be hindsight. She was never exactly communicative. Some women chatter all the time. I'm afraid I was just grateful she didn't.'

'Yes. That's all you can think of then? Nothing else?'

Only Holly and I knew about those letters. I couldn't bring myself to tell Felix. Shame on my behalf, or on hers?

I said, 'I suppose it's odd she didn't tell me how he was behaving.'

'She'll have to see a doctor.'

'She didn't seem ill, though. Not till last night. Then I thought . . .' What had I thought? I sat down and at once wanted to stand up again. I couldn't go on, pacing about. I stayed sitting, reached for my cup and put on a judicious expression. 'I suppose I was frightened that if I fetched a doctor she'd blurt it all out and he'd have to do something.'

I smiled at Felix, stretching my mouth: one ordinary, well-balanced man appealing to another.

He was fiddling with the venetian blind, making a snapping noise.

'Suppose she does go to the police?'

'Her mother says she won't.'

'How on earth does she know?' He looked amazed. 'Henry, you've got to face this.'

I felt very calm. 'They won't take any notice of her. Why should they? People are always confessing to murders. I've never understood why. Someone gets killed and police stations all over the country are besieged by these people. Snowed under.'

I laughed loudly. I was laughing so much that my hand shook and cold coffee slopped out of my cup and onto my lap.

Felix said, 'Shut up, Henry.'

'Sorry.' I felt for my handkerchief and dabbed at my trousers. 'Why do you suppose people do it?' I said.

Felix sighed. 'It's a way of searching for identity, I suppose. Who am I? *I* am the person who's done *this*.'

He snapped the blind once more and came to sit opposite me, on the other side of the gas fire. His plump hands perched on his plump knees. He was scowling ferociously.

'Henry – I said we had to face this. All the possible con-

164

tingencies. Suppose she does want to go to the police? Ought we to stop her? If we could, I mean. If she comes home first, or Holly finds her.'

'Of course, we would have to stop her. She's ill. She must be ill. What would be the point?'

'There might be one.' Two red spots had appeared on Felix's cheeks. 'I mean, just for the sake of argument, if there had been this – this *accident* – what would be the right thing to do?'

'From a moral point of view?' I was impatient. This was just an argument; undergraduates discussing the morals of imaginary situations.

'No. From hers. Yours too, if you like.'

'You mean, would I want her punished? Oh, for God's sake, Felix.'

This was ludicrous.

'Well. Look at it this way, then. If you'd done something like this . . .'

'*What?*'

What did he mean? If I'd had a row with Emma's mother and pushed her down the stairs? I thought – This is terribly funny. My chest was heaving like a bellows. I wanted to laugh but Felix was deadly serious. Leaning forward, the whites of his eyes inflamed. I composed my face.

He said stiffly, 'If you'd killed someone in an accident, what would you do?'

'I don't know.'

'Suppose no one believed you. Me, Emma – how would you feel?'

'Desperate, I imagine. Unreal.'

'What would you do?'

'I don't know. How can I possibly say? This is just hypothetical.'

'Would you give yourself up?'

'I might. Oh, I probably would.'

'Why?'

'For Christ's sake! Truth. Expiation. . . .'

'Then why should you stop her?'

'That's different.'

'How, exactly?'

He was cross-examining me. This pedantic little man. He was stupid beyond belief. I hated him.

I shouted, 'Because she didn't do it, you bloody fool.'

I knew what had happened. Emma was ill, the letters proved it. She had left them for me to see, so I would understand. She had retreated into this fantasy world, she no longer knew what was true. I didn't know why this had happened to her. Did there have to be a reason?

I began to shake. Where had she gone?

'You mean that? You're quite sure?'

Felix was watching me. I thought – Of course, this is what he's been after. Therapy. I had to be forced to make up my mind about this.

'Of course I'm sure. I was just so bewildered.' Relief made me babble. 'You know, when she came out with this last night, it was like – like stepping into a *novel*. I thought – This is something that only happens in the imagination. *Last night*. I wonder – I've just thought of this – could it have been something to do with what happened to Ginny? It being Rufus's fault? She couldn't bear that, you know, couldn't bear to think he was in any way to blame, she wanted to blame herself – She couldn't do that, so she built up something much worse that *she'd* done, to shelter him, distract attention – Unconsciously, of course. . . .'

A bird hopping away from the nest, pretending to trail a broken wing. The sentimental image made me want to cry.

Felix said gravely, 'A kind of transferred guilt?'

I said, 'Well. . . .'

*Emma and I were talking with a psychiatrist. Eminent, silver-haired, perhaps a slight Viennese accent. He was saying, We know so little about other people's minds, so little even, about our own. . . .*

I said, 'Well, a bit far-fetched, maybe, from here and now.

But perhaps in the state she was in? The oddest things go on. And in a sense, not unreasonable – not *mad* – I mean if you accept the fact that she'd quarrelled with my father, been in that way instrumental – she'd be bound to feel guilty – *want* to be punished. . . .'

Felix nodded. He was staring at the gas fire. His face had a veiled look. Or I thought it had. I wondered if he really believed this. I thought – I *have* to believe it.

I said, 'Felix, tell me . . .'

The front door banged. My heart knocked in my chest as if someone had kicked it. Footsteps came thudding up the stairs. The little house shook.

Felix said, 'Holly.'

She came in, flinging the door wide, letting in a gust of cold air. She looked extraordinarily healthy; clear-skinned, bright-eyed, like a woman athlete. Action was a tonic to her.

'No luck,' she said. 'I went everywhere I could think of. I even bought a ticket for the cinema and charged up and down the aisle. What a hideous fug in here, you must be mad.'

She strode across the room and crouched between us to turn off the gas fire.

'Henry was cold,' Felix said.

'But it's like a hot-house! What *have* you been doing?'

'Talking,' Felix said.

# 10. *Emma*

Emma sat in the station buffet. The coffee she had ordered was made with tinned milk; she had drunk one mouthful and abandoned it. She looked at her transparent reflection in the window and watched herself waiting. A girl in a film. She took a packet of cigarettes out of her handbag, remembered she had no matches and sat, dully.

A match flared under her nose. She said, 'Thank you,' and he said, nervously. 'The tea is better, you know. They don't make a bad cup of tea here.'

He was a little man; thin, middle-aged, his neck crimson and baggy above a tight, respectable shirt collar. He wore a navy pin-striped suit that hung on him loosely, like his skin.

He said, 'Are you waiting for someone?'

*. . . She is sitting at this table and Lucas comes in. Haggard, desperate, his coat undone. He has been searching for hours. Thank God, my darling. . . . He collapses onto a chair, his hand creeping forward over the formica table top but not daring to touch hers, afraid to speak, to declare his penitence, his love. She sits, waiting sad-eyed and silent, not to torture him, she is too fine, too generous, but because the pain is too deep for words; beautiful in her exhaustion, her lack of coquetry, pale lips and spiritual, ivory pallor classically perfect. Age cannot wither her, nor the years condemn. She is wearing the coat with the fur collar, the simple lines setting off her small, elegant body; her silky, pale hair loosened like a young girl's but her eyes a grown woman's, a little wistful, yearning for what might have been, but infinitely understanding, hauntingly sad. She touches his hand lightly, a world of pardon in her marvellous eyes, and then gets up quietly and leaves without looking back.*

*Leaving a tip for the waitress beneath the saucer . . .*

Emma laughed, then stopped short. *Was* this a parody?

The man said, 'Can I get you a cup of tea, then?' The offer was faintly reluctant, as if he realized now that he had made a mistake, but could not see how to get out of it.

Emma stood up, stubbing out her cigarette. She smiled warmly and said he was very kind, but she had a train to catch. She left the café, still smiling, aware of his eyes on her back.

168

The station was a grey, Sunday waste, more pigeons than people. Snow, pressing on the high, glass roof, hushed and filtered sound. The canned music coming over the tannoy seemed soft and solemn: an organ playing in a cathedral.

She walked towards the News Theatre, which was closed. Standing outside the shuttered box office, she stared at advertisements for other cinemas. Lord Jim. On one birthday – which, fifteen, sixteen? – her mother had given her a book by Joseph Conrad. It had fallen open at a page on which she had underlined a sentence. *Every lie has a bit of death in it*. Emma thought – But I wasn't a liar. No more than other girls, bored and dreaming. *She* made me a liar, often. That time she said I had stolen the sugar biscuits and refused to speak to me, shutting me out with an annihilating silence until I confessed to it. And I was glad to confess to this lie, weeping and blotchy – as I sat on my bed I could see my face in the mirror. She kissed me then. 'There, it's better to tell the truth, isn't it? Now it's all over and forgotten.'

Emma thought – I am running away. Using the past to escape from the present.

As if she could physically do this, she turned from the cinema entrance and walked fast out of the station. A weak sun shone, yellow slush trickled in the gutters. The snow that still lay on rooftops was turning blue at the edges. It was four o'clock in the afternoon.

She descended the steps, crossed the road, came down to the river. A police launch chugged by, parting black, silky water. She sat on a bench but the wind was cold and after a little she got up and began to walk, swinging her arms. By the time she reached the bridge, her limbs were less numb but her stomach remained chilled and there was a warning pain in her back: her period was due. She recognized the accompanying feeling of panic almost before the cause of it: she had always been terrified of this happening when she was away from home and unprepared, remembering with shame an occasion, years ago now, when she had danced all evening, unaware of the small stain on the back of her dress. She quickened her pace crossing the bridge, and hurried into a public lavatory.

Nothing had started yet, but she bought a packet of Tampax from the machine and felt more at ease with it in her handbag. Walking round Parliament Square, she was appalled that she had allowed such a commonplace worry to obtrude upon and obscure, even temporarily, the horror of her real situation. Though had this been, at any point during the day, really plain to her? She had tried to think, she excused herself piteously, but her mind kept sliding away: she had let herself be distracted, as if today were a holiday, listening to the speakers at Marble Arch, walking down Oxford Street, looking at clothes in shop windows and wondering if that colour would suit her or that shape of dress and then, suddenly and ravenously hungry, eating in Soho, taking care with the menu and treating herself to a bottle of wine. And, worst of all, the dreamed encounters: a man's briefly admiring gaze turned into a passionate involvement; Lucas's worshipful sorrow that tightened her throat and made her glance into windows and mirrors, cherishing her sad, beautiful, forgiving face; Henry's – and her mother's – bitter, hopeless remorse as they waited at her death-bed or stood silent, gazing at her drowned body. Lift her up tenderly, so young and so fair. . . .

*I must think*, Emma told herself, recognizing in this injunction the same histrionic determination with which she had tried, when a girl, to concentrate on some particular piece of homework that she found difficult or distasteful. Other people were different, she had always known this, even at school, using their minds like precision instruments to bear on one problem at a time, undistracted, *serious*, as she had never been – gazing out of her bedroom window, wool-gathering, or arranging and re-arranging her treasures in the table drawer, the lipstick, the sea-shells, the lily of the valley scent in the green glass bottle, the red leather edition of *A Shropshire Lad – Be still my soul be still, the arms you bear are brittle –* while her mother, downstairs, correcting school books, cooking supper, ironing blouses, thought only of other people and what she could do for them. Next to putting yourself first, wasting time was the worst sin.

*She* never wasted time. She used it, every scrap and scrag-end, like a thrifty housekeeper. Even times of enforced idle-ness, bus journeys, the wait in the doctor's surgery, were chances to enrich her bubbling stockpot of plans and resolu-tions: she threw nothing away, not one short minute of the precious day, any more than she would have left good food behind on her plate.

In deference, always, to those less fortunate. The time she saved was spent only on those demonstrably in need of it, who could not – could never be – those closest to her. The child, Emma, had known this from the beginning. She had no chance: the outside competition was too strong.

Emma thought – And yet I wanted so little. Or so much? Needing – or greedy for? – love and attention. She walked into Westminster Abbey, tears of sympathy blinding her eyes and sat in a side aisle, beside a marble memorial to some erstwhile defender of Empire, his tomb surrounded by naked men with spears. It was nearly five o'clock, she was tired, cold, and had no more money. Only a return ticket home.

How could she go home? Go back, walk in? She had said to Henry, 'I killed your father.' This might seem no more real to her at this moment – seemed, indeed, less real – than many an imagined situation, but it would be real for Henry.

Had he believed her?

Thinking about this, the blood rose hotly in her cheeks as at some unimportant gaucherie: she felt shame, but only of an embarrassed, almost social kind. Only? Perhaps these things really were, for her, the high-points of horror: the speck of blood on the party dress; Holly in Lucas's flat – not jealous love, she was not capable of it, but silly, shameful

171

mortification; her father-in-law coming out of the bedroom with those foolish letters, her – what would Henry call them? – *shop girl* delusions. *That look* – indescribable – on his sly, old man's face, his cackling pleasure in having caught her out. The inevitable, killing ridicule, the pitiful exposure. . . .

Poor Emma. How sad, but how funny.

Was it this she couldn't face? She thought, with fear – I am empty, trivial, worth nothing.

She dug her nails into the soft part of her thighs; though this movement had been involuntary, it struck her as theatrical, and shocked her. For perhaps three minutes, she forced herself to sit absolutely still, breathe steadily. Then she stood up, buttoned her coat and walked out of the Abbey.

Outside in the lighted dark, it was much warmer now, a fine rain falling. As she came onto the bridge, the wind blew it gently in her face. She stood, leaning against the parapet and watching the river. Reflected light wriggled like yellow snakes in the water.

*Emma stood alone on the bridge. A small, insignificant, yet somehow heroic figure. . . .*

She said aloud, with crisp disgust, 'Oh, I despise you. Always looking at yourself.'

And then thought – Why do I do it? To *see* myself, reassure myself that I exist? How else do you do that, after all? There must be some kind of mirror. Some way to find out who you are, why you do what you do. Why am I doing *this*?

Examining this question, forehead creased, hands clenched on the wet stone of the parapet, she encountered familiar resentment. I want to make myself important, someone to be considered. Make them sorry for disregarding me. To get my own back. All the shabby motives *she* would produce at once if we could discuss this together, never recognizing an honourable, decent impulse in me, her daughter, only in other people, and only *then* merely to show me up, to

172

shame me. . . . And she wouldn't believe me, anyway. She would always believe bad things of me, but only small bad things, lying and stealing biscuits and selfishness. I was too *negligible* for any greater crime, a flimsy creature, no spunk, taking after my father, gassed on the Somme and weak-chested ever after, a poor fish by the time she got hold of him and made poorer: she encouraged his failure because it pointed up her own strength and then despised him for it. I could have talked to him, told him everything, we were in the same boat. Why didn't I? He would have listened, he had time – if he had nothing else, no job, no self-respect, he had time – but I never talked to him about anything. He asked questions sometimes, about my work, my friends; I must have answered, but only out of politeness, briefly, not wanting to be bothered with his shy importunity, brushing him off like a troublesome fly buzzing round and distracting me. Fond of him, of course, covering up for him sometimes – 'Oh no, Ma, Daddy's not been smoking in here, someone must have a bonfire somewhere' – but only in the way you shelter a lame duck, an underdog. Not an equal.

*He wasn't worth impressing.* Was that why I wanted to tell her, then? Or is it just that this is what I know she would say. Am I trying to impress her *now?*

'Oh, for Pete's sake.'

The voice – Holly's – was so live and independent, so clearly ringing with characteristic impatience, that Emma started involuntarily, even glanced behind her. But the bridge was shining black with rain and empty. She was still quite alone.

'Why, why, why – what does why matter? It's what you do that counts. All this self-disgust. Self-indulgence. And this rubbish about giving yourself up? What earthly good would that do?'

Emma gave a grimace, a half laugh: Holly's ghostly voice lent an extra dimension, a shape, to the dialogue in her mind.

*My disordered mind.* For some reason, not to be examined yet, she found the formation of this phrase comforting.

'The publicity, the disgrace, Henry's career ruined . . . ?' She answered without speaking.

'Well, I suppose that might happen, if only in a modified way. At least, you have to think about it.'

No – that wasn't Holly.

'As far as that goes, serve the old bugger right.' *That* was better, an authentic note. 'But that's not what you really want, is it? I mean, he may not be my cuppa char, but you're fond of him, aren't you? Love him, you'd say. Pardon me if I'm wrong.'

'You're not. That's one of the reasons I have to do this. To put things straight between us. Make a proper life, no more of this pretence.'

'It'll be a fine life in the circs, won't it?'

'You couldn't possibly understand,' Emma said rudely. 'You've got absolutely no conception of how decent people think, or of how they behave to each other.' She stopped. Absurdly, her heart was thumping as if she had actually said this to Holly. The idea exhilarated her: there were a lot of other things she could get off her chest while she was about it.

'You ought to know what Henry thinks of you! Oh – not just your sleeping around, though that won't be such an attractive business when you're a bit older, will it? From an aesthetic point of view, to say the least. The quality of the lovers is bound to go down – by the time you're a desperate old bag of fifty-five or so, you'll be just about scouring the gutter. But the worst thing about you, Henry says, the most pathetic thing, is the way you've persuaded yourself that you've got everything worked out so marvellously, that Felix doesn't mind, that he's happy, that *you* are! What a fantasy! I may have been a fool, but at least I know it – know what's real and what isn't – and I've got enough sense to try to get out while there's still time. Of course it'll be hard for Henry in the beginning, I shall expect him to hate me for a while, but it was an accident, not deliberate, and he'll come to see that in the end. And forgive me, I hope. He might even respect me because I had the courage to come out with it. There are easier things to do, you know.'

'Claptrap.' Holly snorted, rather vulgarly, and Emma giggled. She waited for the voice to go on, and when it did not, tried, conscientiously, to think what reply Holly might make to her tirade, but without success. At length she said, tentatively, 'That's all very well, but what would you suggest? I *told* him, remember. I can't just march back home now, as if nothing had happened.'

There was silence for a moment. Then Holly said, 'It should be easy for you. You know what you are.'

No more. Nothing. Only the water, slapping muddily against the piers of the bridge, and the traffic on the Embankment, a moving caterpillar of light and sound.

Emma felt diminished, emptied, as if her body were a sack that had been briefly filled by Holly's more robust vitality and now sagged limply, incapable of independent life. Tension was gone, leaving a heavy listlessness: walking across the bridge, she found it hard to put one foot in front of the other.

Holly was right. She had only to go home. Henry would be half out of his mind by now, ready, even anxious, to believe she had been half out of hers: had blown up the whole, nightmarish story in a fit of guilty hysteria. All that had actually happened was this foolish row – undignified, but not wicked – and the poor old chap turned giddy and fell. Henry had given her the script last night and would be only too grateful to receive it back, unedited. Even the telephone call to Felix, that moment of plucked-up courage, of determination to shore up her resolve, would be tenderly explained, forgiven. 'My poor darling, you were overwrought, hysterical.' Showing up her inadequacy with pity.

Of course it was quite easy, really. She had known this

even last night: lying awake with Henry snoring beside her, she had known he would make it easy for her. Not just for her sake but for his own, for all the good, practical reasons that Holly would endorse without a second's thought: comfort, a quiet life, if what's done can't be undone, at least it can remain unsaid.

*And so debase them both*, she had thought, moving her legs restlessly in the bed and wondering whether to push Henry onto his side to stop him snoring, or to retreat herself to the spare room. For if what she had told him was to change nothing, if nothing you ever did or said changed anything, then either life itself was worthless, a dreary chore to be got through with as little effort and expense as possible, or they were not worthy of it.

The state she was in – her mind generally muzzy from the sleeping-pill, but shot through with unnaturally sharp perceptions, rather as a cloud is pierced by dazzling pinpoints of light – this seemed a piece of apocalyptic wisdom. She had a sudden dread that if she went to sleep it would have slipped away from her by the morning, wasted, forgotten, and longed to wake Henry up to tell him now. But when he did stir, rolling over and grumbling after a louder snore than usual, she held her breath with fear.

It was then that she got up, dressed, and went downstairs. The house was cold: she decided to make cocoa to warm herself up and, while the milk boiled, laid the table for breakfast. That done, she mixed the cocoa and drank it standing by the stove, but remained as cold as before, chilled to the bone. She went to the drawing-room and downed a good slug of brandy straight from the bottle: this, on top of the hot, thick, sweet cocoa, produced disagreeable sensations, indigestion and a steady, hypnotic drumming in the ears. To cure this, she drank some more brandy and sat by the dead fire, smoking.

*Silly girl*, Emma thought, patronizingly, but with a certain affection for this sad, feckless heroine; she should have drunk her nice cocoa, taken another sleeping-pill and gone back to bed. She was too muddled to sort things out – if that had, in fact, been her intention – too muddled, too tired, too drunk. She had known she was drunk. When she closed her eyes, the room tilted.

She had forced herself to sit upright and stare at the wall. What else had she done? What else had she thought about? Emma could not remember now. She seemed to be looking back at something that had happened in another existence and to someone else. Watching, not even a completed film, but a series of rushes, a trailer. . . .

*Poor Emma. At some point a violent fit of shivering had seized her. She had gone to the cupboard in the hall and taken out her coat, dragging it round her with stiff fingers. The clock in the hall had struck six. It was then, or soon after – she had caught the first train at seven o'clock – that panic had taken over. She had run from the house, stumbling in the snow, weeping. . . .*

Walking across Westminster Bridge, Emma recognized what she was doing. Up to her old tricks again, this private cinema unreeling inside her head. Only the weak and foolish did that, improving on life and on themselves.

What harm in that? What *harm*? Edith Thompson, writing to her poor young lover, pretending she was putting ground glass in her husband's porridge. . . . Suppose she had posted one of those letters to Lucas by mistake; sometimes she wrote one to keep and one to send, suppose she had put the wrong one in the envelope, though she had always checked, even opening the already sealed envelope, tearing it at the fold and wasting the stamp. . . .

He and Holly discussing it. Bewildered, amused. Lying there, naked and laughing.

Poor old Emma.

She broke into a sudden, loud laugh, began to run, ran for perhaps thirty steps, almost to the end of the bridge, and then slowed down, pulse thudding, body blushing, facial muscles jerking extravagantly, as if fear and embarrassment could be charmed away by bursts of nervous, physical activity, groans, hideous grimaces.

'Don't be a fool. This isn't important,' she said, aloud; loud enough, anyway, to be clearly heard by a boy and girl approaching, arms round each other, shoulders hunched under the same, black, plastic cape. For a moment, their startled eyes met hers, then slid nervously away: polite children, averting their gaze from this mad woman, muttering. She thought she heard them giggle before they broke into an awkward, high-stepping run, lurching about like ill-matched partners in a three-legged race.

Emma doubled her fists against her chest and ran down the steps onto the Embankment. There was that woman she used to meet on her way to school: harmless, mad as a hatter, wearing – in her seventies – a tight, short, red satin dress with nothing on underneath, the outline of aged breasts and buttocks clearly visible, who talked and laughed to herself, sang songs, gesticulated, tossed back her long, grey hair, *flirting*, pleased and primping, with her reflection in the shop windows that she passed, her inner life so vivid and complete that sidelong glances, sniggers, even the words rude children shouted, the worst they could think of – *Left your knickers behind, Gran?* – meant nothing to her. . . .

'I could be her.' Emma whispered; no sound, only her lips moving. Tears mingled with the rain on her face. She had loved Lucas. He had loved her. That had been – she had let it become – reality for her; clear, sharp, brightly coloured. Beside it, everything and everyone – Henry, his father, even the children – had seemed fixed and faded, remote as figures in an old, sepia-coloured photograph, or in a dream. Emma thought – people don't dream in colour: what you do in a dream isn't real. Was this madness, or simply the borderline, the narrow territory in between? How could you tell? Reality has so many levels. Perhaps all you can do, in the end, is accept what other people see and confirm as real. Lucas did not love her. Nor did he know she loved him. His surprised

178

face at the door of his flat had betrayed no guilt, only surprise – he had been *bashful*, like a child caught out in some naughtiness by a stranger who would not really mind, nor punish him. *Thank God it was only Emma.*

The pain, then, the ache in her heart, was only the reflection of some irrelevant longing. Some shoddy, worked-over emotion. Driving Holly to the hospital, she had faced this. Reality was her father-in-law dead, Holly's child dying: both her fault. She had forced herself to drive carefully – practical, cautious, reliable Emma – while Holly, half-demented, urged her through red lights, to pass an articulated lorry on a blind bend. *Jesus God, can't you go faster?* Then the hospital, the child glimpsed through the door, and Holly on her knees. Felix, who knew what she had done, and rightly blamed her – he had shouted at her, 'What in Christ's name were you doing, you silly bitch?' – and Henry, who didn't know. Henry, who was cut off from her as by a piece of stretched, transparent skin, or a sheet of glass. She had wanted to smash this glass, get through to him.

But he hadn't believed her.

She caught the six-twenty home. Sitting in an empty compartment, she stared out of the window, seeing through her transparent, huge-eyed reflection to the rushing dark and the solid world beyond: the telegraph poles; the lines of narrow houses built close against the railway line; the lights in kitchens, bathrooms, sitting-rooms; a solitary man in shirt sleeves, reading; a family round a table, the television flickering in the corner of the room.

She said, 'I have to go through with it. I have to make him believe me. Holly . . . ?'

But Holly was silent. This trick of the mind would not work here.

Emma sighed a little. Locked in the swaying train, she was helpless, inert, as perhaps she had always been, her life arranged and controlled by other people. Everything predetermined; everyone innocent. If that was true, she thought, then life was the enemy, not death. To defeat it, you had to do something, take a risk. Otherwise you just sat, waiting. . . .

Emma said, 'There's nothing else I can do.'

She took off her glove and drew round her phantom face on the window. Puffed cold breath and drew. She felt quite calm now. Liberated. Guilty, but free.

## 11. *Holly*

I told them I would have thought they could have found something better to do in the circumstances, and swept out of the room. Perhaps I was a bit sharp, but the pair of them got on my nerves, sitting there in that stuffy room and moaning like the chorus in that boring Greek play Emma made me go and see at Syracuse. Ah, alas, alack! Woe is me!

'But what *can* he do?' Felix asked, following me downstairs into the kitchen, and speaking in a hushed, reverent voice as if Henry were on his death-bed and could only hope for a merciful release.

I said I was sure I couldn't say, I only knew that in Henry's place I wouldn't just sit comfortably on my fanny and have a cosy chat with my best friend about my troubles. Then I began peeling potatoes for supper and it struck me that there were some advantages, some of the time, in being a woman: whatever is happening, there are always meals to be got and beds to be made and children to look after.

'He could keep an eye on his kids for a start,' I said. 'How do you think they feel, poor little buggers? Their Mum vanishing into thin air and no one explaining why. At least, I *imagine*
180

dear Henry hasn't given them a blow by blow account of the whole situation!'

Felix said Emma's mother was there, and Henry was finding her rather difficult at the moment. Her attitude towards Emma wasn't exactly sympathetic! Felix spoke in a placating way, as if he felt duty bound to stick up for old Henry, but didn't altogether disagree with me, all the same. 'She seems to think Emma's only done it to annoy,' he said, grinning at me wryly and scratching the top of his head until the hair spiked on end.

'Well, maybe she has, too,' I said, to annoy *him*, and he turned pink at once and looked shocked, as if it was downright insensitive of me to agree with such a petty assessment of his precious Emma's behaviour. After a brief interval of silent disapproval, during which I was supposed to reflect upon, and see, the error of my ways – a little trick I had long ago stopped taking any notice of – he asked me if I could really believe that?

I said, cuttingly, that any alternative seemed to be a good deal more unpleasant for all concerned.

He blinked at me as if he didn't understand what I was talking about. Or didn't want to. It got my goat. 'Mad, or a murderess,' I said, hurling potatoes into a pan of cold water and watching him out of the tail of my eye.

His face had gone poker-stiff. He said he didn't think this was the sort of situation one should joke about.

I laughed at that. Felix on his dignity is enough to make a condemned man die laughing on his way to the gallows. He glared at me for a minute, pop-eyed and red-faced, and then said, 'What do you honestly think, Holly?' He was whispering, in a scared, secretive way, as if he really thought I might have something shocking to tell him.

That shocked *me*. I was so full of contempt that I could have hit him. It must have shown in my face because he glanced nervously at the sharp vegetable knife in my hand and backed away round the other side of the kitchen table. This was so ridiculous that I determined to keep my temper and managed to speak quite calmly, though inwardly I was trembling with rage. I said I had no more idea than he had, and that I thought all this morbid talk and speculation behind poor Emma's back was hideously disloyal and disgusting. I wasn't going to join in, so he needn't think it. But if he wanted my opinion – and whether he did or not, I was going to give it to him – I was horrified at the way Henry was going on, telling all and sundry that his wife had killed his poor old Dad. 'It isn't decent when she's not here to defend herself,' I said, throwing a red cabbage onto the chopping board and looking in the vegetable rack for a lemon.

He looked at me with his mouth open. His jaw was actually hanging down, like a dead man's. He closed it, with a deliberate effort, swallowed, and said in an astonished voice, 'But he's only said what she told him. And only to us. Can't you see he's half out of his mind with worry?'

'Her mother knows, apparently. Fancy worrying the poor old soul! What did he have to do that for?'

'I don't think she is the sort of person one could easily lie to.'

'Oh – *fiddle*. Look – he and Emma had a row and she screamed all this nonsense at him. For heaven's sake! He's a grown man. Or supposed to be.'

Felix said, 'You're sure it's nonsense, then?'

I snorted, as if this was really too ludicrous a question to answer, and began chopping the cabbage. Though my face was still burning with anger, there was a sliver of cold trickling down inside me as if I had swallowed a glass of iced water on a hot day. 'Of course it is,' I said, banging away with the knife. 'I was *there*, you fool. I know the state she was in. I told you, don't you remember?'

And I thanked God I had. I saw now that this was a sensible precaution to have taken.

He said, slowly, 'Yes, you did. I'd forgotten.' He was looking thoroughly ashamed of himself, I was pleased to see. He said. 'Henry says the same. It's a sort of hysterical thing. Though I would never have thought Emma was the type, somehow. . . .' He sighed, reluctant to take the poor girl off her pedestal and stand her on the solid ground with the rest of us.

'I expect Henry knows her better than you do,' I said, looking him straight in the eye. 'And since he's got more to worry about, too, I suggest you wipe that miserable look off your face and take him up a drink and try to keep him cheerful.'

I put the cabbage in the oven, told Felix when to put the potatoes on, and went across the road to give Emma's mother a hand. The boys were in the drawing-room, playing Ludo, and she was getting their tea. She looked terrible. Years older – her eyes seemed to have sunk back into her head and the skin round them had gone dark and crinkled, like tissue paper.

She was a bit guarded when I first came in, but I thought she was pleased, on the whole, to have my help. I offered to take over altogether and give her a rest but she wouldn't hear of it – she wasn't the type to sit down and give way to unhappiness – so we got the boys' tea together, sat them in front of the telly with a tray, and settled down ourselves for a quiet cup of tea in the kitchen.

She said it was good of me to be so kind when I must be so terribly worried about Ginny. I said there was no worry now the old girl would be fighting fit in a day or so and she said she thought it was wonderful that I could be so calm about it. She told me about a woman she had known – a widow – whose only daughter had fallen off her bicycle on her way to school and lain unconscious for three years before she died. The mother had given up her teaching career and taken a job as a ward maid at the hospital to be near the child as much as she could: she spent all her free time by the bedside, talking to her and singing the songs she had liked and bringing her presents and a cake with candles on her birthdays. 'She used to be such a pretty woman, but she fell away to nothing in those three years,' Emma's mother said, and though I knew that if Henry were to hear this story, he would only laugh and say his mother-in-law had an insatiable appetite for disaster, it seemed to me that she had genuinely felt this poor woman's tragedy as something real, in her heart. And, in a queer way, envied her for it. 'Of course, she was closer to that child than she could ever have been to a normal one,' she said, and sighed a little, as if she wished she could have had a chance to show such selfless love and sacrifice.

Then she looked at the clock and asked me if I would like a glass of sherry. I said I would get her one, of course, but I never touched the stuff myself.

She raised her eyebrows at that, as if she would have thought I was a natural tippler. 'Principle, or inclination?'

'My mother drank,' I said. I was a little surprised to hear myself saying this.

'And that affected you?'

'*Not* at-tall,' I said, because although I had disliked the way it had made her look and behave, the mouth going sloppy and the features blurred, the weeping and the shambling run, I had always known it wasn't really the drink that was to blame, but her own weakness that made her turn to it. 'I just don't like the taste,' I said.

I went to get the sherry. When I came back, she was sitting with her hands folded on the table and staring at the kitchen clock. She said, half to herself, 'There's no chance – I suppose she won't do herself any harm?'

'Emma? Lord – not her. She's too good at taking care of herself.'

She looked at me with sudden, sharp attention. '*You* know that, do you?'

'It simply wouldn't cross her mind,' I said, speaking very firmly, and not just to comfort her. It was something that I was completely sure of.

\*　　\*　　\*

184

I was bathing the boys when the telephone rang. Henry must have come in: I heard his voice in the hall, answering it. I closed the bathroom door and made a great fuss and noise getting the twins out of the bath. I was towelling their heads when Henry opened the door and beckoned to me. I told them to finish drying, and went onto the landing.

He said, 'She's at the police station. They won't say anything. Just that they want me to come.'

He looked groggy. I could smell whisky on his breath.

I said, 'You're not fit to drive. I'd better come with you.'

William and Rufus burst out of the bathroom, stark naked. I said, 'Put your pyjamas on now, and Granny'll read you a story.'

One of them – I could never tell t'other from which, unless I looked closely – wound his legs round mine and clung on. 'I want *you* to. . . .'

Henry was halfway down the stairs. I said Aunt Holly had better things to do at this moment, disengaged myself and followed him. They hung over the banisters. 'You going to fetch Mummy now?' one of them said.

I said, yes, if they were very good and no trouble to Granny. Henry was looking as if he couldn't stand this. I took his arm and marched him out of the house. He didn't speak until we were in the car. Then he said, 'For God's sake, what am I going to do?'

'It depends on what she's told them. What they say.'

He said, 'I don't know what to do.'

I drove fast, faster than Henry liked: he kept braking with his foot on the floor. From time to time, he gave little grunts, or groans: either at my driving, or the situation.

I said, 'Henry, it might be best to pretend you don't know a thing. Just seem astonished. Not guilty, or anything.'

I thought – Some hope!

He seemed to be thumping his fists against his forehead. He said, 'She's ill. She must be ill.'

'Will they believe that?'

'I don't know. They must be used to this sort of thing. Cranks, and so on. But there *is* something wrong with her. . . .' He stopped. I glanced at him as I changed gear at the traffic lights and saw he was looking wretchedly embarrassed. 'She wasn't having a love affair. She just wrote those letters.'

'How d'you know?'

'Well. I went to see Bligh.' He gave a short, dry laugh. 'I made a right old fool of myself, Holly.'

I thought – I shall look forward to hearing the other side of *that* story.

Henry said, 'What's so funny?'

'Nothing. We're nearly there.'

He said, 'I really don't know what to do.'

A policeman was waiting by the desk. He said, 'Mr Lingard?' and looked at me.

Henry said, 'This is a friend. I thought my wife . . .' and the policeman nodded. We went down a long corridor into a room. There was a man in ordinary clothes sitting on the edge of a desk and swinging one leg in a relaxed and sociable way, and Emma, in a chair, a grey blanket wrapped round her. She looked like a war refugee.

As soon as she saw me, she began to cry. I went to her and took her hands.

Henry said, 'Darling . . .' But she hid her face against me, the way a child might do. Someone gave me a chair and I sat beside her. She smelt of wet clothes and was shivering in spasms.

Henry and the plain clothes policeman were whispering by the desk. Emma closed her eyes and gave little sobs and gasps as if she could neither bear to see nor to hear them. After a minute, Henry pulled a face at me and they went out of the room and shut the door. I caught Emma's shoulders and shook her gently. I said, 'Well, what have you been up to?'

Her eyes stayed closed. Blue veins stood out on the lids.

I said, 'It's all right, old dear, you can come out now. They've gone.'

She said, 'I walked about all day – oh, everywhere – it was so cold – then I sat in the Abbey.' There was a little spit at the corner of her mouth and I wiped it away. She opened her eyes wide. 'Holly – do you know, I had an extraordinary – a *conversation* with you on Westminster Bridge. . . .' She made an odd, choking sound that ended in a giggle.

'I hope I was sensible.'

'Oh, very. . . .' . .

The giggling continued. Her eyes were rolling upwards, so that only the whites were visible.

I wanted to slap her. I said, 'Look, you don't have to put on this great act with me. Pull yourself together for a minute. What have you told them?'

She didn't answer. The giggling stopped; she was rigid and trembling. I wondered if I *ought* to slap her. She said, 'Oh, I did try . . .' She gave a long sigh and went limp in my arms. I said, 'Emma, duckie,' and she murmured, so low I could hardly catch it, 'Holly, help me. . . .'

She began to cry again. There was nothing I could do except hold her tight and try to comfort her. Under the blanket, her clothes were sopping wet: she must have been walking in the rain for hours. I said, 'It's all right, love, it's all right.' I knew I was being a fool and taken in, but all the same, an aching tenderness seemed to swell up inside me.

Henry and the policeman came back. As soon as the door opened, she began to tremble again.

Henry squatted on his haunches in front of her and said, 'Listen, sweetheart . . .'

Her head jerked back and she began to moan, rolling her eyes in that awful way, like a horse.

Henry said, 'She made a statement. Insisted. Then she broke down like this.' Sweat had started up along his hair line.

I said, 'I know. She's told me.' It seemed easiest to pretend this. I said, very loudly and firmly, 'Of course the whole thing is quite ridiculous.'

Henry nodded. Behind him, the policeman was watching Emma, standing with his head thrust forward. He was picking his nose. When he saw me looking at him, he stopped at once and grinned self-consciously. He had a nice, rugged face, with a blue, pitted chin. I wanted to smile back but decided it would be unsuitable, in the circumstances.

Henry said, 'Emma, my dearest . . .'

She gave a long sigh and slumped against me. I pushed her head down onto her knees.

The policeman said, 'Has she fainted?' He sounded hopeful.

Her hands were pawing in front of her. She made a noise in her throat and struggled up. I leaned her head against my shoulder. Her eyes were closed again.

The policeman said, 'She's clearly in no condition . . .'

I said, 'That's the understatement of the century.'

He said, 'We can see her tomorrow.' He was looking very unhappy indeed, as if he did not know how to deal with this. I wondered if he was married.

I looked straight at him and said, 'Whatever for? This idiotic nonsense.'

Henry said, 'You see, they can't just ignore it.' He was standing up now, mopping at his forehead. The electric light was directly above him and made his face look all planes and hollows.

I said, 'But haven't you explained?'

I tried to sound totally bewildered. I had no idea what happened when you walked into a police station and said you had killed someone. Henry was a lawyer. He ought to know.

He said carefully, 'She's unwell, of course. They understand that. But there are formalities. They want her to see a doctor.'

He looked helpless.

Emma began twisting in the chair, throwing herself about. I put my arm behind her to stop her hitting her head against the wall. She was breathing in little gasps, panting, with her mouth open. I thought – 'Well, one thing is certain, she can't keep *this* up much longer!'

The moment I had thought this, I felt suddenly braced up: the skin round my forehead seemed to go tight with excitement. I could only see one thing to do. I said loudly, almost laughing – in fact, I did want to laugh – 'Oh Lord, Henry, I didn't mean that. Anyone with eyes in their head can see she's ill! But as far as your father goes – oh, for Pete's sake! Haven't you told them I was there?'

My voice was clear as a bell. The room seemed to be ringing with it. I held my breath. No one said anything. Emma lay quiet in my arms, making no sound or movement now. Henry was staring at me.

The policeman said, 'No, we hadn't realized that.' He sounded so relieved, it was comic.

He looked at Henry. I looked at Henry. He cleared his throat and I felt the room begin to spin round me. I knew that I had done the only possible thing, and that whatever happened I would never have a bad conscience about it, but I can't deny that I was scared for a minute.

But give the devil his due, Henry was quick enough in the uptake. Though his eyelids flickered a bit, he said, calmly enough, 'Hadn't you? Oh, I'm so sorry, I should have made that clear. I suppose I was so worried about my wife's health that nothing else really registered.'

We put Emma in the back of the car and tucked the rug round her. She was submissive and quiet and seemed more drowsy than anything else. She didn't speak or look at either of us.

Henry came to open the driver's door for me. He said, in a stiff voice, 'Thank you, Holly.'

That cost him something, I could see. Having to thank me.

'Don't mention it,' I said. 'Any time. Any little thing.'

He put his hand on my arm. 'Please, Holly, don't make a joke of it.' In the light from the street lamp, his mouth looked thin and dark.

'No post-mortem,' I said. 'So morbid.'

'No. All right. I just want to say you mustn't – I mean, I hope you won't ever feel bad about this. In a way, it was a sort of short cut to the truth.'

I shrugged my shoulders. Why not? If it cheered him up to see things this way. 'I shan't lose any sleep, don't worry yourself,' I said.

'*I* might, though.' He grinned, his whole face lighting up as if he had suddenly seen through himself and was highly amused by what he saw. Then he said, 'Seriously, though. They'd have had to question her. Doctors' reports, that sort of thing. It would have been ghastly for her, and for what? After all, we know the truth, don't we?'

'Yes.'

'Well, then.' He was smiling at me. '*Dear* Holly,' he said, and kissed me – a sudden, inexpert dive, like a shy boy. Our noses bumped together and he laughed. He opened my door and then got in the car himself, in the back, with Emma. She lay with her feet up and her head on his shoulder, and soon after I started the engine she began to cry, softly and drearily. Henry put his arms round her and talked to her as if she were a baby, saying it was all over now, she would be all right, she was not to cry, or to cry if she felt like it, it didn't matter, nothing mattered, they would soon be home and she could go straight to bed and sleep. . . .

She said, 'Forgive me.'

Henry said, 'Oh, my love, there's nothing to forgive, don't you understand that? You're not well, my mouse, my Emma-kins. That's all.'

'I'm not mad,' she said, almost angrily, and then. 'Henry, you don't think I'm mad, do you?'

There was a quaver in her voice that the best actress in the world couldn't have bettered. Like a piteous child afraid of the dark. Good old Emma, I thought. That was a bloody marvellous performance!

It had certainly taken Henry in. He was talking to her now with more honest gentleness and feeling in his voice than I had ever heard before. I said to myself, 'Well, she's got him where she wants him now!'

For a minute, I felt what was almost a kind of envy. Or irritation, perhaps – it was a queer, mixed-up sensation. *I* could never have got away with an act like that; nor, to be honest, would I have ever tried. All this fantastic tarra-diddle when she could quite easily have kept her mouth shut in the beginning! I know I would have done, and if that makes me out to be insensitive and crude, well Amen to that: it would have caused less trouble. But I knew, even while I was thinking like this, and feeling this sudden, bitter resentment against her – which was probably mainly caused by the lie I had been forced into which went against the grain because I am not a liar by nature – that Emma could never have done that. Where I would have said, 'Well, what's done is done, this could have happened to anyone, and after all, it was pure accident, I meant the old man no harm,' she would have to go on, rootling about in her mind like a pig after truffles and turning up a wicked thought here, a bad impulse there, until she couldn't bear the burden by herself any longer.

But for Emma, of course, it couldn't even be as straightforward as that! She would not only have to have the relief of doing what she thought was the right thing, but she would have to be loved and admired for doing it, *and* let off the consequences as well! And the only way to do that was to make sure that no one could really believe her, so she could always say to herself, 'Well, at least I did try to tell them,' and put her conscience to sleep that way. A tall order, in the circumstances, you might think, but not beyond our Emma! Go off your rocker a little, not enough to land yourself in a straitjacket or anything unpleasant like that, but just enough to make sure everyone is really sympathetic and sorry and falling over themselves to explain that you couldn't possibly have done this dreadful deed. 'Poor pet – you're just so fine and sensitive that you feel you have to take the blame for everything, heave all the sins of the world on your delectably frail shoulders. Of course we don't believe you – which is just as well, by the way, since it would be extremely inconvenient for us, as well as for you, if we did – but we revere you for your wonderfully tender conscience, just the same.'

Not that it was all straight bluff, of course – she could never have put on that inspired act if she didn't almost believe it herself – though leaving those letters about for old Henry to find came pretty near it. On the other hand – this struck me suddenly – *that* could have been a kind of double bluff! Suppose what horrified her most, more, even, than giving an old man a shove in the heat of a quarrel, was the fact that she, *Emma*, had actually fallen in love with a man not her husband? Oh – unthinkable, unbearable. Peerless, virtuous Emma! So what to do? You have to confess and be forgiven but not – God save the mark! – not *blamed*. You leave those letters about, but at such a time and in such a situation that they will only be taken as a sad and touching sign of temporary derangement, a confession, not of guilt, but of innocence – and on both counts: neither of your sins are *real*.

The mind plays odd tricks. Driving along, I worked myself up into such a state that by the time we had reached the house and Henry had got out to open the drive gates, I turned round half-expecting to see some kind of monster in the back seat. But of course, there was only Emma, her sweet face damp and blotchy, looking so scared and exhausted that I despised myself. For though everything I had thought might be true, it was not fair. It wasn't Emma's fault that she was always trying to be better than she possibly could be, strapping herself so tightly into a kind of corset of old-fashioned beliefs about how a 'nice' woman should think and behave, that something was bound to give in the end. And, after all, the high standards she set were for herself, not for other people. She'd never blame me for going to bed with Lucas, only herself for falling in love with him. And though that could be a sickening kind of pride – *my little sins are worse than other people's big ones, because I aim high, not like that old tart, Holly* – it could also be real goodness, and that was something I wasn't really qualified to speak about!

Not that it would ever occur to her to think like that. She was too humble. She looked at me now with her sad, swollen eyes, and said, 'Holly, you must hate me.'

It was on the tip of my tongue to say something like, 'Come off it, old dear, you can't fool me,' but she was looking at me so pitiably and so trustingly that I knew it was beyond my power to say anything to hurt her. I remembered how she had said, in the police station, 'Holly, help me,' and I thanked God I had been able to, and suddenly a wave of affection seemed to flood my heart as it had then, washing away all my spiteful thoughts and feelings. I felt, I suppose, a little the way you must feel when you have rescued someone from drowning: once you have saved their life, you are bound to be responsible for them, from that moment on!

I said, 'For Pete's sake, you thumping idiot, you know I love you!'

And as soon as I had spoken, I felt relaxed and at peace with myself and the world. As if just saying that, had released some tension in me.

# 12. *Henry*

'Emma's mother said, 'Is she all right?'

I thought – This is the hardest nut to crack. Her belief that she 'sees through' everything. But she was looking frightened. She loved Emma. I thought – *That* breaks down the old defences.

I said, 'Terribly tired, of course. And very confused. I don't think she can take much more.'

She said, 'The boys are in bed. I can tell them poor Mummy's ill.'

Holly was backing the car down the short drive, much too fast for prudence. Emma's mother stood at the front door, peering out. There were lines round her mouth. I had never thought of her as old before.

I went to the garage. Holly was out of the car. She gave me the keys, said, 'Bye, now,' and patted the top of my arm in a comradely way. I thought – Good old Holly!

I opened the door for Emma. The rug had slipped, tangling round her feet: she tripped over it as she got out of the car and stumbled into my arms. I stepped backwards to regain my balance and trod on the teeth of the garden rake that was leaning against the wall of the garage. The handle shot forward and hit the back of my head. I thought – This is a scene from a comic film.

Emma was leaning against me, her face pressed into my coat. She said, 'I don't want to go in.'

I put my hand to the back of my head and felt the bump coming up. Like a shelled egg. Then I tightened my arms round her.

'Not much more,' I said. 'There's my brave girl.'

I felt as if I could lie down on the cold ground and go to sleep. So tired. My head throbbed and I had a pain in my stomach. I said, 'Come along, my honey bee.'

The hall was empty. Her mother must have gone upstairs to the boys. How tactful! The drawing-room door stood invitingly open; the fire danced in the hearth.

I said, 'Straight to bed? Or would you like to get warm first? Sit by the fire and have a drink?'

I had put the letters back into the Queen Anne bureau where she had, presumably, kept them. She knew that I never used the bureau. I had thought – She will find them and assume she must have left them there, after all; believe them untouched, unread. . . .

Or at least know that I want her to believe this.

I thought – What a fool! Off my bloody nut! I had wanted an excuse to be jealous of Lucas, who was a writer. *I* could have been a writer if it hadn't been for my family commitments, my highly developed sense of responsibility. What a fantasy! I had never even finished my play. How foolish, once one knows!

I thought – Was she really so lonely?

Emma said, 'I don't really think I want a drink.' She swallowed, and smiled at me.

'Bed, then.'

'Where are the boys?'

'Your mother's with them. Don't worry.'

'No.'

She started up the stairs, dragging herself, one hand on the banister rail. I held her elbow, steered her across the landing into the bedroom. She collapsed on the Victorian nursing chair my father had bought for her when the twins were born, her legs sticking out stiff, like a doll's. She looked up at me, hair streaked across her face.

She said, 'Henry . . .'

'Don't talk.'

*For God's sake, don't talk.*

'I don't know what to say.' She sighed; the breath seemed to rush out of her. She looked broken, ashamed.

I said, heartily, 'Come along, now.'

I helped her undress. She was wet to the skin. I fetched a towel from the bathroom and rubbed her dry. She was shivering as if she had malaria. I wondered if she would get pneumonia and die, and how I would feel about it. Saw myself at the graveside, weeping. I got her nightdress and she put her arms up like a child, her breasts pointing upwards, the nipples stiff with cold. I wanted to make love to her and was ashamed of this impulse. Like lusting after a nun or an invalid. She would, if I wanted to. She never made excuses: she only liked the light to be out. But her mother might come down. If I locked the door, she would know. *Men are such beasts*. I thought – Emma's mother is too intelligent to have said that, but did she ever imply it? I put my arms round my wife and held her briefly and gently. A fatherly embrace.

The bed was warm. Full of hot water bottles.

I said, 'Who would have imagined we had so many hot water bottles?'

I helped Emma into bed, turning the sheet down and smoothing it neatly, like a fussy nurse. I still wanted to make love to her.

She moved her head fretfully on the pillows. Her hair lay stranded, like seaweed.

She said, 'Henry, say something. . . .'

Her voice shook. I sat beside her and stroked her arm.

'Henry, please. . . .' Her eyes were huge, pleading.

It had all been said before, but I said it again. Only one new angle occurred to me, possibly because of my present preoccupation. My father's unfortunate behaviour had distressed her, naturally, but what was important, and *interesting* – I stressed this word pedantically as if this was an academic discussion – was her own reaction. She had clearly been too embarrassed to tell me. Why? Was sex something you couldn't talk about, something you only did in the dark? Of course she

196

wasn't repressed on the surface – 'Don't misunderstand me, *I'm* not complaining,' I said, smiling my wise, lop-sided smile – but perhaps deeper down? Not her fault – Heaven's above! – but the way she'd been brought up. Her mother! Oh – she needn't protest, I'd known the old girl long enough! Flowers and bees, perhaps even the occasional mammal to illustrate the reproductive processes, but not men and women! This sort of thing was old hat, of course, a joke now, and Emma knew it *rationally*, but reason wasn't enough. Practice always lagged behind theory: impossible to shake off a puritanical background by taking thought! Though she knew her mother's attitude to be ridiculous, Emma had been conditioned by it. Nothing to be ashamed of: we were all trapped by our beginnings. The only escape was to admit this. Emma knew how her mother would react if she had complained about my father. Disbelief, disgust. '*That type* of woman will say anything. Of course it's all in their own dirty minds.' So when she finally lost her temper and he had the stroke and fell, she was too ashamed to explain what they had quarrelled about. Anything was better than that. Anything. . . .

I said all this. She listened, watching my mouth like a deaf person lip-reading. She nodded slowly, rather bemused. Her hand moved towards mine over the turned-down sheet. I took it and thought – Of course, this is what happened.

There was a scuffling noise on the landing. A giggle. Her hand gripped painfully; the fingers trembling.

Emma's mother peeped in. Just her head, round the door. 'William and Rufus want to say nighty-night. I've read them two stories, but they say they won't go to sleep until they've seen Mummy. I told them she had a little temperature.'

Lower down the door, their faces appeared, solemn and pink. Emma smiled and said she would be quite better tomorrow: they must be good boys and do what Granny told them. Their heads vanished, whipped away like glove puppets. The door closed.

There was more colour in Emma's cheeks. If it had done nothing else, my didactic lecture had given her time to recover. I said, 'My darling, do you want something to eat? Anything you fancy – well, not caviar, perhaps, but I could make scrambled eggs. It might do you good if you could manage something.'

I thought – The ways we express love! Hot water bottles, scrambled eggs. Holly had lied for her.

I said, 'We all love you, you know.'

She chewed at her lower lip. She said, 'Oh, *don't* . . .'

Bangs and thumps on the ceiling. We both stared upwards.

I said, 'You'd think – a pair of elephants. Not small boys.'

Her eyes creased, smiling. 'Have they really been all right?'

'Fine. It was lucky your mother came, of course.'

She stopped smiling.

I said, 'I expect she'll want to see you. Do you feel up to it?'

She nodded.

'You don't have to, you know.'

'I've got to sometime, haven't I?' She jerked her hand away, almost petulantly, and began plucking at the bedclothes. Then she looked at me. 'I'm all right now. Honestly.'

I said, 'There's my brave girl.'

We waited. I yawned. I couldn't think of anything to say. I took her hand again and squeezed it, to reassure her.

Her mother came in, head round the door first, and then her body, insinuating herself into the room like a dog unsure of its welcome. Her colour was high and she was breathing deeply. Like Emma, she was determined to get this over with.

'How are you, dear? Feeling better now?'

'I'm all right,' Emma said.

'Good.' Her mother smiled rigidly. Her face was a bright mask, crowned with heavy hair.

She moved round the room, picking up Emma's clothes. She clucked over the dress she had been wearing. '*Soaking wet.* You silly child. I think I better just go and hang it up in the kitchen.'

Emma said, 'Do leave it, Ma. It doesn't matter.'

'It wouldn't take a minute . . .'

But she put the dress down on a chair and sat on the end of the bed in a casual, schoolgirl's attitude, hands clasped round plump knee.

Emma said, 'I'm so sorry all this had happened.' She spoke in a clipped, clear, bright voice, as if apologizing for some minor failure in hospitality that had been quite beyond her control.

'Well, dear.' Her mother caught her breath as if she had been running. She said, 'To tell you the truth, I don't really understand what did. . . .' She gave a little, hurried laugh, admitting that she was a foolish old woman. I found that I felt sorry for her.

Emma said, in that same, bright voice, 'Henry has explained it all very well. His father made a pass at me. He was always doing it, Naturally, gently nurtured as I was, this upset me a great deal. So much so that I went off my head for a while. I suppose that could happen.'

I protested. 'Darling love, I didn't say it was as simple as that. . . .'

But she wasn't listening to me. I didn't exist for her. She was watching her mother, who had begun to blush.

She said, 'Emma, dear.' Another of those quick, nervous laughs. 'You know, I really do find this a bit hard to believe.'

Emma said casually, 'Yes. I rather expected you would.' She half-smiled, as if some memory amused her. 'You didn't believe me about Uncle George, either.'

'George?' My mother-in-law's cheeks were deep purple now, like an elderly, choleric, Brigadier's. She made a little snorting sound. 'Really Emma, your *imagination*. . . .'

'It was true, though,' Emma said. She seemed quite calm now.

Her mother bent her head and began picking bits of fluff off her tweed skirt. I recognized the colour of this fluff: there was a new green carpet in the boys' room and it was shedding

surplus wool. Her hand was shaking. I thought suddenly –
This is cruel. I said, in a humorous voice, 'Have a heart, now.
Who's Uncle George?'

Emma's mother turned to me. She looked surprised and a
little relieved as if she had forgotten I was there and was now
glad of it. As she spoke, she kept her eyes on my face as if I
could protect her from something.

'He lived at the bottom of our garden. George Stiller. He
was in a bank. A manager, as a matter of fact. Emma used to
call him Uncle George because he was in and out of our
house such a lot. His wife was dead, and he often came to us
for his evening meal, poor man. He had two children. A girl –
what was her name, now? Deborah? No – that was another
friend of Emma's. Sylvia? Yes, that was her name. Sylvia.
She was a bit younger than Emma, but they were the greatest
friends.'

'I don't remember,' Emma said. Her mouth was gathered
up like a purse.

'Oh, surely, dear . . .' The painful blush had faded: now she
had diverted this conversation from what was clearly a dangerous topic, she seemed garrulously at ease. 'Plump, rather
jolly little thing, though not much to look at, you know. Took
after her father, which was a misfortune, really. I believe her
mother had been very pretty. Sylvia had warts on her hands.
Isn't it funny, the things you remember? I know I hoped you
wouldn't catch them, though you said you wanted to, I really
can't imagine why! And of course there was her brother, that
tragic boy. . . . You must remember *him*, Emma. You were so
fond of him. When he went into hospital you used to write to
him regularly and send him books – poor George was always
most appreciative and said how sweet it was of you, but it
must have been heartrending for him, really, because of course
the poor child couldn't read towards the end.'

'Gordon.' Emma said.

'That's right. I can't think why I forgot! Old age taking its
toll, I expect. *My goodness* – the terrible things that happen to

people! Poor George. His wife dying of cancer and then his son getting this tumour on the brain. He was absolutely devoted to that boy.'

Emma said, 'Would it have been any less terrible if he hadn't been?'

Her face was still and cold. It frightened me. I said. 'Darling . . .' I put out my hand but she brushed it away.

'Of course not, dear.' Her mother's voice was gentle, almost humble. 'One just says that sort of thing. Silly, but there it is. I'm sorry I brought this up now. I'm afraid I'd forgotten how much that sad business upset you. You were such an impressionable child.'

'Twelve,' Emma said, 'I was twelve.'

'Well. Old enough to be upset, of course. And you were certainly fond of the boy, though I think you exaggerated a bit afterwards. I remember I blamed myself for letting you read too many romantic novels. But you were such a bookworm you gobbled everything up!'

She laughed, throwing back her head. Showing fine, even teeth.

Emma said, 'I remember Gordon dying. His father held a mirror to his mouth. It was all my fault.'

She began to cry. Her face contorted helplessly, like a weeping child's. Like a child, she thumped clenched fists on her raised knees.

'You knew it was my fault, you *told* me so,' she said.

Her mother caught her hands. Emma pulled away and lay back against the pillows, shuddering and sobbing.

Her mother said, reproachfully, 'Oh Emma. As if I would ever say such a dreadful thing to a little girl.'


Emma's mother said, 'It's not true, of course. Emma wasn't even there. The poor lad died in hospital.'

She was clearing the drawing-room, making a neat pile of games, putting a collection of small, model cars into a white, cardboard box. She straightened up now, one hand to her back. She looked handsome, but tired.

She said, 'You needn't look at me like that, Henry. I took his sister to see him before he died.'

I said, 'Then why does she feel like this?'

I thought – Why ask? I know the answer. Or think I do. We all want to be guilty. Guilt is power. It means you have made something happen.

I said. 'But there must have been something at the time. Some reason. . . .'

'Jealousy, perhaps.' She made an impatient movement of her head. She had so much to do: tidy the drawing-room, make some sort of supper. These things were more important. She said, 'Sylvia stayed with us when the boy went into hospital that last time. Her father was so broken up, the house was no place for a child. We made a fuss of her, naturally. I daresay Emma resented it, dreamed up some story to attract attention.'

I said, 'You can't believe that.'

I meant – I can't. Not because I loved Emma, but because she wasn't so simple. No one is. I thought – Not even my honest, down-to-earth mother-in-law.

She shrugged her shoulders. Pitying my innocence?

I said. 'What I don't understand is, why she never told me about it before.'

'Perhaps she's only just thought of it.'

She appeared unaware of the implications of this remark. Calmly adjusting a pin in her hair.

I said, 'I don't know whether you are being unbelievably callous. Or merely absurd.'

She frowned. 'I didn't mean anything unkind, Henry. Just that she probably feels ashamed of all the trouble she's caused. So she's dragged up this old story. As a kind of red herring.'

I was suddenly shaking with anger.

I said, 'Do you despise the whole of the human race? Or only Emma?'

She stared at me. Astonished. I thought – Perhaps no one has ever spoken to her like this before. Cracking the shell.

I said, 'It's so degrading.'

She said, 'Henry . . .'

She looked as if she couldn't bear this. Perhaps she couldn't. She had had a long day and she was tired. Not young any more. Her mouth was trembling. She put up her hand to hide it.

I said, 'My dear, you have to take people seriously sometimes.'

She sat down on the sofa. Her hands folded in her lap, staring at the carpet. Her bent head shamed me. I like to think of myself as a kind man.

I told myself – I have to be sorry for Emma, not for her: she can look after herself.

I *was* sorry for Emma. She wasn't cruel. Not a liar. My sweet, precious girl. This was an article of faith. Everything else could go, all the pretences, but not this. I needed her to look after. How could I live, otherwise?

I said, 'Listen. What I mean is, where – or when – this boy died isn't important. You know that. I didn't think Emma had taken an axe to him. What matters – what's *real* – is that she blames herself in some way. She said you blamed her. Why should she think that?'

She said nothing. To give her time, I moved round the room, shaking cushions, straightening a picture. Not looking at her.

She said, to my turned back, 'I can only tell you, Henry, that I have no idea. No idea at all.'

Emma said, 'Well . . . ?'

She was sitting up in bed. She had been reading. She put the book down on the bedside table.

I thought – What shall I say? Your mother is a liar? Harsh. Perhaps not even strictly true. We all remember what we want to remember. On *that* count, I am as guilty as she is. This myth about my charming old rake of a father! And his death – a myth in the making? Perhaps the truth doesn't matter much. Only the way we look at it and we have choice there. We have to protect ourselves, survive somehow.

I wanted to be happy. To forget all this.

I said, 'Are you all right, my mouse? That's all that matters.'

She smiled at me. She looked quite different. Her face smoothed out.

I thought – She has carried this around with her all these years. Now it is exorcized.

She said, 'Henry . . .'

I said, 'Darling, we don't have to talk about it any more. As long as you're all right. Nothing else matters.'

She said, 'Henry, hold me. . . .'

## 13. *Emma*

They were laughing at my letters. She and Uncle George. They were drinking coffee after supper and laughing. She said, 'Oh, that child's got such an imagination!' I was outside the sitting-room door, listening. They didn't know I was there. They thought I was out, playing with Sylvia, but she had a headache and had gone home to bed.

He said, 'No one ever wrote letters like that to me. I'm quite envious.' She laughed, and I wanted to die.

I hated them both. I went into the kitchen and started to wash the supper dishes. Uncle George carried in the coffee cups and said he would give me a hand. He said my mother had some school books to mark. 'I don't know how she does it all, a wonderful woman, your mother.'

He dried the plates. He was talking to me, but I wouldn't answer, or look at him. He said, 'What's up, Em? Tell your old Uncle George.' He put his hand on my back and rubbed my spine up and down. I could see his face in the little mirror above the sink. It was pale, with a sort of sweat on it, like cheese. He moved his hand up to my neck and tried to turn my head around. He said, 'Come on, give your old Uncle a kiss.' He was holding me tight and wriggling against me.

I was a bit embarrassed, but I was mostly just angry because he had read my letters. Later on, I knew he had only read them because Gordon couldn't read them for himself, but I didn't know that then. I jabbed him in the stomach with my elbow and said, 'Let me go, you fat beast.'

I ran out of the kitchen, upstairs to my room. I lay on my bed, on my face. My mother came up. She said, 'What's the matter, dear?'

I couldn't say – You were laughing at me. I felt so sick and ashamed. I threw myself about, kicking at the end of the bed, and she said, 'You really must try to control yourself, Emma.' She took hold of my shoulders and made me look at her. At her traitor's face. I had to say something. I said, 'He put his hand on my neck. He tried to kiss me.'

She was very angry. She said she knew girls often had strange fantasies at my age, but she couldn't feel that excused me. She hoped I understood the damage this sort of dreadful invention might have done an innocent person. She frightened me. Her not believing me frightened me. It made me feel I couldn't be sure what had really happened. Like waking out of a dream and finding it still going on.

I hated her. When Gordon came out of hospital, I hated him, too. I had made a fool of myself, writing those letters. He was *so* stupid and ugly. I used to look at him and think – Why don't you *die?* I didn't want to play with him and Sylvia, but my mother made me. She said I must try not to think of myself and my own feelings all the time. I did try, I wanted to be good, like her, but I was so selfish. And so full of hate: it was like a blackness, blotting out the sun. When I pushed him over that day, I went home, crying, and told her, and she said, 'You wicked girl, you might have killed him.'

After he died, I thought she would remember that. I couldn't understand why she didn't tell everyone, shout it from the rooftops. Sometimes I wished she would, then it would all be over. They would take me away and hang me, with something black over my head.

Even a long time afterwards, when I knew I couldn't really have hurt him, I would see her looking at me when we sat quiet in the evenings, and I would start to tremble.

I loved her. She was strong, like a tower. I could hammer on the door and say – Let me in, this is Emma. I could hide in her and be safe.

But she wouldn't let me in. I was so wicked, I wasn't worth loving. It was this that frightened me. Not anything I had done, but what I knew I was capable of doing.

I was frightened by my own, black heart.

And my own insignificance.

Someone listen to me.

## THE BIRDS ON THE TREES

'Nina Bawden gets inside the skins of all her people and shows them as paradoxical, crotchety, adulterous, ambitious and completely human . . . A beautifully sustained impression of the impossibility of family life' – *New York Times Book Review*

## A WOMAN OF MY AGE

'Rarely have the workings of a woman's mind been revealed with such clarity' – *Daily Telegraph*

## FAMILY MONEY

'Nina Bawden's marvellous new novel . . . funny, subtle, sympathetic' – *Observer*

## WALKING NAKED

'*Walking Naked* is a book about influences – friends and enemies, parents and children, pains and pleasures and the vagaries of fate. And in the way of all the best writing, it is relative to ourselves. Her heroine stands before us . . . a looking glass through which to see ourselves' – *Cosmopolitan*

## THE ICE HOUSE

'Nina Bawden's great talent is to be able to take you along a perfectly ordinary street, rip the façade away and show the strange and passionate events that go on behind closed doors' – *Daily Telegraph*